'Am I you

'For the time [obscured]
Emma stiffene[obscured]
across her abd[obscured]
overboard, Mr M[obscured] a display of
affection for the c[obscured], so that he doesn't follow
his perfectly natural impulse to slit your throat.'

'Is that so?' Without warning he jerked her towards him, so that she collided against his chest.

'How dare you!'

'I was only displaying my affection.'

Victoria Aldridge is a fifth-generation New Zealander. She married young and happily, and spent some years travelling before settling down with three children. Her husband has his own company, and due to his unfailing support she has been able to complete her BA and begin writing.

BEN MORGAN'S MISTAKE

Victoria Aldridge

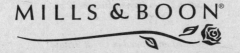

MILLS & BOON®

All the characters in this book have no existence outside the imagination of the author, and have no relation whatsoever to anyone bearing the same name or names. They are not even distantly inspired by any individual known or unknown to the author, and all the incidents are pure invention.

First published in Great Britain 1998
Harlequin Mills & Boon Limited,
Eton House, 18-24 Paradise Road, Richmond, Surrey TW9 1SR

© Victoria Aldridge 1998

ISBN 0 263 81285 5

Set in Times Roman 10½ on 12 pt.
04-9901-71515 C1

Printed and bound in Great Britain
by Caledonian International Book Manufacturing Ltd, Glasgow

Chapter One

1840

They buried Thomas on a Sunday.

There had been no rain for weeks, and the soil was little more than dust, floating lightly, blackly through the air as Kahu threw one last shovel of earth over the mound that was the Reverend Thomas Augustus Johnson's last resting place.

'It's not right, Mrs Johnson.' Kahu leaned on his shovel to survey his handiwork. 'The reverend always said no work on Sundays, just Church. He wouldn't have liked you doing this.'

Her late husband would certainly not have liked the unmistakable ring of satisfaction in his servant's voice, Emma thought. 'Burying the dead isn't work,' she said defensively. 'Besides, we had to do it today. With this heat…'

It seemed too indelicate to finish the sentence, even with Kahu's interested dark gaze upon her. She knew he was wondering why she was not crying.

Perhaps she should try to pretend, perhaps she should pull out a handkerchief and bury her face in it until Kahu went away and left her, satisfied that the mourning rituals were complete. But today she seemed to lack the energy to do even that. She turned her head away from his curiosity.

She was standing now on top of the hill where Thomas had wanted his church to be built. They had already cut down a few of the heavy-fronded *ponga* trees in preparation for the foundations and it was in this clearing, with the Whanganui River sliding quietly by below, that they had put Thomas to rest. He would have approved of her choice of site, she knew. For the first time in her life she had done the right thing, and he wasn't here to witness it. Burying him—that was the easy part. Carrying out his life's work, now—that was quite different.

'The church,' he had said, in a voice that was halfway between a wheeze and a whisper, and which had frightened her terribly. He had made a feeble gesture and she had taken his hand, careful not to show her revulsion at his hot, dry touch. His fingers had clutched at her as if clawing at her own health and strength, his bones brittle beneath the pale, stretched skin. 'The church... Promise me!'

Emma had nodded quickly, anxious not to upset him, but it had not prolonged his life. 'So much left undone...' he had said in a whisper so faint that she barely caught his words, and then he was gone.

Leaving her here, alone. She turned away from the grave and looked out over the hills, steep, tree-dark, endless. How many miles to the nearest European settlement? Fifty miles? One hundred? Were there any inland at all? No, the only way to leave was surely back down the river, although it had taken them over a week to get this far upriver, to the Place-With-No-Name. That was what she called it in her head, although the Maoris had a name for it, a name in their beautiful, melodic language that meant something like 'The Place Where Three Chiefs Met and Ate Fish'. She had tried to learn it, but Thomas had decided that the site of his new church was going to be called Redemption, and so there had been no point. It no longer mattered what name the place went by—now it would always be The-Place-Where-Thomas-Is-Buried.

Kahu was treading down the earth over her husband's grave, half-humming, half-singing 'The Lord is my Shepherd' under his breath. They had sung the psalm, she and Kahu, and she had found the relevant passages in Thomas's bible to read over the blanket-wrapped body. None of the native people had come to the funeral.

It was not as if they didn't know of Thomas's death: Emma was certain they knew everything about her and Thomas, down to the most intimate details. From the moment they had arrived at the village there had been a swarm of enthralled observers watching everything they did. Day and night the Maoris squatted around the campsite, commenting cheerfully to each other on the white-skinned strangers' clothes, food and ablution habits and making off with whatever they thought would not be missed. It would have been so easy then to have befriended them. Emma was fascinated by the language, their openness, their dark beauty. Beguiled by their smiles, drawn by their beckoning fingers, she would have wandered into their village at once, but Thomas would have none of that!

'Tell them, Kahu,' he had ordered on that first day, as he carefully drew a line in the soil around his and Emma's belongings. 'Tell them that within this line is our property. Not theirs. Tell them.'

Kahu looked surly. 'They won't understand, Reverend.'

'Perhaps Kahu is right,' Emma ventured nervously. 'This is their village, after all, and we don't want to impose…' She looked at Kahu for support and was taken aback by the hostility in his eyes. She, too, did not understand. But, oh, how she wanted to! Instead, the opportunity to learn was lost, and Kahu gracelessly translated Thomas's directives to a bemused and uncomprehending audience. Enough of Thomas's intention had got through, however, to ensure that offence was taken, and the open-handed offers of friendship were tacitly withdrawn. That was why there had been no other mourners at Thomas's funeral today. She knew enough about the Maoris to know that they were a people with an elaborate set of mourning rituals. Yet the only acknowledgement of Thomas's death had been a lessening in the number of observers that day, and that unsettled her. No, Thomas had not been liked here. Not even respected.

Kahu, who had been with them ever since Wellington, had not liked Thomas either. He would never have come this far up the river with them had Thomas not promised him good wages. But they had needed an interpreter, and someone to help with the heavy work, and Kahu had seemed willing enough in the beginning. Emma watched him stamping hard on the grave, the soft earth puffing up between his toes. At any moment she expected him to break into a little dance.

'What am I going to do, Kahu?' she asked suddenly.

'Do, Mrs Johnson?' Kahu lifted his heavy shoulders in a shrug. 'Go back downriver. That's the only thing to do.'

She hugged Thomas's bible closer to her chest, trying to conjure up his presence. Tall, thin, slightly stooped from a lifetime of study. Grey hair worn a little too long, because Thomas had not cared for the vanities of the body. And his eyes. Dark, intense eyes that had seemed to penetrate to one's very soul, seeking out any evil that might be lurking there, and always finding it...

She shivered. 'I could go back downriver, I suppose,' she thought aloud. 'Or I could stay here and build the church. Thomas wanted it so much, and I wouldn't want to disappoint him.'

Kahu made a noise of disbelief through his nose. 'How can you disappoint him, Mrs Johnson? He's dead now. With his Maker.'

'Yes, he is, but I'm sure he's still watching us.' And he knows what I'm thinking, she thought with a rising sense of dread. He knows that when I woke up this morning, the first thing I felt was free. Free and young. I'm only twenty-three, after all. My life is only just beginning...

Your life of service is only just beginning. She had to stop herself from glancing back over her shoulder, so clearly did Thomas's familiar words sound in her head. How often had he had to remind her of the enormous debt she owed: to the Lord, to the Church and, most of all, to himself. He had been right to do so, of course. She had so much to atone for, and she owed Thomas so much. But did she have to repay the debt here, all alone?

'Kahu, if I go back downriver, will you come with me?'

He shrugged again, his eyes sliding away from her. 'Maybe, Mrs Johnson.'

'I can pay you, Kahu,' she said steadily and completely untruthfully. If Thomas had any money left over after purchasing the materials for the mission, she could not find it. Kahu had not been paid since before they left Wellington—she had heard the men arguing about it. Once she had dared to ask her husband about funding for the mission, and Thomas had haughtily reminded her that—if she only had faith—the Lord would provide everything they would need. But not, it seemed, a little hard cash with which to bribe Kahu.

'Maybe, Mrs Johnson,' Kahu repeated stonily.

Her heart sank. If not Kahu, who else? She dared not ask any of the local men to take her. She knew nothing of their language, and what guarantees did she have that they would not find it less bothersome to simply tip her into the river, or worse? The Maoris who had rowed them up here had left as soon as Thomas had paid them, taking the canoe with them. How long would it take to make the return journey? If she walked, it could take weeks. And there were all those native villages they had passed. What if they weren't as friendly as this tribe had been? What if she became lost, or injured, or…

Oh, this was not fair! she found herself thinking. How could Thomas have put her in such a position? Why had he refused to listen to her pleas and that of the other churchmen in Sydney that they go to one of the Missionary Society's settlements? They would have been safe then, with others of their own kind, in a part of the country where the Maoris were known to be friendly. But Thomas had denounced the Missionary Society as spineless and lacking in dedication. And of course she, as his wife, had to meekly follow where he led…

Guiltily, she thrust her disloyal thoughts from her. Thomas was dead now, and this situation was for her alone to resolve. Anger would change nothing.

Her head was aching with the heat and the worry, so she went back to her hut and made herself a pot of the sweet *manuka* leaf infusion that had to pass for tea. The sun was approaching its zenith now, and under the heavy black folds of her voluminous dress the perspiration was trickling down her back and between her breasts. Paler colours would have been so much more suitable to these temperatures, but Thomas had insisted that she dye all her clothes black the day after their marriage. Black was the colour of sobriety and penitence, he had told her, the colour of humility and duty: all the virtues she had to learn. It was also the colour of mourning, now perfectly appropriate.

She sat in the shade of the fragrant, white-flowered *manuka* trees surrounding the little hut, made of wood and *raupo* reed, that she had built herself and had so recently shared with her husband. Around her a few brown shadows flittered under the trees and then she heard the padding of bare feet along the track to the village in the hilltop. It was too hot for missionary-watching today, especially when the one remaining missionary was doing nothing more exciting than sitting still. Why not find somewhere shady to lie down by the cool river and sleep away the midday heat? So they went away, leaving Emma alone for the first time. A light breeze had sprung up and she loosened the strings of her bonnet, wishing she could take the whole thing off and let the air ruffle though her hair. Thomas had never let her bare her head, maintaining as he had that a woman must never immodestly flaunt herself so. Now that he was dead... Her hand dropped to her lap. How long would it be before she was free of the feeling that he was hovering somewhere overhead, watching her?

Despite that, it was soothing to be able to sit in peace, with no one to tell her to collect firewood or prepare a meal or gather for prayers. Yet again she had to clamp down hard on the restless tide of freedom surging within her. Thomas had constantly had to warn her of her natural inclination towards sloth and irresponsibility. She must be strong without his surveillance and finish what he had not been given time to do. But how?

She tried to make some sense of the turbulence in her mind. Staring down at the river helped, watching the play of light on the smooth, green ripples. She found herself focussing on the soothing, surging rhythm of the water, the quiet roaring sound that surrounded her, feeling the chaotic threads of emotion gradually sort themselves into strands of coherent thought. It was hard to think for herself again, after a year of marriage. Thomas had told her when to eat, sleep and work. What to wear, who to speak to, what to read and what to think. It had been such a struggle in the beginning to accept his discipline, but in the end she had submitted, just as he had always known she would.

Now she was alone, with no hope of immediate rescue. The Maoris had an extraordinary reputation for savagery and cannibalism, and although they seemed friendly, it was impossible to tell what they really thought of the white-skinned foreigners with their strange ways. And Thomas had set himself against the chief from the very first…

She saw that her hands, wrapped around her cup, were shaking. But I must be strong! she told herself firmly. If the Maoris had not been especially welcoming, at least they had not been hostile. Even on the day of their arrival, when Thomas had gone to Tawhai, the chief, and berated him for the open licentiousness of his tribe, they had not taken offence. In fact, Tawhai had nodded and smiled and listened attentively to Kahu's translation of Thomas's words. The chief would think about what the Reverend said, Kahu had told them briefly, although Tawhai had responded in a long, measured speech. Emma had wondered at the time just what Tawhai had said, and how accurate Kahu's interpretation had been. She would have liked to learn Maori, but Thomas had forbidden it, saying that the sooner the natives learned English, the sooner they would be able to read God's Word.

'Thomas was wrong!' she said aloud, and then stopped, horrified at her boldness. But no thunderbolts descended upon her head; the earth beneath her did not open up to swallow her whole. The birds continued their drowsy twittering in the high trees, the cicadas trilled on in competition with the whispering water. 'Thomas was wrong!' she said again, louder. And then jumped at the sound of a high giggle, hastily broken off.

She turned her head slowly, so as not to alarm her observer. The little girl she had noticed before was there again, only the white of her teeth giving her away against the darkness of the ferns she hid under.

'Hello,' Emma said softly. *'Haere mai.'* Welcome. Come to me. They were the only words of Maori she knew. The white teeth disappeared as the little girl ducked her head, considering. Emma held out her hand and sat still, waiting. After a minute she began to think that the child wouldn't come after all, but then the fern fronds shook as the girl stood up.

She could have been no older than seven, although her thin arms and legs testified to a short lifetime of malnourishment. Under a wild thatch of black hair her eyes were huge and meltingly dark. As Emma leaned forward encouragingly the child cowered back, looking ready to run at the slightest threat. The other children here were quite different: inquisitive, confident and endearingly cheeky.

'Haere mai,' Emma said again and smiled.

Like a small, wild animal the girl approached, testing each step, always poised to take flight at the first sign of danger. But Emma sat patiently, her hand outstretched, her smile never fading even as the sunlight revealed the child's pathetic state. The child came closer, until she dropped to her haunches just out of Emma's reach, her face wary.

'Would you like something to eat?' Emma reached over and pulled the protective cloth off the bread she had set to cool on a stone beside the hut. She had baked it yesterday shortly before Thomas had died and had forgotten all about it. Taking one of the loaves, she deftly tipped it out of its tin and broke off a piece.

'It's good,' she soothed, as the child shrank back. 'Look… ' She put the piece of bread in her mouth, chewing vigorously and with an expression of great enjoyment, and the girl shuffled closer, fascinated. Delicately, she took a little piece, tasted it, and her face lit up with a huge smile.

'*Kapai!*'

'*Kapai*? That means "good", does it?' Emma laughed and held out the rest of the bread. 'Good heavens, you're hungry, aren't you? I wonder if you've ever had enough to eat.' She touched herself on her chest and said slowly, 'Emma. I'm Emma.'

The little girl swallowed a huge mouthful of bread. 'Hemma,' she said, and giggled. Emma pointed at her.

'And your name?'

The child hesitated and then understanding dawned. 'Rima!' she said firmly, and tapped her bony ribcage. 'Rima!'

'Well, Rima,' Emma said, 'and what are we to do with you?' The girl was naked, as were all the children in the village, and her arms and back were covered with small, weeping sores. A large, un-healed wound on her upper arm concerned Emma—she guessed that the injury had occurred some time ago but that the child's fragile body was unable to adequately fight off infection. It took a little persua-sion before Rima allowed her to clean her sores and put an antiseptic salve over them, but when Emma wrapped a small bandage around her injured arm it was plain that Rima thought she had been given the most marvellous gift imaginable.

'Keep it on,' Emma told her, trying to commu-nicate her meaning in sign language. 'Tomorrow I'll change it for you. No—' she brushed away the small, inquiring fingers as they plucked at the knot she had made '—leave it on, Rima. Oh, how I wish you could understand me...'

She suddenly knew then, without a shadow of doubt, just what she had to do. She had seen other children here like Rima—not in such poor condi-tion, but with injuries and infections that she had longed to treat. From childhood she had assisted her father in his medical practice in London, and later in the shanties of Sydney. Although unable to openly practice medicine because of her sex, she had been taught most of what her father knew by the time of his death. Thomas had never made much of her skills, but it had made her valuable to him as a wife, none the less. She had accompanied him to New Zealand to provide schooling and medical care for the Maori, while Thomas was to look after their souls. And now the strongest possible evidence of the need for her skills was squatting just inches away, devouring the last of the bread.

After Rima had left, one hand possessively over her precious bandage, Emma made her preparations. In one of the trunks she found pen and ink, and a blank journal, and these she put into a satchel. Then, hands clenched tightly to steady her nerves, she took the track along the hill up to the village. Kahu was there, talking to the local woman he fancied as she strung eels on a pole, ready for smoking. When Emma told him what she planned to do, he stood up reluctantly.

'What do you need to learn Maori for, Mrs Johnson? Better that you go back downriver, eh? Safer.'

'But if I go, will you come with me?' she asked, and when he hung his head she sighed. 'Then I must have the protection of Tawhai. Perhaps he will help me. Will you speak to him for me?'

Kahu glanced at her in quick surprise, and then recovered himself to shrug carelessly. 'All right, Mrs Johnson. I will speak for you.'

She had only seen Tawhai from a distance, as it had been Thomas who had made all the contact with the Maoris. But now, as a lone woman, it seemed logical to Emma to ask for the protection of the local chief. The last thing she could afford to do at this time was to unintentionally make any enemies.

Tawhai was sitting in the sun outside his hut, deep in conversation with other men of the tribe. As Emma and Kahu drew near, he rose to his feet. He was a solidly built man with a fierce face made even more fearsome by the tattooed whorls on his forehead and cheeks. His long black hair was tied back in a knot, giving him even more height and, as he pulled his dogskin cloak around him, she caught a glimpse of heavily tattooed, muscular thighs. She knew that the Maori spent much of their time fighting between themselves, that a chief must possess courage and skill to protect his tribe, and Tawhai looked every inch the warrior. As their eyes met he threw his head back a little, arrogantly, and spoke to Kahu. It did not sound particularly friendly. Too late she remembered that the Maoris considered it discourteous to look a superior in the face, and she bowed her head humbly and sank into her best curtsey. When she peeped up from under the brim of her bonnet she saw with relief that Tawhai's expression had softened a little.

'Kahu, can you please tell the chief that I would like to speak to him?' she said quietly, still not rising. Kahu said something and Tawhai grunted. He held out a hand, indicating the flax mat beside him and she took her seat, arranging the folds of her dress with care so as not to touch the chief accidentally. From under her lowered lashes, she saw one of Tawhai's wives hovering in the background, proudly bearing Rima's prized bandage around her arm. Appalled as she was, Emma resisted the temptation to say anything and kept her eyes lowered in an attitude of submission.

Tawhai spoke, obviously a question.

'The chief says, what will you do, now that your man is dead?' Kahu translated for her. Emma took a deep breath and answered, her voice low and soft.

'I would like to stay here for a while, with the chief's permission.'

'Na te aha?'

'Why?' Kahu said.

'Because I have nowhere else to go. And because I have some healing powers—I can help his people.'

Tawhai laughed at that.

'The chief says that your healing powers did not save your husband. The tribe have their own ways of healing,' Kahu translated and then added, 'You would not care to anger the *tohunga*, Mrs Johnson—the priest of the tribe. To do so would be most dangerous.'

Emma nodded, aware of the keen brown gaze of the chief upon her. 'I understand that. But I am also a healer among my people, and I would like to share my knowledge with this tribe. My husband died of an illness—I think it was an illness borne by the water—and I was powerless to save him. Perhaps with the knowledge of the Maori that would not have happened.' She spoke in bursts, giving Kahu time to translate between each sentence, and for once she believed that he was phrasing her words accurately. Tawhai said nothing when she had finished speaking, only staring at her thoughtfully. She kept her eyes firmly averted to a spot by his left elbow.

'Kahu, could you also tell the chief that I would be honoured to learn his language. I want to make a dictionary of it.'

Kahu shifted his weight awkwardly. 'Dictionary? There is no word for that, Mrs Johnson.'

'A book, then. I want to make a book with all the

words that the Maori speak in it.' At Tawhai's sound of incomprehension she produced the satchel and brought out the pen, inkpot and journal. She opened the journal to the first page, dipped the quill in the ink and carefully wrote her name.

'Emma. That's my name.' Kahu translated, but Tawhai looked blank. She wrote another word. 'Tawhai. That's your name, see?' The chief shrugged, scowling. Emma sat back, looking around her, and then pointed to the hut behind them.

'Kahu, what is the name for a house?'

'*Whare*, Mrs Johnson.'

She wrote the word 'house' and then alongside it wrote '*whare*', saying the words as she did so. Tawhai was delighted, and the journal was handed around everyone present to be admired. When Emma got it back the ink was smudged, but she was sure that her intention was now clear.

'He says you can stay,' Kahu told her, and she sensed that he was almost as relieved as she was. 'You can put words into the book and you can learn from the healers of the tribe. You are an honoured guest and are welcome.'

'Tell him thank you,' Emma said gratefully, and noted that the words in Maori were '*Tena koutou*'.

Once taken under the protection of the tribe, Emma found life to be quite different. Each morning the women left food outside her door: eels, fish, watercress and sweet potatoes ('*puha*' and '*kumara*' she noted in her dictionary), and she felt free to walk around the village, or '*pa*'. She had little difficulty adapting to the protocol required—simply by watching and listening she soon learned what was appropriate behaviour and what was not. It didn't take long to realise that she had acted correctly in approaching the chief so submissively—women, especially young women, had a low status in the tribal hierarchy.

Much to her relief she found Maori relatively easy to learn, and soon filled her 'dictionary'. She could find only fourteen letters with which to reproduce the soft sounds, but it was a subtle language, with rich layers of meaning and inference beneath what superficially appeared to be a basic vocabulary. Surrounded by the language every minute of her waking day, she had learned enough to be able to hold a reasonably fluent conversation within six weeks. It was as well that she could, as Kahu quietly disappeared one morning with the local woman he had been courting. His defection did not take Emma completely by surprise, and by then she was becoming so adapted to her new life that it was not the worry that it once would have been for her.

Understanding the language enabled her to learn from old Kaharangi, the *tohunga*. At first she was a little apprehensive of the holy man, but he had wisdom and a keen sense of humour and—once he had judged her sincerity—he was happy to share some of his knowledge with her.

The Maori relied on plants for their medicines; poultices of flax reduced septicemia in wounds, and infusions of *manuka* reduced fever. *Kaukau* bark purified the blood. The barks of trees, the grasses, even vegetables, all seemed to have a specific use. Emma learnt that the spirit was regarded as being as important to treat as the body, and the concept of faith as an aspect of healing intrigued her. But, as she demonstrated her own skills, she found Kaharangi just as keen to learn from her. She showed him how to pull teeth, set broken bones and lance boils. Her cough remedies and mustard plasters soon became very popular, and each day she had an increasing number of Maoris squatting patiently beside her *whare*, waiting for the 'medicine' they so loved.

There was an ongoing battle with the bandages, however—they were regarded as desirable pieces of adornment, and it was not until Emma became fluent enough in Maori to strongly state why they should not be handed around from person to person that she was able to use them for their correct purpose. Like all her possessions, her medical supplies often seemed to simply vanish. At first it had infuriated her, walking up to the *pa* and seeing one of her bonnets on one of Tawhai's wives, or her buckets being used as playthings by the children. But such was the tribe's own generosity that she came to understand that their attitude to personal possessions was quite different to that of the Europeans. It had been such a misunderstanding that had set Thomas at odds with the tribe on the day of their arrival.

Every day Rima came to squat beside Emma as she worked, seemingly happy to just be beside her and to watch. She quickly learned to hand Emma the items she needed in her medical preparations, and showed considerable intelligence and wit. At first Emma had not wanted to encourage her too much, in case she inadvertently offended the child's mother, but as she learnt more Maori, she discovered that Rima had no mother—she was a slave, spared her life when her tribe lost in battle to Tawhai's tribe, and now destined to a life of servitude. Her father had been eaten after the battle, she told Emma matter-of-factly.

Emma grew very close to the child. It pleased her to watch how the extra food she gave her added visibly to her height in just a few weeks, and how well the painful sores on her skin responded to cleaning and treatment. Whether by accident or design Rima slowly became her full-time assistant, and Emma welcomed her company.

As each day passed she felt more a part of *pa* life, and more accepted. The days ran one into the other—long, hot summer days filled with hard work and a growing sense of fulfillment. She was needed here, just as she had been needed in the slums of London and Sydney. Using her healing skills had always given her the greatest satisfaction and here, in this place, her knowledge seemed doubly valuable. If she was lonely sometimes, or frightened about what the future held for her, she took strength from the quiet nights. Lying drowsily in her cocoon of warm blankets, watching the brilliant display of stars above her, listening to the rustle of the river and the owls that were called *ruru* calling in the trees... Then her world seemed made of magic.

Christmas came and went uncelebrated, and on the first day of 1841 she sat quietly in the clearing that would one day be Redemption's church, listening to the song of the cicadas throbbing in the warm air. She had placed fresh *rata* flowers on Thomas's grave, winding the scarlet branches around the wooden cross she had erected. Already small ferns were thrusting their way through the soil, covering the turned earth, and she was reluctant to pull them up. The soft growth made Thomas's grave more permanent, more respectable, somehow.

She pulled up her skirt to knee height and let the sun warm her pale, outstretched legs. They were much more muscular than they had been, and marked with bruises and cuts. She had long since given up wearing stockings—Thomas would have been horrified at her immodesty, but they were heavy, impractical things to wear when one was living outdoors. Often she had to wade out into the river to empty an eeltrap, or kneel on the ground to pound a herbal mixture. Her stockings were already heavily darned, and would not last many more wears. She would need them, though, when the winter came, if she were still here.

She envied the Maoris their easy acceptance of their own bodies—clothing was worn only for warmth or adornment; if it was easier to work or fish naked, then they discarded their clothes without hesitation. Thomas had at first tried to shield Emma's eyes from the sight of large men calmly working in the *kumara* gardens without a stitch on, but she had soon grown used to it, and could not but think of it as most sensible. She had made Rima a couple of little shifts, one for day and one for nightwear, although the child wore them only when she was with Emma—they would have been torn from her back if she had dared to wear them to the *pa*. Emma supposed that she should try to put the women into something more decent, but she had brought very little material with her. Besides, how could she say to these women that their beautiful strong bodies were something to be ashamed of, and should be hidden? Thomas had had no qualms about saying exactly that but—as in so many things, she thought sadly—she lacked his convictions.

She threw a guilty look at Thomas's grave. She had been a widow for seven weeks now, and had still to shed a tear. It was true that there had been no love in their marriage, but she had committed her life to her husband, and she should be grieving for her loss. Was she really so shallow and selfish that she could not even cry for Thomas?

'So, Hemma, you have legs,' said an amused male voice in Maori. Emma blushed violently and pulled down her skirt—she had not heard Tawhai approach over the racket of the cicadas. She went to stand but already he had settled himself companionably beside her, his arms crossed over his knees. He nodded thoughtfully. 'You have legs, you are a woman. I was not sure—under your…' He brought his hands out to his sides.

'"Dress".' Emma shifted uneasily. What on earth could Tawhai want from her, that he should seek her out alone like this?

'Dress. Ah.' The chief nodded again and looked down, beyond the trees, to the river where it flowed on relentlessly, with a powerful life of its own. The heat shimmered in waves above it, like a twin river. 'So now I learn your language, just as you learn ours. Do you know the name of the water there?'

'*Whanganui,*' she said. It meant 'The big wait'.

'Do you know why it is called thus?' he asked. She shook her head. 'Ah. The great chief Hau was pursuing his wife Wairaka, who had been unfaithful to him. When he came to the water here he did not know how to cross. He thought, too wide to swim, too deep to wade. I will wait for the water to turn.' Tawhai smiled. 'A big wait, eh?'

Emma chuckled. 'And did he find his wife, Tawhai?'

'Yes. He found her by the sea, a long way from here. He made her go into the water to fetch him *paua* to eat, and when she did so he turned her into a rock. She stands there still, as a reminder to all wives that they belong to their husbands.'

Emma sat very still. This was the Maori way, she knew—their laws, their history, were all derived from an oral tradition of story-telling, and Tawhai was using the ancient myth as a warning. But of what, exactly? The chief said nothing more, only stretching himself out in the sunlight with a grunt of satisfaction, like some great brown cat. The silence stretched on until she could stand it no more.

'Tawhai, my husband is dead. Why have you told me the story?'

The chief opened one lazy eye and looked at her. 'Is it not a good story, Hemma?'

'Yes, but you told it to me for a reason,' she said doggedly.

'Ah.' Tawhai closed his eye again, 'You are a woman without a man.'

'Yes…' Emma said dubiously.

'You need a man,' Tawhai said firmly.

'No, I don't,' Emma said just as firmly.

He pushed himself upright and looked at her in surprise. 'You need a man,' he repeated, and used a word she had never heard before. At her blank look he extended his hand and made an explicit motion in the direction of her skirts, one that left her in no doubt at all about what he meant. She felt her face scorch, and yet there had been no obscenity intended in his gesture. 'You need a man,' he repeated, simply.

She wet her lips and found her voice again. 'I...I am in mourning for my husband, Tawhai.'

'Ah, yes. The God Man.' There was another long pause, while Tawhai plucked a blade of grass and began to pick at his teeth. Emma gained the distinct impression that the real reason for the chief's visit was about to be revealed. 'There is another white God Man I have heard of,' he said at last. 'He is living where the river meets the sea.'

Emma's heart skipped a beat. Another missionary? A man who could take over from where Thomas had left off?

'This God of yours, he is greater than all the others, this man says. Is this true?'

'Yes.'

'Ah. You will teach us the ways of this God? How to please him?'

'I could,' Emma said hesitantly. 'But I think it would be much better if the other missionary could come and tell you—'

'No!' Tawhai slammed his fist down, making her jump. 'No, Hemma, there is no time. One day soon the Ngati Tuwharetoa come down the river to do battle. We need your God on our side if we are to win. You understand?'

She stared at him in dismay. 'Tawhai, that is not how it is—'

'Hemma, that is how it is. This God that you tell us is the greatest God, he will win the battle for us, eh? You come and tell me tonight how we worship him, so that he will lend strength to our arms and give us victory.'

'But, Tawhai—'

'Tonight, Hemma. I will hear no more argument.' He got to his feet and began to walk away. Passing her little *whare*, however, he slowed, then stopped. 'Hemma? What are these things?'

She had washed her undergarments that morning, and now they lay spread over the bushes, drying in the sun. He fingered the fine material of her chemise, picked up the heavy square that was her corset. His face puckered in a frown of curiosity.

'My…my clothes,' she managed, resisting the impulse to grab the garments from his prying fingers.

'Ah. And this?' He held up the corset. 'What is in this?'

'Bones. From a very big fish, called a whale,' she said.

'Whale.' He tried the unfamiliar name on his tongue. 'Ah. A *taniwha*?'

The *taniwha* were magical monsters of the deep, great fish-spirits that possessed wonderful powers of good and evil. The river was filled with them, according to the Maoris, and they must be avoided or appeased according to tradition if the river was to

be travelled in safety. Emma tried hard to think of
another description of a whale, but the right words
failed to come to mind. After a moment she nodded.

'Yes, from a *taniwha*. Well, a kind of a *taniwha…*'

'Ah.' He smoothed the corset with an envious
hand. '*Taniwha*. I like this.' She said nothing as he
waited and at last he put it regretfully back down
across the bush. 'Tonight you come and teach us,
eh?' And away he went, leaving Emma with her
mouth agape.

What would Thomas have done? She went over
to the little wooden cross on his grave and placed
her hand on it, hoping for some sort of direction.
She knew nothing about teaching the bible—that
had been her husband's work. She was only a wife,
useful for her labour and her healing skills. That was
all. How could she set about converting a tribe, especially when their sole motivation for learning
about Christianity was to give themselves an advantage over their enemies? She should have known
better—the Maori were a proud, aggressive race, to
whom warfare was as natural as eating and sleeping.
Old slights, ancient grievances, were nurtured and
remembered even under the guise of friendship, and
retribution was always taken. Oh, she had been
crazy to have stayed on here! She should have taken
Kahu's advice at the very beginning and fled back
down the river to the town of Whanganui, where
there were other Europeans and some degree of protection!

But it was too late now for such regrets. Tawhai

would be unlikely to let her go now, while he thought she could be of such use to him.

She slumped down on Thomas's grave in despair. What had she got herself into?

Chapter Two

Ben studied the *pa* on top of the cliff with growing unease. From down here on the river the palisades looked huge, great walls of wood that spiked the sky. The other settlements downriver had been peaceful enough, although the inhabitants had come running out to stand on the riverbanks and stare at the big canoe as it passed. Some had waved, some had called out to them, but no one had made any move to impede their steady progress up the river. At night his Maori crew had pulled ashore, choosing deserted stretches of riverbank rather than settlements, and they had never had any problems. But this *pa* was built for war.

He quickly estimated the height of the hill and sketched it, before securing his survey map in the waterproof bundle under his feet that contained all his instruments. There was tension evident in the backs of the rowers in front of him, and they had picked up speed—something told him that he might need both hands free in the next few minutes.

A quick pat of his jacket pockets reassured him

that his revolvers were still there—only one shot apiece, unfortunately, but he hoped that even that would be enough.

'Eru,' he said quietly to the sturdy rower alongside him, 'what is the problem?'

'Problem?' Eruera shrugged. 'This is a bad tribe, like to fight. They get hold of you, you end up in the cooking pot.' He grinned broadly, although his face was strained. 'You scared, eh, *pakeha*?'

'What do you think?' Ben picked up a paddle. 'Let's get past here as fast as we can.'

But already they had been spotted and a warning shout echoed across the river. Almost at once a horde of people poured from the gates of the *pa* and down the hillside to where canoes were tied up at the river's edge.

'Speed up!' Ben shouted to the crew, but enough of them had already decided to turn back to ensure that the canoe did nothing but start to spin slowly around. Within minutes they were surrounded by the canoes from the *pa*. They might be friendly, Ben kept telling himself optimistically, resisting the urge to produce his weapons. He smiled and nodded and tried to look relaxed—until a warrior in a canoe alongside gave a mighty shout and clubbed the rower sitting directly in front of Ben. His body fell into the water with a splash.

'You bastards!' Ben yelled, and started to stand up. Eruera tugged him back down into the canoe.

'Quiet, Ben! It is not you they want!'

'But…'

'Quiet!'

Against all his instincts Ben stayed sitting until

his canoe was towed to the bank. There were maybe a hundred Maoris on the bank now—warriors, old men, women, children… Not one of them looked or sounded remotely friendly.

'Can you tell them we only want to pass by in peace,' he shouted above the noise. 'Tell them we mean them no harm, we only want to go upriver.' Looking doubtful, Eruera began to rise to his feet, but had spoken no more than a single word before a spear was thrust forcefully upwards through his throat. He gave a horrible gurgle and toppled heavily across Ben's knees and into the water.

Oh Lord, Ben thought, I'm next. His fingers closed over the revolver and he fired a single shot into the air. Like magic, the crowd backed off, all eyes riveted to the gun in his hand. He held it up for them to see. He knew it was highly unlikely that any of this tribe had seen a gun before—if he could keep them afraid of it, at least until he and what was left of the crew could get away…

A movement on the hill caught his eye. Someone running down fast towards them, pushing through the crowd. Ben stared at the apparition in amazement. It's a woman, he thought blankly, a woman in European clothes. No—it was a European woman! Middle-aged from what he could see of her face under the shading bonnet, rather dumpy… He caught the glint of a crucifix swinging free from the ample folds of her black-draped bosom. There must be a mission here of the French nuns whom he knew to have established themselves in the northern part of New Zealand. Well, that was a stroke of luck! The men beside him shifted uneasily in warning.

Sure enough, the warriors on the shore had begun
to surge forward again. At least three spears were
aimed directly at his heart, the others ready to pick
off his terrified, unarmed crew.

'You!' he said quickly. 'Do you speak English or
French?'

'I'm English,' the woman said, her voice breathless and well-spoken. 'Please, I beg you! Put away
those guns! Don't you understand what you're doing?'

He risked a quick glance of surprise at her before
realising that from where she stood she could not
see Eruera floating face-down in the river, his body
trapped between the canoe and the riverbank. Short
of a miracle, he and the rest of the crew would be
lying there too in a matter of minutes. He took a
deep breath and steadied his remaining loaded revolver. His hands felt cold, the metal too slick in
his wet palms. One wrong move, one second's in-
attention...

'Do you speak their language?' he demanded.

The nun moved forward, her hand outstretched.
'Please give me your guns,' she said in the same
calm, matter-of-fact voice that she might use to a
recalcitrant child. 'I don't think you know how
much harm you can do here. Believe me, these people will not hurt you.' Behind her, a warrior took
careful aim at Ben's heart with his spear.

'I'm not putting down my guns,' Ben said tersely.
'If you can speak their language, tell them to get
back. Now!'

'But there are children here, and...'

'Listen, lady, I don't give a damn about the children. Just tell them to back off or I'll shoot. D'you understand?'

Her mouth shut tight. Her face, under the ugly black bonnet, went white. 'How many shots do you have left? One? You can't kill all of them with just one bullet. Do you want me to tell them that? I will, unless you put your guns down.'

'You bitch,' Ben said under his breath. She was over ten paces away. If he leapt ashore and grabbed her, held the gun to her head, would the savages back off? For a moment he contemplated doing it. But if the canoe shifted under him at the crucial moment, if she backed away, then his only advantage would be lost. And what if the savages couldn't care less what happened to his white hostage? That was a very real possibility.

He had no choice.

'Ah well, what the hell…' he muttered and very, very slowly replaced his pistols inside his jacket. The woman gave a small nod of approval before turning to speak to the warrior beside her. The Maori answered rapidly, shaking his spear in emphasis in Ben's direction, and she turned back to him with a frown.

'You have someone with you from another tribe. I don't quite understand why they are so angry with him, but his tribe have taken something from this tribe…'

'Heads,' Ben said abruptly, inwardly cursing his carelessness. He looked down the length of his canoe. All his rowers were afraid but one of them, a small wiry man he had brought up with him from Kapiti, was rigid, his eyes glazed with terror. 'It's you, isn't it?' Ben said softly. 'You're the one. Well, you'd better get going. Right now.'

The man dived over the side of the canoe, striking out wildly as the current dragged him swiftly downstream. With a great shout the people on the shore, even the children, surged forward into the water after him. As they did so Ben took careful aim with his pistol just above the bobbing head and fired. The swimmer threw up his arms and sank beneath the water as the current swept him around the bend and out of sight.

'I've killed him,' Ben told the woman. 'Tell them that.'

'How could you?' she said hoarsely. 'To shoot a man like that, a defenceless man trying to get away. He'd committed no crime…'

'He was from a tribe that has headhunted from around here. Obviously that's crime enough to these people,' Ben snapped. 'Tell them that I've killed him, dammit! Now, before they jump in and try to capture him!'

Her eyes widened in comprehension and she turned to the tribe, her voice raised over the hubbub, waving her arms in the air to attract attention. Those already in the water began to scramble back onto the shore. She was obviously held in high regard, Ben realised, despite her lunacy; he could have used her as a hostage after all. He wondered if all the other nuns were as bloody-minded as this one. The woman turned back to face him.

'You must come ashore. Your men are safe, and the chief has promised me that you will not be harmed either.'

He eyed the warriors on the riverbank. They looked no less dangerous than they had a minute before. 'All I want is to be allowed to continue up-river. If they'll just let go of the canoe, we'll be on our way.'

'No.' She shook her head emphatically. 'Tawhai wants to speak with you. You must come ashore.' Then, as he opened his mouth to argue, she added, 'I've told them that you have no more bullets left.'

'You've what?' he demanded incredulously.

'You haven't, have you? Not in your pistols, any-way. I suggest you come ashore immediately. To delay any longer will make them suspicious and of-fend Tawhai. Believe me, they mean you no harm.'

'No?' he said, with a cynical lift of his brow. He nodded towards where Eruera's body bobbed in the current, his blood streaking the water darkly. 'And what about him?'

She looked and then screamed, her hands flying to her mouth. 'Oh, my Lord!'

After that, everything happened too fast. Taking advantage of the distraction that the nun's scream created, the men in the canoe thrust themselves away from shore, using their long oars to shove against the bank. The sudden lurch under his feet made Ben lose his balance, and for a moment the sky, the trees, the river lurched in a wild circle be-fore his eyes. He heard rather than felt the crack of his head against the wooden side of the canoe…and then there was nothing but blackness and the rush-ing of water—or blood—in his ears.

A long time later he slowly awoke to other sen-sations. Something comfortable underneath him, the soft rustling of leaves above him, a woman's gentle, deft touch as she lifted his head from the ground. He lay somewhere between sleep and conscious- ness, unable to remember what had happened, un- able to open his eyes. The woman…yes, it was a woman. He could smell the sweet, sun-kissed fe- male scent of her skin. Her hands were gentle as no man's could be, and her slight intake of breath as she carefully moved his head was the most feminine sound imaginable. As she lifted him her breast pressed momentarily against his cheek and he wished he had the strength to turn his mouth against its soft firmness. Through the dark haziness of his mind, the desire to see what this ministering angel looked like grew compellingly strong. It took an al- mighty effort to raise his eyelids.

The darkness cleared to reveal a dappled roof of leaves against the clear, blue sky. And, watching him, a pair of serene, green eyes.

'You're beautiful,' he told her. The angel's lips curved into a smile, changing the flawless oval of her face into something even more perfect. To his wonderment Ben found that his hand was obeying him as he reached up and touched the smooth cheek, inches from his face. Then he slid his fingers behind her neck and brought her face closer. His lips brushed hers so very gently…before the angel pulled back with a gasp and Ben's head hit the ground hard.

'Ouch!' The pain at the back of his skull rever- berated through his body.

'I'm sorry, but you shouldn't have done that,' a

voice said severely, and Ben watched aghast as the angel transformed into the nun. Obviously embarrassed, she picked up her hideous black bonnet and began to stuff the glorious red fire of her hair under its folds. He moaned aloud in protest and she stopped at once, a frown marring her forehead. 'Are you in much pain?'

'Yes,' he muttered, although in truth the pain was receding now to nothing more than a dull throb. But he did not want her to leave him. She might be a nun, but the bulky black gown could not entirely obscure the lush curves beneath, and even her stern expression sat oddly on a face made for passion. It was her bottom lip, he decided. Sensuous and full of promise… What a waste, to be buried out here in the wilderness when she could be gracing the bed of any man she chose. His, for example… He closed his eyes to block out the sudden and all-too-clear image of her spread wantonly beneath him.

'What happened to me?'

'You hit your head on the side of the canoe as you fell into the water. From what I can make out, you have a shallow cut and some bruising.' She was observing his reactions carefully as she added, 'Do you remember anything of that?'

'No.'

'You will, in time, I'm sure.' She raised her hand. 'How many fingers am I holding up?'

He opened his eyes again and looked. 'Three.'

'Good. You're focussing well and your co-ordination seems unimpaired.' She flushed slightly, looking at his lips. 'Do…do you remember being in a canoe? You were stopped along the river-bank, and two of your men were killed.'

'God, yes, I remember!' He went to sit up and groaned at his protesting body. 'The others…?'

'The others in the canoe got away downstream,' she soothed. 'The tribe gave chase, but fortunately had no chance to catch up with them.'

'Damn,' he said. 'Damn and blast.'

She blinked. 'They'll be halfway to the coast by now, at the rate they were travelling. I'm sure they'll be quite safe.'

'Oh, I'm sure they'll be safe enough, gutless bastards that they are,' Ben snapped. 'It's my equipment I wanted. I suppose it's lying at the bottom of the river by now.'

Her wonderful, kissable lips compressed into a disapproving line. 'Was it a long, thin package?'

'That's it. How did you…?'

'Your men threw it overboard as they left. I have it safely in my hut, although I'm afraid it got rather wet. I haven't had a chance to see what kind of condition it's in, though, I'm sorry.'

His shoulders slumped in relief. 'It'll be all right. It's all wrapped in sealskin.' He could see that he had upset her, and so gave her the special smile that always worked on women. 'Thank you. Thank you for everything.'

It worked on her. She flushed and looked away, charming in her innocence. 'I've done nothing, simply bandaged a little cut on your head, that's all.'

'I suspect you've done a great deal more than that, and I'm grateful. I owe you my life,' he said softly. He stirred and became aware for the first time

of the harsh abrasion of woollen blanket on bare
skin. 'My clothes. What happened to them? Did
you...?'

'The warriors who brought you up here undressed
you,' she cut in quickly. 'Your clothes were soaking.'

'Oh?' He grinned wryly. 'That'll be the last I'll
ever see of them, then.'

She gurgled with laughter and somewhere in
Ben's mind a memory prodded uncomfortably. Another woman had laughed in such a way, deep in
her throat—a sensual, earthy laughter that had
stirred his senses...

'No, I have them safe, and almost dry now, although I admit that I had to argue for their return!'

He touched her arm as she turned away. 'I do
know you, don't I? We've met before.'

'No.' She shook her head. 'We've never met.'

'I think we have.'

'No!' she said sharply, her voice rising.

'How can you be so sure?' Ben persisted, curious
now.

'Because I would have remembered you,' she replied and then broke off, a becoming flush rising
from her collar. 'I mean...well, I don't even know
your name, do I?'

'Ben. Benedict Morgan.'

The woman lowered her eyes and deliberately
moved her arm from under his fingers as if he were
unclean. 'Mr Morgan. My name is Mrs Johnson.'

'Mrs!' He stared at her. 'Then you're not...'

She waited. 'Not what?'

A slow smile lifted the corners of his mouth. 'It

doesn't matter. So—what brings you all the way out here, Mrs Johnson?'

She bent her head and began to wind up a length of unused bandage at lightning speed. 'My husband and I came here to establish a mission. Now, Mr Morgan, would you like something to drink? I have some boiled water, or perhaps you would prefer tea? It's not the real thing, I'm afraid, but quite palatable…'

'Sydney,' Ben said suddenly. 'That's where we met, I'm sure of it.'

The woman visibly paled. 'No, you're quite mistaken. I've never been to New South Wales. Please—lie still for a while and I'll bring you something to drink.' She got to her feet, almost stumbling over the heavy folds of her dress in her haste to be gone, and hurried away out of his vision. Ben settled back against the blankets. That had been stupid of him. He hadn't meant to imply that the missionary's wife was some Sydney-side lightskirt, but that was plainly how she had taken it. He must have hit his head harder than he had thought to have made such a blunder.

There had been so many women over the years, and he hadn't always been sober enough to take in their faces, let alone their names, but he would have remembered a face like hers for certain. So gentle and innocent and good, untouched by the grime of experience… Hell, she would have stood out a mile on the Sydney docks! Still, some small, elusive memory nagged away in his subconscious, something he knew he should remember. His head began to ache with the effort. Well, it was of no consequence; no doubt he would recall in time whatever or whoever it was that the missionary's prim and proper wife reminded him of.

He carefully turned his head and watched her standing motionless by the fire. Even the hideous black bonnet and dress could not hide the perfect lines of her face and voluptuously feminine body from his practised eye. She was a lovely little thing, and the sixth sense he could always draw upon when it came to women told him that there were depths of sensuality there that he could easily tap into. For a second he toyed with the idea of pursuing her. A little light dalliance... She might welcome a bit of fun, imprisoned as she was out here. But he dismissed the thought as swiftly as it had arisen. She would succumb quickly enough, of course—they always did—but it wasn't worth the risk. He needed the assistance of these missionaries much more than he needed a quick roll with the missionary's wife. Besides, for all her earthly promise, she could well prove to be a disappointment—how did one set about corrupting an angel, with a face like that of a stained-glass saint? Poor woman, he thought in amusement, as he closed his eyes. If only she knew what a sinner she gave succour to...

He knew! He knew about her! Emma felt as if her lungs would burst from her chest with the tight constriction of panic. Of all the people to meet here, of all the places on Earth, why someone who knew her? He would remember in time, she was sure of that. And then... Oh Lord, what could she do? What would he do? What would he expect of her? The can of water slipped from her unsteady fingers and she stood staring blindly at the streaks of water soaking into the dry ground.

Nothing. He could do nothing to her. The wild thumping of her heart slowed and steadied as she began to reason it out. What could he prove? Even if he was right, even if he had known her in Sydney, he would never be able to prove it. It had been a bare-faced lie, certainly, but she had been right to deny to him that she had ever set foot in New South Wales. She was the respectable widow of a missionary, and this was nothing more than a test of her courage and resolve. Besides, as soon as he was recovered, he would be on his way and she would never see him again.

Unless... She held her breath, scarcely daring to form the thought in her mind. What if she went back with him? Why, in Whanganui she would be sure of finding a ship back to Sydney! For one long, thrilling moment the memories warmed her. She missed her house so much, the beautiful house that Thomas had brought her to as his bride. And how she would love to see her little sisters again, to make sure that they were happy in the foster home she had found for them. She even missed Charlotte. Thomas had banned her eldest sister from his house after their marriage, but she would love to go back and set things right between them, to put the past behind them once and for all.

Absently, Emma scooped up another billycan of water from the pail and set it over the fire. Yes, leaving here would solve all her problems!

'You are sad, Hemma?'

'What?' Emma started at Rima's high voice beside her. After only a few minutes of conversation with a man of her own race the Maori words returned with an effort to her lips. 'Oh, no, Rima, I'm not sad.'

'But you are frowning. It is the white man, eh? He makes you angry? Was it what he did to your face—that strange thing?'

'Strange thing…?' Comprehension dawned and she laughed to hide her embarrassment. 'Oh. That was what we call a "kiss", Rima. You know how when your people greet each other you press your noses together in a *hongi*? Well, white people press their lips together instead. Sometimes.'

Rima screwed up her face in disgust. 'Eeeeh!'

'Yes, I suppose it is,' Emma said thoughtfully. She added some more twigs to the fire and sat back, pulling Rima's warm little body against her own. As she sat there, staring into the flames, the enormity of the dilemma she faced dawned on her. She would have to leave Rima here, as well as the child she was treating for a skin infection, and the woman who was due to have a breech birth any day now. If there was going to be a battle with another tribe, there would most certainly be many injuries to attend to. And then there was the promise she had made to Thomas. How could she desert these people, when they had taken her in and treated her like one of their own? When they needed her so much? She sighed and then managed a smile for Rima.

'You were right, after all, Rima. I am sad.'

'It is the white man, eh, Hemma? I don't like him.'

'No? Why don't you like him?'

Rima darted a quick look at the man across the clearing. He looked to be asleep, his harsh profile turned away from them. 'He has strange eyes.'

'His eyes are light blue,' she explained. 'In my country—England—only some people have beautiful brown eyes like yours. Lots of other people have grey eyes, or green—like mine—or blue...' But not that ice colour, she thought. Pale and yet intense, the coldest eyes she had ever seen.

Rima shook her head firmly. 'His face says one thing, his eyes say another thing. He does not care for anyone but himself, Hemma.'

As if he heard and understood them, Ben stirred and threw one arm free from the restricting blankets. He was powerfully built, a man who had spent perhaps his entire life in manual labour. The joking comments the warriors had made about his size had been so obscene that Emma had been forced to busy herself elsewhere while he was being undressed, but there was no denying that he was a big man. He frightened her, physically and emotionally, and she wanted nothing more than to see him gone.

As if in protection she gathered Rima close. 'You're right, little one. You're very clever.'

The child twisted in her arms to stare up at her. 'Clever?'

'Yes, because you've made up my mind for me.' She laughed and pulled Rima's hair over her puzzled little face. 'Now, go and collect *manuka*, Rima. I want to make Mr Morgan some tea before he leaves us.'

Chapter Three

Mr Morgan slept on through the afternoon, so still that several times Emma bent low over him to check his breathing. A short negotiation with Tawhai ensured that a canoe was made ready for him and it lay tied up and waiting, together with his dried clothes and a few provisions. The mysterious package that was so important to him was still in her *whare*, safe from curious fingers until Mr Morgan left.

'His weapons,' Tawhai had said flatly. 'They stay.'

'But they are useless without the ammunition,' Emma protested. With a casualness that she was far from feeling she picked up one of the pistols from the mat in front of Tawhai. 'Look. I pull the trigger, so. And nothing. They don't work, Tawhai, not without the powder and the balls that go inside them.'

Tawhai grunted and examined the other pistol. 'Then we need this "ammunition". Ask him where it is.'

Emma shook her head. 'He has none left. If he had, do you not think he would have used it? No, Tawhai, the guns are useless to you now.'

'Hmm.' He thought for a moment, weighing the heavy pistol in his hand. 'Then I will keep the weapons for giving him a new canoe.'

'But, Tawhai, the pistols belong to Mr Morgan!' Emma said desperately. The chief grinned at her.

'What does it matter, if they are useless now, eh, Hemma? Of course, if he finds that he had some ''ammunition'' left…'

He was much too pleased with himself to listen to Emma's common sense. Heavy-hearted, she returned to her patient. The day was beginning to close in, and soon it would be too dark to send Mr Morgan on his way, and he would have to spend the night. She didn't want that.

She knelt beside him. 'Mr Morgan? Mr Morgan, wake up.'

When he did not stir, she rapped hard at the rug covering his chest. Still he did not wake up. With a sigh she sat back on her haunches and studied him in exasperation.

She guessed Mr Morgan to be somewhere around thirty. He was passably good-looking, she supposed. Not in the conventional manner, but she could imagine that some women would find him attractive. He was darkly tanned for a white man, with the kind of tropical tan that distinguished the men who worked in New South Wales's harsh interior lands. But he had not been there recently—his eyelashes were dark and only the ends of his hair were bleached almost white. He was in dire need of a haircut, although his smooth chin indicated an excess of vanity—Thomas had required only that Emma give his beard and hair a quick trim every month or so; more than that required constant preening in mirrors and was therefore unmanly.

Her medically trained eyes detected a slight thickening at the bridge of his nose—it had been broken at least once—and a barely distinguishable network of scars on his forehead looked suspiciously as if a smashed bottle had been ground into his face at some stage. He had a distinctive way of speaking, with his mouth closed and tight, and yet when he had smiled at her—oh, so confidently!—she had noticed that one of his front teeth had been chipped.

So, he was an outdoors man. And a brawler. And a womaniser. With her index finger she prodded him unchristianly hard in the ribs.

He sat bolt upright, taking her by surprise.

'What?' The pale eyes focussed on her. 'Oh, Mrs…Johnson.'

'Mr Morgan,' she acknowledged tightly. 'How do you feel?'

'Much better.' He ran his hand cautiously over his bandaged head and she averted her eyes as the blanket slipped to his waist. 'Have I been asleep for long?'

'A few hours. While you were asleep I dried your clothes for you, and a canoe has been prepared. You can leave as soon as you wish.'

'Thank you,' he muttered, making no effort to move. He was still pale under his tan, she noticed with a twinge of guilt at forcing him to leave so soon after his accident. He looked past her to the campfire where her dinner simmered. 'Is that chicken stew?'

'Pukakho,' she corrected him automatically and then hesitated. To send him off in such haste that she did not even offer him a meal would surely be a mistake. Less than graciously she said, 'I…I suppose you would like some dinner before you leave, Mr Morgan?' She sounded too abrupt, she realised at once. She did not want to make him suspicious.

He began to struggle to his feet and she kept her hands behind her back, resisting the impulse to help him even when he staggered. He stood for a moment, knotting the blanket around his waist, waiting for the world to stop spinning around him.

'This friend of yours—the chief—he wanted to see me before I left, didn't he? I've got a few things I want to say to him, in any case. And I must thank your husband for your kindness. Where is he?'

'He's…' Her eyes darted to the small, *rata*-adorned cross at the edge of the clearing. She should have pulled the thing out while Mr Morgan was asleep, she thought, and then was appalled at herself for the very thought. 'He's not able to see you, I'm afraid. Look, here are your clothes—' she seized them from the ground and threw them into his arms '—and if you put them on and have something to eat, I'll take you to see Tawhai. Then you can leave.'

Hurriedly she turned her back on him and bent over the fire to ladle out some stew. It was imperative that she be rid of him as soon as possible! In her haste the ladle clanked against the edge of the bowl and a splatter of hot stew burnt her wrist. She dropped the ladle in the stewpot and knelt back, sucking her burnt skin and blinking back sharp tears of pain.

'Mrs Johnson?' he said quietly, from a few inches behind her. 'What is the matter?'

She swallowed hard. 'Nothing, Mr Morgan.'

He took the bowl from her shaking hand and placed it to the side of the fire. 'Why can't I see your husband, Mrs Johnson?' He was so close that she could feel his breath on the back of her neck. His voice was gentle, but there was a thread of insistence beneath it that terrified her.

'Because he is…unavailable,' she got out somehow.

'Unavailable…permanently?' He jerked his head towards the cross in the clearing. 'Is that him?'

She nodded tightly as she fought an absurd compulsion to cry.

'Are you alone here, Mrs Johnson?'

She nodded again. There was a long silence, filled only by the quiet roar of the river and the sounds of the birds nesting for sleep. Finally Ben turned away, shaking his head.

'This is unbelievable,' he said flatly.

The memory of the fear and confusion she had felt at the time of Thomas's death suddenly welled up inside her and now no amount of blinking would stop the hot tears smarting in her eyes. 'It was a quick death, and he died believing in what he was doing…'

'He was a madman.'

Her jaw dropped. 'I beg your pardon?'

'And what the blazes did the Missionary Society

think they were doing, sending you all the way up here alone? Nobody's been this far upriver before— maybe only a trader or two, and not all of those made it back out again! So why did they think that you two would have any chance of surviving, let alone setting up a mission?'

Emma swallowed hard. 'My husband did not completely agree with the direction that the Missionary Society was taking. He was a *fine* man, Mr Morgan, a *good* man.'

'Then I have to admire your loyalty, if not your intelligence, Mrs Johnson. Do you have children?'

'No.'

He looked at her steadily, analysing her white face. His eyes dropped to the voluminous skirts gathered about her as she knelt.

'Are you expecting?'

'*No!*' she spluttered indignantly. Good heavens, was nothing sacred from this man? He stood there, demanding the most personal information about her and yet, to her horror, she heard herself stammering on in self-justification, 'We...well, we were only married for a year. It wasn't long enough...'

'Obviously not.' He abruptly walked away to look down to where the river rolled by into the gathering dusk. He was still wearing nothing but the blanket knotted around his hips and—as used as she was to Maori warriors wandering around naked— Emma found her eyes drawn to the long sinews of his back, the hard-packed muscles of his shoulders and arms. Despite his brawler's face, his body was a study of male perfection, so different to Thomas's pale thinness. Not that she had ever seen Thomas undressed, even in intimacy... She gave a small, inaudible gasp of horror and turned away, her face scarlet at the direction of her thoughts.

'Mr Morgan, would you mind dressing, please, sir?'

He turned with a frown, his thoughts obviously elsewhere.

'What? Oh...yes. I'm sorry.' He picked up his shirt and began to pull it on. Out of the corner of her eye she could see him still watching her.

'So,' he said. 'You've been here...how long?'

'Almost two months now.'

'And your husband died...?'

'A week after we arrived here. From some sort of fever.' As she watched his lips twist in derision she clenched her fists. 'At least he died doing what he believed in! I'm sure you have no comprehension of what that means, but it's true, none the less. Oh, I know what you're thinking! But how dare you belittle him, just because he might have made an error of judgement! And what about you? Two men died today because you were foolish enough to choose your crew from a warring tribe! They might still be alive if you...'

'D'you think I don't know that?' he flared at her. 'One of those men was my closest friend, and his death is something I'll have to learn to live with. I had no idea what the situation is like up here. I don't speak Maori...' He broke off, his eyes lighting with sudden intensity. 'But you do, don't you?'

She shrank back, wishing she had never spoken. 'A little, perhaps...'

'Rather more than a little, madam. You're as fluent as any European I've ever heard.' He nodded slowly. 'So that's the solution. You can come with me upriver. If this chief of yours can lend me a canoe—'

'No!' she burst out, horrified. 'I won't! I can't!'

'Why won't you?'

'Because…' She hesitated. Because even had she wanted to—which God alone knew she did not!— Tawhai wouldn't let her go. But she knew she couldn't tell Ben about the Ngati Tuwharetoa's planned invasion; then he would be even more insistent that she accompany him. She took a deep breath. 'Because I can't leave these people, Mr Morgan.'

'Why not?'

'Because my skills are needed here. I heal their sores, tend their illnesses…'

'With all due respect, madam, I'm sure they were doing very nicely for themselves before you and husband came along to interfere in their lives.' He stared down at her obstinate face in irritation. 'Can't you see that you can't stay here? There'll be other missionaries up here soon enough—this country seems to be swarming with well-intentioned fanatics at the moment.'

'Like those of the New Zealand Company?' Emma sprang to her feet. 'I take it that's who's employing you. You're a surveyor, aren't you, Mr Morgan? So just what are you doing here? Drawing up neat little plots so that your company can sell land that isn't theirs to would-be colonists at a tidy profit?'

She was pleased to see that her words had stung

him. His dark tan deepened as he flushed, but his eyes did not drop away from hers for a second.

'It's either the New Zealand Company or the Missionary Society who are going to own this country, Mrs Johnson. Just how much land are your people taking in the name of the Lord?'

'That's quite different! The Missionary Society has to take the land in trust for the Maori, to keep it out of the clutches of predatory companies like yours—' she broke off abruptly, aware that they were no longer alone. 'Yes, Rawhiri?' she demanded of the young Maori man squatting beside her hut. *'He aha mau?'*

Rawhiri grinned widely. 'Is this man giving you trouble, Hemma? Do you want me to split his belly for you?'

'No, thank you,' Emma said hurriedly, with a quick glance at Ben. However, he looked quite uncomprehending at the rapid exchange of Maori and began to button his trousers. 'What is it that you want, Rawhiri?'

'I have come to see if our guest is well enough to come to the *pa* now. Can he walk? Or perhaps he is so blown up with his own importance that I must carry him?' He rose slowly to his feet, mischief gleaming in his eyes, and Emma knew a moment's panic. Tawhai had been calm enough when she had last spoken to him, but Rawhiri was one of the younger, hot-headed warriors, and it would seem that the afternoon's massacre had only whetted his appetite for more blood. The impending battle with the Ngati Tuwharetoa was something that the warriors were looking forward to with great relish—the anticipation in the *pa* was almost tangible, with tempers on a hair-trigger. The two lives lost that day on the river had meant nothing, and it was possible that Ben's life would be no more important. Unless…

'You've got very pale, all of a sudden,' Ben remarked as he tucked in his shirt. 'What's the matter, Mrs Johnson?'

'The chief wants to see you now,' Emma told him, her mind still whirling with possibilities. 'Do you feel ready?'

'I certainly do.'

Rawhiri spun around to head up the track towards the *pa* and Ben followed him, walking with a sense of purpose that struck fear into Emma's heart. 'I'm looking forward to telling this Tawhai bastard what I think of him for murdering two of my men,' he flung over his shoulder. 'Are you coming along to translate for me?'

She gasped and ran after him, bundling her skirts in both hands in her haste to catch up. 'Mr Morgan! Sir! Wait!'

'Why?'

'Because you mustn't upset Tawhai! Or any of them! Your life depends on it!'

He slowed down slightly to allow her to run alongside. 'If they were going to kill me, Mrs Johnson, they've already had plenty of opportunities to do so. I'm still alive, I've still got all my body parts, and I'm still bloody furious!'

'But that's just what you mustn't be, don't you see? Things are so tense here at the moment…'

'Why? Are they preparing for war?' He disconcerted her by abruptly stopping and she almost ran into his shoulder.

'N...no! Why should you think that?' she said quickly.

'Because this lot always are. And it would account for why they were so quick off the mark in killing my crew. Look at me, Mrs Johnson.' Puzzled, she looked up and immediately regretted it as she found her eyes held in unwilling captivity. The calculation in his strange glacier-pale eyes sent a shiver down her spine.

He gave a quick nod of satisfaction. 'I thought so. You're a bad liar, Mrs Johnson. So if they're going to war, you can't stay here. You're going to have to come with me.'

Like hell I will! she thought fiercely as they walked through the *pa* gates, but it was no time to argue.

Once within the gates Ben, as a visitor, was challenged by a warrior in the ceremonial way of the Maori. Every occupant of the *pa*, it seemed, had come to watch. To Emma's relief Ben appeared to know the protocol to follow and he stood quietly enough through the challenge and subsequent welcome. Tawhai was waiting for them outside his *whare*, splendidly dressed in his chief's cloak of feathers, his eyes alight with the anticipation of barter. Before him, on a mat, lay Ben's two pistols.

To Emma's dismay Ben's patience seemed to abruptly run out at the sight of his pistols. 'I want those back,' he said, pointing to them. 'Tell him.'

Tawhai did not need an interpreter for that. 'Tell

him, Hemma, that he can have a canoe and food if he leaves me the ammunition for the guns.'

Emma looked helplessly from one implacable man to the other. 'Tawhai, I've told you he has no ammunition. The guns are useless to you.'

'Then why does he want them back?' Tawhai snarled. 'Tell him, Hemma! Tell him to give me the ammunition or I will feed him to the eels!'

'He wants the ammunition, does he?' Ben was watching the interchange intently.

'In exchange for a canoe,' Emma said carefully, wondering how she could tone down each man's demands.

'Tell him he can stuff his canoe up his...'

'Mr Morgan!' she broke in, shocked. 'You're not helping matters by shouting!'

'I'm not shouting!' he shouted. 'Just tell the thieving, murdering bastard that I want my pistols back!'

'Aiee!' With a hiss of rage Tawhai leapt to his feet, his fingers closing around the ornate club hanging from his waist. While he had not understood one word, it was plain that he had the gist of Ben's speech. 'So this is how he rewards our hospitality? I shall send him to join his friends in the river mud! I shall tear out his heart and throw it into the midden! I shall slice his nose into tiny pieces and make him eat it! Tell him, Hemma! Tell him what I shall do to him!'

'Tawhai, please!' Emma threw herself imploringly between the two men. 'Don't hurt him!'

'Why not?' Tawhai stared at her, his eyes slowly narrowing in comprehension. 'Ah. You like him?'

'Yes.' It was the opposite of the truth, but she was desperate.

'Ah.' With insulting deliberation Tawhai walked around Ben, pretending to study him from head to toe. Emma held her breath, convinced that Ben would flatten him any second. Tawhai nodded his head. 'Very well then, Hemma, if he pleases you then you may have him. He is stronger than your last man.' He waggled his club in the direction of Ben's trousers. 'Bigger, too. You can take him back to your *whare*. And perhaps then he will tell you where his ammunition is.'

'What is he saying?' Ben demanded tensely. 'Why was he waving his club at me like that?'

'It's nothing!' Emma said quickly, her face scarlet. She linked her arm through his and looked up at him appealingly. 'Please come with me now.'

His mouth thinned and he removed her fingers from his arm. 'Not without my pistols.'

'The pistols are no good to anyone without powder and shot,' she began, and then the light dawned. 'Of course! That's in your sealskin package…'

'So it is,' he said, his eyebrows rising as he pretended to be impressed at her stunning powers of deduction. 'But I'm not going to get anywhere upriver without a weapon, so just be a good girl and get my pistols back for me, will you?'

Tawhai made an impatient motion with his hand, a scowl deepening the tattoos on his forehead. 'It seems your chosen man does not want you, Hemma. I told you he was ungrateful.'

'He…he is just overcome by his good fortune.' Deciding that matters had gone quite far enough, she turned to face Ben, placing the palm of one hand on his chest with a pressure that defied him to remove it. Beneath her fingers she could feel his heart pounding fast.

'Come with me now, please, Mr Morgan,' she said firmly. 'And it would help if you put an arm around me as we leave.'

For one dreadful moment she thought he would refuse, but then she saw amusement gleam in his eyes. He slipped an arm around her waist without further ado.

'Am I your property?'

'For the time being, and for your own safety only.' She stiffened as she felt his fingers brush across her abdomen. 'There's no need to go overboard, Mr Morgan—this is only a display of affection for the chief, so that he doesn't follow his perfectly natural impulse to slit your throat.'

'Is that so?' Without warning he jerked her towards him, so that she collided against his chest. She was immediately and disconcertingly aware of a barrage of sensations—the heat of his skin under his shirt, that thin-lipped, infuriatingly smirking mouth just inches away, the hard muscular length of his body pressed against her, even through her thick skirts...

The inappropriateness of his arousal here, in this most dangerous of situations, horrified her just as much as the outrageousness of his announcement of it. She shoved him away violently.

'How dare you!'

He looked at her in wide-eyed innocence. 'I was only displaying my affection.'

Emma glanced at Tawhai but he, along with everyone else present, seemed to have understood perfectly what had just taken place between them and was grinning broadly. Abruptly deciding that she no longer gave a damn what happened to Mr Morgan, she gathered her skirts and strode out of the *pa*, her head high. So let Tawhai cut him into little pieces and throw him into the river! See if she cared! And as for his accursed ammunition, that could follow him into the water too!

Ben caught up with her as she reached her *whare*.

'Are you angry with me, Mrs Johnson? Or should I call you mistress?'

She took a deep breath as she struggled to control herself. 'Of course I'm angry! Don't you realise how close to death you came? Don't you care?'

'We've all got to go one day, Mrs Johnson.'

She stared at him, incredulous, and he stared right back.

'You're insane,' she said at last. 'I should have realised it before. I should have let them kill you and put you out of your misery.'

He looked slightly affronted at that. 'Hardly Christian of you, madam. All I wanted was my pistols back, and I was reasonably sure that your Maori friends wouldn't kill me with you around.'

'I wouldn't be so confident about that.'

'I would. Now, why don't you sit down—' he took her elbow and somehow she found herself forced on to the log of wood that served as her fireside seat '—and let your humble slave serve you your supper. That poor chicken will have died in vain if we don't eat it soon.'

'*Pukakho,*' she corrected him futilely as he stirred the pot over the fire and ladled the stew into the two waiting bowls. One of the bowls had been intended for Rima. Emma stared hard into the shadows of the trees around the clearing but could not see the child in the dark. No doubt she was hiding somewhere in the ferns, waiting until the loathed Mr Morgan had gone permanently.

'Good stew,' Ben said, scooping up the last morsels of food with his finger. In the darkness the leaping light of the fire made him look almost satanic, the blonde ends of his hair above the bandage glowing like flames. She watched him in disgust, wishing with every fibre of her being that he would simply vanish into thin air and leave her in peace again. Everything about him, everything he did, was so much larger than life, so…so excessive. She very much doubted that he would know what the word 'moderation' meant, let alone how to spell it.

'Can I have yours, if you're not going to eat it?' he asked, and she handed him her bowl in silence. She had to get rid of him as soon as possible. The only problem was that he wasn't going to go without his pistols, and the tribe was not going to let him go until Tawhai had the ammunition. Which she had. She allowed herself a small smile at the ease of the solution. Tonight, when Ben was asleep, she would take the source of all their problems from his sealskin bag and throw it in the river. Once Tawhai realised that their visitor had no ammunition to give him, then Ben could be forced to leave.

'That's better,' said Ben. He propped himself up

on one elbow and studied her. 'Yes, you look much prettier when you smile. I'd begun to think that the snarl was permanent.'

'What snarl?' she said indignantly, but he simply grinned and stretched his alarmingly huge arms behind his head. He had, it seemed, the ability to make himself at home anywhere. Rather like an annoying stray tom-cat that didn't know where it wasn't welcomed.

'So, Mrs Johnson. Tell me about yourself.'

The small knot of panic began to turn in her stomach. 'I have nothing I wish to say to you. You ridiculed everything I told you this afternoon...'

He sighed. 'Then I apologise. I guess it came as a shock, realising that you were here all alone, with no man to protect you. I'm sorry if I was rude—I really didn't mean to be.' He studied her averted profile for a moment. 'At least tell me where you're from.'

'No.'

'That accent of yours sounds like a London one.'

She hesitated as anger warred with courtesy, and then she nodded briefly. There was no harm in admitting to that much. And, despite herself, she was drawn to the warmth in his voice, the slight smile he was wearing as he watched her in the firelight. In fact, he could be positively charming when he chose to be.

'I'm from New South Wales. Ever been there?' She shook her head quickly, not trusting herself to speak.

He studied her response with close-lipped amusement. 'I'm not a convict, Mrs Johnson.'

'I didn't think you were,' she responded primly, although to be strictly honest the thought had crossed her mind, at least until she had seen his bag of surveying instruments.

'You're lying again, Mrs Johnson,' he said, the laughter apparent now in his voice.

She regarded him coolly from under lowered lashes. 'To tell the truth, I'm not in the least interested in where you're from or where you're going, Mr Morgan.'

'Fair enough—I guess it doesn't matter a damn, really. We've both ended up here.' He pulled a face at the darkening forest around them. 'Whatever this godforsaken place is called.'

'Thomas—my husband—called this place Redemption.'

'Did he? Bit rough on the people upriver, wasn't it?'

'What do you mean?'

'Well, they'd all be beyond Redemption, wouldn't they?' He started to laugh and then saw her face. 'Sorry.'

'As you should be. My husband was worth ten of you.'

'I'll take your word for it. Was he from London, too?'

'Yes.' She threw some more branches on the fire and rose to her feet. It was time this conversation was terminated.

'It's just that…I couldn't help but notice…that the cabin labels on your trunks are from Sydney.'

She felt herself go cold and she sat down again quickly. Lying had never come easily to her—

hadn't this obnoxious, prying man pointed that out to her just an hour before?

'My husband spent some years in New South Wales, I believe. But…but we met in London.' Her heart was pounding so fast that she could barely get the words out. 'It's getting late, Mr Morgan.'

'I knew a Reverend Thomas Johnson in Sydney,' Ben mused. 'He ran a ministry down by the docks, saving the souls of sailors and sluts…if you'll pardon the word, madam. That wouldn't be him, would it?'

She had to lie. She tried to lie—oh, how she tried! But her head nodded, seemingly of its own volition. To deny Thomas would have been to deny his whole life's work, and she could not do that to his memory.

'Really? So you married old Thunderbolt Tom?' He seemed caught somewhere between mirth and amazement. 'But—hell!—he was *ancient*!'

'He was a little older than me,' she allowed tightly.

'He was a little older than *God*!' He shook his head in disbelief. 'Well, I guess that explains why you haven't any children—'

'Now that's quite enough!' She leapt up, her fists clenched. 'I've had enough of your insinuations and insults for tonight, Mr Morgan!'

'I should save some for tomorrow, shouldn't I?' he agreed, getting lazily to his feet. 'So, which side of the bed do you prefer? Not that I suppose it really matters…'

She was grateful for the darkness that covered her violent blush. 'You can sleep down by the river, or in the bush, or anywhere you want to, but you are not sleeping in my hut!'

He blinked. 'But I have to. I'm your property, aren't I? Didn't you trade me for my pistols with the chief?'

So that was what he was so angry about! 'If I had a dog it would sleep outside,' she said coldly. 'And so can you, if you insist on hanging around my hut.'

He was looking quite put out, she was pleased to see—plainly he was not used to women turning him down.

'But if I sleep outside, I'll probably have a spear in my back by dawn. You wouldn't want my death on your conscience, would you?' he said plaintively.

'I could live with it.'

He shook his head sadly. 'You're a hard woman, Mrs Johnson.'

Mercifully he made no further comment as he took the bedroll she handed him and laid it out by the fire, and Emma was careful to ignore him as she made her own preparations for bed. She was satisfied that she had resoundingly put him in his place, but an uncomfortable suspicion kept nagging that his intolerable behaviour might have been due to more than just his annoyance at her failure to retrieve his pistols for him. It was almost as if he wanted to deliberately shock and provoke her.

That night she lay sleepless and tense for a long time on her bed of woven flax. Outside the occasional flap of blankets indicated that Ben was also lying awake. I wish he was gone! she thought. I wish he would just disappear overnight, so that in the morning I wouldn't have to face him and his questions and his horrible, sneering comments! Her hands were aching and she realised that she had been clenching them so hard that she had broken the skin with her nails.

To think that he had wanted to lie here, beside her, where Thomas had once lain. He had even expected that they...

She rolled over on to her stomach, squeezing her eyes shut to drive away the image of him above her. How could he? She had given him no encouragement, none at all. And yet when he had smiled at her, when the ice in his eyes had thawed just that once, when he had kissed her... It was almost as if he knew, as if he had seen through the black widow's weeds to the woman beneath.

Oh, don't be so stupid! she told herself. There was no way he could know anything about her that she didn't tell him. And the sooner he left, the less information he could prise out of her.

Comforted by her own reassurances, she was almost asleep when Rima crept in like a tiny black shadow and curled up beside her. With the child's reassuring presence against her back, she at last fell asleep.

Chapter Four

The sound of the rising wind through the trees brought her to a state of semi-consciousness. The searing flash of lightning which split the sky, followed almost immediately by a heavy *boom*! of thunder, had her wide awake and sitting bolt upright. There was a flurry of raindrops and then the rain turned into a steady tattoo on the roof of the hut. But Emma had built the hut carefully and it was covered with a heavy tarpaulin—they would remain dry and comfortable, no matter how hard it rained that night.

She relaxed and was preparing to snuggle back into Rima's familiar warmth when a huge black shape pushing its way in through the narrow doorway had her screaming in fear. Like a little feral cat, Rima hissed and lunged at the intruder, her fingers curved. There was a curse of surprise, a short struggle, and then Rima yelped in pain, a sound that made Emma feel sick as she realised what had happened.

'Stop it!' she cried, groping in the darkness as

she tried to sort out the tangle of limbs. 'Let her go!' Her fingers skimmed across the wet, naked shoulder of a man, tangled briefly in the hair on his chest, closed carefully around the tiny, trembling arm of the child. '*Haere mai*, Rima. It's all right, you're safe, little one!'

'Ouch!' Ben recoiled into the wall, and she felt the whole hut shudder. 'What is it? Some sort of an animal?'

'It's Rima,' Emma said defensively, pulling the terrified child out of harm's way. 'She's a little girl. She lives here, with me, and you don't! Get out of my hut!'

'In this rain?' As if to give emphasis to his words, there was another roar of thunder directly overhead. He was right, she supposed—he could hardly go out and spend the night under the trees in this torrential downpour. She felt for the lamp and tinderbox and a few seconds later the hut was filled with flickering light.

Apart from her obvious shock, Rima appeared to have survived the encounter unscathed. Ben, with blood dripping down his hand, had not fared so well. A neat set of teethmarks on his wrist bore testimony to Rima's ferocity.

'I should give you some salve for that,' Emma said grudgingly.

'If you please.' He jerked his head at Rima, who met his glare unflinchingly. 'By the looks of her, it'll be poisoned by dawn.'

'She was only protecting herself—and me.' Emma opened her medicine bag and placed a cloth and pot of healing salve on the mat in front of him.

Nothing on earth would make her apply it to any part of his detestable anatomy. She wrapped a blanket and then her arms around Rima, poignantly aware of the tremors that still shook the tiny, defiant frame. 'You terrified both of us, barging in like that, without a word…'

'I asked if I could come in—twice. I guess the thunder drowned me out,' he said curtly, swiping away the blood from the palm of his hand. 'What's she doing in here, anyway? Is she your servant?'

Emma looked down at the little upturned face that she had come to love so dearly.

'She's my adopted daughter,' she said after a slight pause, and the words seemed exactly right.

'Hmm.' Ben stopped swiping and opened the lid of the jar. 'And what was that you called her? Rat?'

'Rima!'

'Rat is more appropriate.' He took a dollop of salve and liberally daubed his wrist. 'Is she all right?'

'Are you all right now?' Emma asked in Maori, and when Rima nodded she smoothed the girl's hair back from her face with tender hands. 'But you terrified her horribly!' she told Ben severely.

'Good.' He screwed the lid back on the jar. 'So where is she going to sleep?'

'She sleeps here, with me.'

He was obviously about to protest, but the look on Emma's face made him think better of it.

'She can stay,' he said magnanimously. 'But I don't like children. Tell her to sleep on the other side of the mat, will you?'

It was not worth arguing about. Wordlessly

Emma arranged a wall of blankets down the middle of the sleeping mat, between her and Mr Morgan.

'Is he sleeping here?' Rima demanded in horror. 'With you?'

'He can't sleep outside in the rain, Rima.'

'Is he…is he your husband, now?'

'Rima, no!' The very thought was enough to make Emma blanch. 'But he must sleep somewhere, out of the rain. It's only for tonight, and when we lie down like this, we can't see him, can we…?'

But the slightest movement from Ben and Rima slithered over Emma's restraining arm and glared down at him from the top of the wall of blankets.

'For God's sake!' Ben complained. 'She's gnashing her teeth at me!'

'Rima, stop that!' She pulled the child back and tried to secure her with blankets. 'Let him sleep in peace.'

'But I want to kill him.'

'Well, you can't. I'm not allowing it,' Emma said firmly, pleased that their conversation was in Maori. 'Now, go to sleep.'

There was a silence of some five minutes, then— 'She's still looking at me,' Ben complained.

'Oh, for goodness sake, stop whining!' Emma sat up and turned off the lamp. 'Now no one can see anyone else. Rima, go to sleep,' she instructed in Maori. 'Mr Morgan, I don't want to hear another word from you, or I'll set Rima on you again and you'll sleep outside for the rest of the night. Is that understood?'

He made a comment that—while it did not sound in the least civil—was at least muffled by the blan-

ket over his face. She lay rigid for some time, waiting for his next move, but there was only the re-
lentless beat of the rain pounding on the roof, and
very slowly she allowed herself to relax into the soft
warmth of her bedding.

She didn't expect to go back to sleep quickly, but
she found there was something oddly familiar about
another adult body lying beside her in sleep. It
seemed that she had only just become used to sharing a bed with her husband when he had died, and
yet she had missed the feeling of…of security, she
decided it was, at last. She smiled wryly as she
drifted off to sleep. Of all the people in the world
to feel secure with, Ben Morgan would have to be
the most unlikely.

Gently, soothed by the sound of running water,
she eased into a beautiful dream. She was floating
on her back, not in the deep, cold fast-running
Whanganui but in a warm, languid, buoyant pool.
The feeling of peace was indescribable. Her limbs
felt heavy and relaxed, and as she felt the sun caressing her skin she knew that she was naked. The
knowledge did not worry her in the least—on the
contrary, she felt powerful and beautiful, like a god-
dess. Her body was sleek and strong, an instrument
of delight as the water ran over it, around it, between her thighs. Her breasts were glowing under
the warm touch of the sun's rays, they tingled and
seemed to swell, rising up voluntarily to the source
of all pleasure. Up and up, and she followed, her
mouth opening in greed…

She sat up abruptly, her heart pounding. Had she
cried out? She must have—she was sure she had,

but on either side of her Rima and Ben slept on
undisturbed. The sky lit with lightning, silent now
as the storm moved away, and in the momentary
light Emma could see that Ben was lying with his
back to her. His breathing was light and slow, that
of a man deeply asleep. Shakily she lay down again,
pulling her thin nightgown up to her chin. The top
button had come undone, and the chill air on her
chest—her chest, not her breasts, she told herself
firmly—had given her the odd sensations that had
woken her.

Even so, she slept uneasily, waking up to a still,
fine dawn. She gathered her clothes and quietly
crawled out of the *whare*. It had been her habit for
a long time now to bathe down by the river's edge
before the *pa* woke up for the day when, apart from
Rima's occasional company, her only observers
were the thousands of birds giving rowdy welcome
to the morning.

She had already taken off her nightgown when
she noticed the smear of blood on the collar. She
stared at it, while the possibilities raced through her
horrified mind. It wasn't hers or Rima's. Ben had
been the only one bleeding last night, and she hadn't
touched his injured wrist—she had been careful not
to touch him. Unless he had touched her...

He wouldn't! He wouldn't have dared! She would
have woken... But then, she had, hadn't she?

Her whole body seemed aflame with embarrassment and she scarcely felt the chill of the water as
she plunged in. She could not swim, but a fallen
tree made a safe pool for her, despite the swollen
river. When she climbed out, cold now and physi-

cally tired, it was to find Rima sitting huddled on the riverbank. Emma quickly grabbed her towel, but it was plain that Rima was alone.

'What's the matter, Rima?' Belatedly noticing the child's tear-streaked face, she knelt beside her. 'What's happened?'

'Nothing.' Rima shrugged her away.

'I see.' Emma began to pull on her clothes over her damp body. 'Does "nothing" mean Mr Morgan?'

Rima picked up a stone and began chipping erratically at the bank. 'Your husband.'

'He's not my husband, Rima. I've told you that.'

The chipping became more vicious. 'You lie with him.'

'But not…not like a husband and wife,' Emma said carefully. It was strange, talking to a child so young about such things, and yet of course Maori children knew all about birth and death and the making of babies. She could not make the mistake of treating Rima's fears lightly.

'You will lie with him like a wife, though,' Rima said savagely. She threw the stone into the river, narrowly missing Emma's face. 'He wants you to.'

'Rima, he does not—'

'Yes, he does!' Rima stormed. 'I hate him! I want to kill him!'

Emma took her by the arms, shocked to find that the child was literally shaking with rage. 'Rima, that is enough! No one is going to kill anyone else! Now, I want you to promise me that you'll leave Mr Morgan alone…'

'Then make him go! Why won't you make him

go?' The tears welling up in Rima's big brown eyes tore at Emma's heart.

'I can't make him go away,' she explained patiently.

'Do you want him to stay?'

'No, no, I don't. But I can't make him go away. He wants to go away too, Rima, but he won't go until he gets his guns back.'

Rima perked up at that. 'Guns? The loud thundersticks? Then give them back to him!'

'I haven't got them—the chief has.'

'Then ask Tawhai to give them to you so that you can give them to him.'

Emma wished life was as simple in reality as it seemed to a child. She tried to hug Rima, ignoring the stiff little shoulders. 'But even if I asked the chief, he wouldn't give them to me—they're much too valuable. Look, little one, I know you don't like Mr Morgan being here, but for the time being we have to put up with him…'

'I won't! I hate him and I hate you!' With one quick wriggle Rima slipped out of her grasp and ran away up the bank. 'I hate you!' she shouted again, over her shoulder, before disappearing into the forest.

Emma followed her slowly up the track, feeling as helpless in her way as Rima did. Life before Ben's arrival had been so uncomplicated… No, her innate honesty reminded her, it only seemed that way in retrospect. There still remained the worry of the impending battle with the Ngati Tuwharetoa. The thought of the inevitable deaths and injuries among the tribe that had made her so welcome depressed her far more than the mere irritation of Mr Morgan's presence.

There was no sign of Rima or Ben at the *whare*. Emma built up the fire and hung a billycan of chopped *kumara* over it to cook for breakfast. It was not until she was pulling out the bedrolls to air in the light that she registered that Ben's sealskin package was missing.

'Damn!' she hissed to herself. 'Damn, damn, damn!' She should have taken it down that very morning, opened it out and thrown the ammunition into the river, just as she had planned to do all along! How could she have forgotten to do so?

'Tut, tut, Mrs Johnson. Language,' Ben said breezily from where he stood at the doorway of the *whare*, watching her.

'Where is it?' she demanded, crawling out to face him.

'Where's what?'

'Your ammunition!'

'Oh, that.' He smiled. 'That's safe.'

'Where?'

'I can't tell you that.'

'Why not?'

'Because I think you were planning to throw it in the river. And if you didn't—' he nodded towards her *whare* '—then the chief would find it. They've already been in there this morning, looking for it.'

'They haven't,' she said automatically, even as she realised that that was exactly what Tawhai would do. 'But when…?'

'While you were down at the river.' He watched the colour rise over her face as the implications of that sank in. 'But you needn't concern yourself, Mrs Johnson—they won't find it where I've put it.'

'The only safe place for it is in the river,' she snapped. 'Don't you understand that? These people have never seen a gun before! Think of the damage it could do!'

He smiled politely, as if he were dealing with a difficult child. 'Look, Mrs Johnson, we're talking about my guns and my ammunition. In a couple of years—in fact, I'd make that a couple of months— I'll bet you that this tribe will be armed to the teeth, and a couple of small pistols is not going to make one hell of a difference. But, right now, it could make all the difference to my survival. And, to be perfectly honest with you, my survival is pretty important to me. Do you understand that?'

She stood in stunned silence and he nodded. 'Good. Now, how about getting me some breakfast? I'm starving.'

A shrill scream shattered the air and, with a frown, he turned to look up at the *pa*.

'By the way,' he said, 'where's Rat?'

Chapter Five

'She must die, Hemma. You know that.'

Emma's hands were clenched so tightly under her chin that they hurt, but it was the only way to stop their frantic trembling.

'Tawhai, she's only a baby! She was trying to please me by taking the pistols, I've explained that...'

'Ah, indeed?' Tawhai stared at her imperiously down his nose. 'So the pistols belong to you now, Hemma? It was not enough that I generously gave you the man you wanted, now you want the pistols as well? I am saddened beyond words!'

'I didn't mean it like that—of course they're not my pistols! I don't want them! Rima just thought that giving them to me would make me happy...' Her words trailed away as Tawhai's frown deepened. It's true that I'm a bad liar, she thought despairingly; Tawhai can tell that I'm not telling him the whole truth, but—dear God!—how can I?

At her feet, Rima cowered in the dirt outside the chief's *whare*. Her shift was torn and filthy, her eyes were glazed with fear, blood matted her hair. Every instinct in Emma's body was screaming at her to pick up the child and hold her close, yet Tawhai's huge, ornately carved wooden club hovered just inches away from Rima's head. One more blow and the little girl would be dead.

Ben strolled up behind her, his hands in his pockets.

'What's happening?' he asked, in the same tone of voice that he might enquire about the weather. Emma scarcely trusted herself not to spin around and claw his eyes out—this was, after all, his fault! Instead, she clenched her hands together even more tightly.

'Rima was caught trying to steal the pistols from the chief's *whare*. Now Tawhai is insisting that she be killed for doing so.'

Ben regarded the chief and the child with interest. 'That's reasonable enough, I suppose. Even I know that anything belonging to the chief is sacred. Even if they are my pistols in the first place…'

Emma took a deep, sobbing breath. 'If that's all you can think of, Mr Morgan, I suggest you go away and let me sort this out.'

He looked at the tears shimmering in her eyes. 'Why don't you offer him an exchange?'

'W…what?'

'What is it that he is saying now?' Tawhai thundered, eyeing Ben with dislike. 'Your new husband seems to have far too much to say for himself, Hemma!'

The knowledge that she risked the lives of all three of them if she made an error somehow kept her in control of the blind panic clutching at her insides.

'He has suggested that we trade, Tawhai. If I can exchange something of value for Rima's life…'

'Ah! Yes, indeed!' The chief looked exasperated at the length of time it had taken Emma to reach this stage of negotiations. 'The ammunition!'

She looked imploringly at Ben. 'He wants the ammunition, Mr Morgan!'

'So?'

'So give it to him, *please*! Before he kills her!'

His eyebrows lifted in mock surprise. 'And what about all the principles you were browbeating me with yesterday, madam? Are you really suggesting I jeopardise the lives of so many for the life of one child?'

'Please!' Emma choked in anguish.

Ben looked at Tawhai's triumphant expression and shook his head. 'No.'

Crestfallen, Tawhai lowered his club. 'He says no?' he demanded of Emma. 'Even though you ask it of him?'

The tears were now pouring down her face and she wiped them away viciously with the back of her hand. 'He doesn't care, Tawhai. Oh, please, don't kill her!'

Ben turned to leave and then stopped, appearing to have a thought. 'Haven't you got anything else he wants, Mrs Johnson? Really wants?' At her blank look, he added helpfully, 'None of your possessions? It's always been my experience that the Maoris are very keen on bartering.'

Inspiration struck her. 'Tawhai, my corset—my

taniwha corset. Would you take that in exchange for her life?'

The chief swung his club back and forth as he considered the offer. 'Perhaps,' he said at last. 'Until your husband gives me my ammunition. Until then…yes, I will accept it.'

'Oh, thank you, thank you! I'll go and get it now for you!' Emma spun around and ran out of the *pa* gates, back to her *whare*. Ben turned to follow her, scooping up the bedraggled child from the ground almost as an afterthought. Some of the warriors moved to bar his path, but he merely smiled at them amiably and kept on walking, Rima tucked firmly under one arm.

By the time he reached Emma's *whare* she was ready to return, the whalebone corset clutched to her bosom.

'So that's what he wanted!' He let Rima slip to her feet. 'Can you tell Rat to go and hide somewhere safe in the forest? Somewhere where no one from the tribe will find her.'

Emma brushed past him impatiently. 'Tawhai gave me his word.'

'Did he?'

Some note in his voice made her stop and look at him uncertainly. 'He said that he would spare her life until…' She knelt and brushed the hair back from Rima's face, her heart aching at both the gash on the child's forehead and her stolid acceptance of her fate. The thought of how close Rima had come to death had shaken her immeasurably; she was shocked to realise how much more than her husband's actual death. Common sense told her to wrap the child up warmly, to clean and bandage her fore-head. Instinct told her that Mr Morgan could well be right.

'Go quickly to the place where I keep my eeltraps and stay there until I come for you,' she whispered in Rima's ear. 'Show yourself to no one, little one. Only me. Do you understand?'

Rima nodded and then was gone, only the small-est rustle of leaves to show where she had gone. Emma got to her feet and for a moment the world spun around her. Only Mr Morgan's hand on her elbow stopped her from falling.

'Are you all right?'

She looked up at his peculiar pale eyes, wonder-ing how he could even pretend to care about her well-being. She shrugged him off without a word and took the track to the *pa*, where Tawhai was awaiting her return impatiently. Beside him stood Kaharangi, and it was he who took the corset from her shaking hands.

'The *taniwha* belt!' Tawhai said triumphantly.

Through the cotton Kaharangi felt the bones as-sessingly while Emma held her breath. 'Perhaps,' he said at last.

Tawhai scowled at him. 'They are the bones of a *taniwha*!'

Kaharangi pulled a sceptical face and handed it back. 'Perhaps.'

Visibly deflated, Tawhai flicked a quick glance at Emma and then looked away. 'I want the ammuni-tion, Hemma.'

'But you promised…'

He spun around and glared at her so ferociously

that she stepped back. 'How dare you argue with me, Hemma! I have spared you the child's life for now, so bring me the ammunition!'

'All right.' Emma nodded quickly. 'But I have to ask Mr…ah…my husband for it.'

'Then do so.'

She turned and left. Mr Morgan would never hand over the ammunition. Rima's life would be over almost before it began. The unfairness of it all rose in her throat as if to choke her. Why, oh, why had he come here? It was all his fault, all of it!

She stumbled into the clearing around her little camp, almost blinded by tears. Ben looked up from where he sat by the fire, eating a plate of the *kumara* she had cooked for their breakfast.

'Good, you're back. You'd better eat now.'

'I'm not hungry.'

'You will be.' He nodded to where a plate of steaming *kumara* stood beside the fire. 'That should sustain you through the day. But I'd eat it fast.'

She ignored him and the food, sitting down on the opposite side of the fire, arms crossed over her knees.

'I've taken only what we can easily carry,' Ben said between mouthfuls. 'A change of clothes from your husband's trunk, a billycan, some cups… But you'd better look through what I've packed first.'

She stared at him as if she had never seen him before in her life. 'Why?'

'In case I've overlooked something. And you'll need a change of clothes too.'

She shook her head sullenly. 'I don't know what you're talking about.'

He took another mouthful and stared at her through narrowed eyes, and suddenly she did understand. And she felt a thin thread of fear down her spine as she realised that—whatever he did— she would be dragged alongside him, willingly or not.

'I'm not leaving! I can't.'

'But you can't stay, not if you want Rat alive, you know that.'

Emma rested her forehead on her knees in utter exhaustion. 'So what do we do? Do we go back down the river?'

'That's what they'd expect us to do. There's a canoe ready and provisioned for me, I understand. I'll launch that, and with luck they'll follow it downriver. But we go inland, to the source of the Whanganui.'

She stared at him wearily. 'Which is where you wanted me to go with you all along.'

'As it happens, yes. And we go now, Mrs Johnson, before they come for Rat. Because they will.'

He was right, she knew. And yet she hated him for being right. She hated him for the position he was putting her in, for removing any element of choice she might have in the matter. She reached for the *kumara* and began to eat, not even tasting what she chewed.

Ben got to his feet. 'Right. Now pack a change of clothes and then go and find Rat. In about fifteen minutes I'll create a diversion down on the water. When you hear it, make your way upriver as quickly as you can, making sure no one sees you and that you leave no tracks. D'you think you can do that?'

'But there are dozens of people around!' she protested. 'How can you possibly imagine that I can escape from here without being seen by someone?'

He grinned. 'They'll all be busy elsewhere in fifteen minutes, believe me.'

She waited until he had gone and then packed swiftly, putting as many of her medical supplies as she could together inside her medical bag. Utensils, her dictionary and a change of clothes were wrapped inside two bedrolls. Outside her *whare* she stood uncertainly, her arms full. The rolls and bag were easy to carry, but far too bulky to disguise. How was she to walk past the guards that always stood on lookout, loaded down as she was, without raising suspicion?

Her question was answered minutes later by a loud crash down by the water. Through the trees she saw the flash of bodies as every man, woman and child in the *pa* ran down to the river. And she saw the canoe, with what looked like two people in it, being paddled swiftly away. She didn't hesitate, but ran down to where she kept her eeltraps.

'Rima?' she whispered.

The child shot out of the forest and into her arms, hugging her with all her strength. Together they made their way along the riverbank. Emma resisted the compulsion to run, and instead she moved cautiously, taking care to replace the ferns they brushed past, and avoiding the muddy banks where they could leave footprints. The tribe would be more likely to chase Ben, she reasoned, thinking that he had the ammunition. And if they caught him...

Just for a moment doubt seized her and she

stopped in her tracks. Rima stared up at her, puzzled. What if they caught him, as they surely would! And if they didn't, and if by some miracle he escaped and came back upriver, how would he ever find them if the Maoris couldn't? How had she ever agreed to such a stupid plan?

'Hemma? What is the matter?'

Emma shook her head, too breathless to speak. Whatever happened, the most important thing was to put as many miles as she could between Rima and the tribe—the direction wasn't important!

They followed the river for hours, pushing through the thick, clasping bush. Emma tried as best she could to clear a way for Rima. Wet branches caught at her bonnet and slapped against her face, but she scarcely noticed them. After a while Rima started to flag and Emma piggybacked her, struggling to keep her balance on the slippery soil. The land began to rise steeply, until Emma found herself literally crawling on her knees, clutching precariously on to the bedrolls and bag, with Rima's skinny arms knotted tight around her neck. She was at a point beyond exhaustion, her legs shaking like jelly, when she finally collapsed on a bed of ferns that could have been featherdown for the comfort it gave.

She could find nowhere safer than here, she thought. They were in a small clearing, surrounded by dense forest, on the top of a cliff overlooking the river. From here she would be able to see anyone approaching from up or down the river, and she would be able to spot someone walking through the bush below them. She must have walked for many miles—not one of the hills she could see from her vantage point looked familiar.

The sun was directly overhead now, the air humid, with no trace of a breeze. With the enviable ability of the very young, Rima had fallen asleep. Emma pulled her under the shade of some flax and tucked a bedroll under her head.

Emma's thick black dress was unbearably hot and prickly, and was plastered to her legs with mud. Even out of the sun she felt dizzy with the heat and the residue of the terror that had dogged every step of her escape. It was impossible to believe that they had not been followed. Any minute Tawhai would appear from the forest, demanding to know why she had run away. Ben was sure to be dead by now, and when the tribe caught up with them, Rima would be killed too… It was all too much to bear. She put her hands over her face and finally allowed herself the luxury of tears.

'That's enough of that,' Ben said firmly, if a little breathlessly. 'You can't afford to go falling apart at this stage.'

She gave a small squeak of shock at the totally unexpected sight of him squatting beside her, wet and muddied, but very much alive. She struggled up to a sitting position.

'Where did you come from? I didn't hear you…'

'You weren't supposed to.' He sat down and began to take off his boots, his fingers tugging impatiently at the sodden laces. 'You made pretty good time up here, though—and I don't think your Maori friends will be able to track you if they decide to look up this way.'

'You seemed to have no trouble finding us.'

'Yeah. Well, I spent a lot of my earliest days in the interior of New South Wales where, if you couldn't track your dinner down, you got pretty damn hungry. Here, in the forest, there are broken twigs, footsteps in the mud…it's even easier to hunt.'

Emma shivered at the thought. 'As it will be for Tawhai and the tribe.'

'I don't think so,' he said confidently. 'They'll find the overturned canoe a couple of miles down-river. With this flood, they'll believe our corpses will have been swept even further downstream. The last place they'll expect to find us is safe and well upriver.'

She watched as he upended his boots to pour out water and sand: Where his shirt and trousers clung to his body the material was already starting to dry in long streaks. She tried to raise a hand to wipe away the perspiration trickling down from her hairline, but somehow even that much energy was beyond her. A dip in the river would be so nice, she thought blearily, vaguely aware that he was saying something to her. So nice and cool…

Ben had been watching her out of the corner of his eye and was half-expecting it when she slowly slumped over in a dead faint. He had been surprised at the distance she had covered in just a few hours— she must have run all the way, no doubt lugging the bedrolls and the child too. Under her bonnet her face had been scarlet when he had caught up with them. And no wonder—the ugly heavy dress primly buttoned up to the neck must be intolerable in the heat.

He untied the strings to her bonnet and pulled it off before deftly unbuttoning her dress to the waist and slipping it off down her legs. Underneath she wore several light cotton petticoats, which left her arms and the tops of her breasts bare. He ran his hand down her ribs, feeling nothing but the soft curves of womanhood, confirming that her figure owed nothing to the strictures of a corset. Not now. He grinned, remembering the ransom she had paid to Tawhai.

Her hair had come loose from its bun, spreading over her shoulders and the ferns like a fiery river. Something in her relaxed face, her outstretched bare arms and her tangled hair arrested him. Again, he had that same strong sense of *déjà vu*. He had seen her like this before, surely...

Then, like a dowsing from a bucket of cold water, he knew where he had seen her before. Sydney, almost two years to the day. He had been celebrating—oh Lord, had he celebrated!—and he had been so drunk that he had thought himself to be all but useless to the whore the hotel manager had obligingly sent up to his room. But she had known exactly what to do. Even he had been pleasantly taken aback by her audacity, her knowing hands and mouth. He remembered her astride him, laughing down at him with her hair flying over her naked breasts. Why had he recalled her hair as being blonde? Maybe it had been a trick of the candlelight.

He had cupped her breasts in his hands, wondering at how perfectly they fitted in his palms. She was made for him!

'I think I'm in love,' he had told her and she had given that oddly wicked laugh and wriggled her hips, making any further speech from him impossible...

Of course, in the morning she was gone, with his purse of hard-won coins. No matter that he had hidden them carefully under the mattress, she had known where to look. All she had left him was the scent of roses on the sheets, an almighty hangover, and his shattered dreams.

Two years it had taken to claw back what he had lost. Two years of planning every punishment in hell for that thieving slut. And here she was now, lying unconscious before him, completely at his mercy...

But was it her? As the red mist of rage cleared from before his eyes, Ben took a good, hard look at Mrs Johnson.

Damn, but she looked so defenceless lying there, his po-faced, pretty little missionary's widow. So soft-spoken and so prim that he felt guilty about even his mildest cursing. So modest that she would not take off her bonnet in front of him, so righteous that she blushed when he reminded her occasionally that he was a man and she was a woman.

No. He sat back on his heels with a frown. It couldn't be her. And yet, if it wasn't, she was a dead-ringer for the bitch. And the Reverend Thomas Johnson had worked the docks of Sydney town for his converts...

There was one way to tell. Carefully, so as not to

bring her to, he slid the hem of her petticoats up over her legs to her waist. Her knee-length drawers were roomy enough to be able to be eased up to her crotch...

It wasn't there. He let his breath out slowly, more relieved than he had realised. The whore had had a mole on the very top of her right thigh. He remembered kissing it. And that was another thing—the whore had been a natural blonde. Mrs Johnson was very definitely a redhead.

Feeling almost ashamed of himself, he rearranged Mrs Johnson's clothing to a state of modesty. Then he snatched up her dress and strode with it down the hill to the river.

The dress was so heavily caked in mud that it would be nothing but an impediment once they started walking again.

The dress was like a black lead weight in the water. Ben thought about letting it float away downriver—Mrs Johnson looked so much prettier wearing nothing but her petticoat and drawers—but in the end he simply rinsed off the mud and left it to dry over a boulder. As he took off his shirt and dipped it in the water it occurred to him that he had never had to do a woman's washing for her before. But he was in need of Mrs Johnson's services right now, and that was surely worth a few sacrifices.

When he returned to the clearing on top of the cliff, it was to find Mrs Johnson fully conscious. She was crouching behind the still-sleeping form of the Rat, her eyes wild, her arms wrapped tightly across her breasts.

'What have you done to me?' She had put her regrettable bonnet back on, of all things, but her hair was still tangled about her shoulders. 'Where are my clothes?'

'I've washed out your dress—it's still down by the river.' He saw her staring at the damp shirt in his hand and he held it out to her. 'Here, put this around your head to cool you down.' Instead she seized it and began to pull it awkwardly over her arms, her hands shaking in what he realised in amazement was real fear. Not of the tribe of blood-thirsty savages they had left downriver, but of him. How the hell he had ever thought of her as a whore...

'I want my dress back!'

'It's wet,' he said shortly.

'Where is it?'

'I've told you. I've washed it. It's down by the river.' He waited for her to thank him, but she only continued to stare at him with huge, outraged eyes, and so he turned his back and began to empty out his pack. To his relief his surveying instruments were still intact and his papers—carefully rolled in sealskin—were completely dry. Thank God he had also thought to bring a spare shirt. Behind him he heard the Rat stir and mutter. When he looked around, Mrs Johnson was helping the child to her feet, saying something to her in Maori.

'Are you ready to move on now?' he interrupted.

Mrs Johnson's hand flew up to cover her bare throat and Ben kept his face expressionless as the dark tips of her breasts were revealed through the all-but-transparent wet fabric of his shirt. He couldn't afford to frighten her any further.

'I want my other dress, please. It's in my bedroll.'

'It's the same weight as the other dress. It's too heavy to wear while you're travelling in this heat. Do you want to faint again?'

She swallowed in agitation and, despite his impatience, he felt sorry for her genuinely outraged modesty.

'Then I'm…I'm going to find fresh water. If you can light a fire for us…'

'No fires. Not yet. We're still too close.' He did up the last buckle on his pack and slung it over his shoulder. 'We need to put a few more miles between us and the tribe before nightfall, just to be safe.'

Her fingers worked nervously at the material at her throat. 'You said they wouldn't look for us up-river…'

'They won't. But it's a calm day and I don't see the need to advertise our whereabouts with smoke from a campfire.' Still she hesitated and he clicked his tongue impatiently. 'What's the problem, madam?'

'Rima is tired and I need to tend to her injuries. Can't we rest here just a little longer?' Rat, clinging to Mrs Johnson's petticoats, looked up at him through her matted hair with undisguised loathing. Ben wondered how soon he could get rid of her.

'No. We're safer moving on upriver.'

'To where?'

'I've told you before—to the source. The lake called Taupo.'

'And once we get there?'

'Then my job's done and I've charted the entire length of the Whanganui River for the New Zealand Company. Whether we then go on to the coast or return downriver is something we can decide when we get there.' He caught the odd look on her face. 'What's the problem with going upriver, Mrs Johnson?'

'The Ngati Tuwharetoa.' She wiped the perspiration from her forehead with the back of her hand in a gesture of weariness. 'The tribe from upriver. My tribe were expecting to meet them in battle any day now.'

'Inter-tribal battles are just one of the hazards,' he said lightly. He picked up the two bedrolls and her bag, deftly twisting them into the shape of a pack that could be slung over one shoulder, like the one he carried with him. 'I'll get your dress from the riverbank. There looks to be a small waterfall about fifty yards upriver—you can get a drink and cool down there for a few minutes.' Without allowing her the time for further argument, he strode away downhill.

Emma watched him go, her head thumping in pain. Every muscle in her body ached at the very thought of further movement.

'Is he going away?' Rima whispered hopefully.

Emma shook her head. 'No. We have to follow him, Rima, to get away from the tribe. I know you're tired, but do you think you can walk by yourself now?'

Each step was an effort, but they were encouraged by the cooling sound of water splashing against rock up ahead. Below them she could see

Ben standing silhouetted on a promontory, apparently engrossed in taking measurements with a sextant. At his feet lay his sealskin package, open to reveal his surveying instruments. The sight of them saddened her.

She knew the arguments on both sides by heart now, having heard them on so many occasions over the last few years. No one country had yet claimed New Zealand as a colony, as the French and British governments watched each other carefully to see who would make the first grab for the world's furthermost territory. And within New Zealand, the New Zealand Company and the Missionary Society had clashed time and again over the future of this country. The missionaries wanted the land to be held in trust by the Church for the Maoris, to guard against their exploitation. The New Zealand Company, backed by powerful friends in England, argued for controlled immigration: farmers and tradesmen, servants and labourers—resourceful pioneers who would turn this beautiful, fertile land into a country of unrivalled prosperity and social harmony. Not, of course, that the directors of the New Zealand Company were averse to making a healthy profit from their foresight...

And Mr Morgan, his head down now as he scribbled in a journal, was doing his level best to help them. Emma sighed and turned away from the sight.

The small waterfall tumbled into a pool shaded by ferns and delicate, feathery *toi-toi*. They gulped mouthfuls of the sweetly pure water and then rested their aching feet in the pool while Emma cleaned Rima's forehead as best she could. Like most head

injuries, it had bled profusely and looked worse than
it was. It was Rima's stoical acceptance of the pain
as just another affliction to be borne that affected
Emma the most.

'Are you ready?'

Emma and Rima both started at the sound of his
voice. Mr Morgan looked huge towering above
them, the two packs on his back lending to his size.
His eyes were like the flat, cold river-stones. Emma
reached for her boots, resenting the way he always
flustered her.

'My dress…'

'I've got it.' He spun on his heel and strode away,
as if determined to give her no opportunity to talk.

In fact, with no burden to carry and relieved of
the hot weight of her dress, Emma found it not at
all onerous to follow him at the pace he set. He had
the bushman's ability to pick out the best paths
through the bush, and Emma and Rima found the
going much easier than before. He even held back
the occasional low-lying *ponga* branch for them,
which Emma found an odd courtesy. She had more
than half-expected him to demand that she carry her
own pack, but he seemed to hardly notice the extra
weight, and so she didn't volunteer.

From time to time they stopped while Ben made
more sketches and measurements. At one such stop
by the riverside they could see the long, black
shapes of resting eels mere inches under the shallow
water. Unable to resist such an easy meal, Rima
swiftly fashioned a noose from flax and caught two
of the big fish.

'How clever you are, Rima!' Emma praised. 'What a fine meal we'll have tonight!'

Ben merely raised an eyebrow and turned away. She found herself wondering how someone like him—without the benefit of a gun—would manage to feed himself in these wilds. Even if he had had his guns with him, he couldn't have used them for fear of attracting attention. Did he know how to make a noose like the one Rima had for catching eels? Or how to make a basket for fishing, or a snare for birds? Rima must have thought the same thing— the two of them exchanged a superior smile behind his back as they ran to catch up with him. Emma carried one eel and Rima the other, and they both gathered handfuls of the broadleafed watercress the Maori called *puha* as they walked.

Chapter Six

As dusk fell they stopped under a sheltered outcrop. Below them the river opened out into a small lake, opal blue and deceptively placid-looking, fringed with lush ferns. The fluted canyon walls rose like cathedral spires all around them, and the deep beauty of the place made Emma's heart turn over.

'This'll do.' Ben shrugged the bags from his shoulders. 'We'll sleep here tonight.'

By the time Emma had searched out the billycan he had built a campfire with the aid of his tinderbox. Emma lay the gutted eels over some smouldering *manuka* branches and brought the *puha* to the boil with springwater in the billycan. When she pulled the eels out of the fire half an hour later they were perfectly done. The skin was crisp and fell away, leaving only the strong, smoky red meat. Rima had plaited three small flax squares while she had waited for her dinner, and derived particular satisfaction from arranging the food on the 'plates'.

'I think we should say grace,' Emma said pointedly as Ben reached for his food. Rima obediently copied her steepled hands and bowed head, but Ben merely waited, as Emma made the prayer brief and in Maori.

She could not recall savouring a meal more. The three of them ate in silence until they were full, and then Ben stood to announce his intention of taking a swim. Emma almost told him to be careful but then resisted the impulse. Instead, she and Rima found comfortable niches in the long grass and settled down to let their dinner digest. They began counting the first stars appearing in the sky, but Rima was asleep before they reached double digits.

I should get up and get a blanket, Emma thought. And I should put on my other dress—I can't go on wearing just my petticoats and a man's shirt. It's not decent. But the sun-warmed ground beneath her was so comfortable, and her legs felt like lead, and her eyes were growing heavier… From somewhere below she could hear Ben as he dived into the river. Was he naked? she wondered drowsily, too close to sleep to rein in her errant thoughts.

And she slept, to dream of a naked Mr Morgan lying beside her, warm and smooth-skinned and powerful. His breath was on her cheeks and his hands were stroking her breasts rhythmically, taunting the aching tips until they felt they would burst. The pleasure throbbed between her legs and she welcomed it, concentrated on it until she felt her body clench into spasms of relief.

What am I doing? she thought, even as the intense waves ebbed. What has he done to me? How can I ever face him now, what can I say…?

She opened her eyes to the blackness and the stars

wheeling overhead. A blanket had been laid over her, and over Rima who was sleeping peacefully a few feet away. That accounted for the warmth. And her own hands on her breasts accounted for the inordinate feeling of pleasure that still pulsed through her body. Mr Morgan was just a barely discernible sleeping shape on the far side of the clearing.

Not again! She sat up and threw off the blanket, feeling sick with shame. This time she couldn't blame him for what she was feeling. No, these horrible, lustful dreams were entirely in her own sordid imagination. But why? Why, after years of atonement, was she being tormented like this? And why by the likes of Mr Benedict Morgan?

She knelt by the fire and began to poke it back into life. Perhaps a drink of hot water would help her to get back to sleep. There were herbs she had brought in her medicine bag that would certainly help, but she didn't want to disturb the others by getting them out now.

'Are you all right, Mrs Johnson?'

He spoke softly, his voice sending small shivers through her. She swallowed hard, not daring to look at him.

'Thank you, I'm fine.'

She heard the rustle of blankets on the grass as he propped himself up on one elbow.

'That was quite some dream you were having.'

She flicked a quick, horrified look at him. He was fully dressed, she noted with relief, and seemed to be studying the scattered remains of the fire.

'Did…did I…say anything?' she said as casually as she could.

'Oh, nothing coherent.' He frowned and reached over to lay a precise network of twigs over the emerging flames. 'You were mostly sighing and moaning.'

Her face felt as hot as the fire. 'It was…a nightmare…'

'Was it?' He glanced up at her, grinned suddenly and then went back to building up the fire. 'It didn't sound like one.'

She watched him in hatred as he methodically added to the fire, building it higher and brighter. He would know, of course. How many women had he had in his life? How many women had he pleasured? He would know exactly the private sounds that a woman would make in the throes of sexual pleasure. He must have elicited those sounds dozens—hundreds!—of times. Yet she had never made them before. Not once. Not until now, in her sleep, of all times!

Unable to bear his smug, knowing presence for another second she stood up and left the clearing. He didn't call her back. The moonlight was bright enough for her to see her way clearly until she stood on the banks of the Whanganui. The water whispered by her feet, darkly gleaming, and above her the multitude of stars merged into a great paintstroke of light. She sat on a huge boulder and stared at them for a long time, picking out the familiar shape of the Southern Cross. The stars had never looked so clear in Sydney for some reason.

The old memory came back to her, the one she had tried so hard to forget, the one that would still be haunting her on her deathbed. The nights she had

stood alone in the dark outside the rowdy dockside
bars, waiting for a customer, her stomach clenched
with fear. The smell of rum and beer and salt water.
The sordidness of it all, the utter humiliation, and
all for the sake of a few coins...

The memory never failed to sicken her, and she
had never been able to justify it to herself. She had
sold herself for the very best of reasons—or so it
had seemed at the time. Thomas had made her see
how wrong it was, that there were other options. She
had worked so hard to redeem herself, in his eyes
as well as God's, and when Thomas had asked her
to marry him, all she had felt was profound gratitude
for his forgiveness.

And now it was all for nothing. Her penitence,
her resolution, her hard work to put her past behind
her, all worthless. For two days now she had felt
nothing but disorientation. Her body was so tense
with desire that even the slightest friction of fabric
against her nipples was enough to send her thoughts
flying to subjects no woman should know anything
about. Because, if she looked honestly into her own
heart, all she really wanted to do was lie down with
the despicable Mr Morgan and let him do anything
he wanted to her.

'It's not fair!' she said aloud to the dark hills
across the river.

'Life seldom is,' Ben agreed.

She started so much that she almost lost her seating. Only Ben's hand on her arm stopped her from
staggering into the river. Lord, how she hated his
ability to creep up on her like a cat!

'I didn't hear you!'

'I'm sorry. I didn't mean to startle you.' Again, his voice was oddly unsettling, sending a tingle down her spine at his close proximity. His fingers lightly caressed her arm, setting the fine hairs on end. 'You're cold, Mrs Johnson. Or can I call you Emma?'

'Certainly not!' She removed her arm from his grasp and stood up. 'I'd better go now…'

He refused to move out of her way, baring his teeth in a predatory smile that sent a shudder of excitement through her all the way down to her toes. She stared hard at his chest, too frightened to meet his eyes. After a long moment of silence he sighed and raised his hand to gently stroke the side of her face. As he outlined her lips with a fingertip she had to choke back a sob that was born of both fear and frustration.

'Why don't you just give in, Mrs Johnson?' he whispered.

He leaned forward and kissed her, so lightly that she was barely aware of the pressure, and yet the sensitivity of his lips against hers was exquisite. Then he lifted his head and drew her to him, and the warmth and power of his body permeated her like a strong drug.

She tensed, expecting his hands to slide down to fondle her through her clothes, but to her astonishment he simply held her close against him, as if she were a panicked child in need of comforting. It was like being held in the sheathed paws of a tiger and yet, muscle by muscle, Emma found herself giving into the overwhelming temptation to relax against him. How could she not, when it felt so good to be held like this… For the first time in many months she realised that she felt safe, protected, ineffably feminine. It somehow seemed quite natural to rest her head against his shoulder. He smelt deliciously of grass and clean skin and an underlying scent that was entirely, irresistibly male.

The moments flowed on, like the river running by their feet, and still Ben made no move to seduce her. By the time he began to make small circular movements along her spine Emma could have purred with pleasurable anticipation. The gently, rhythmic motion was soothing and yet somehow most arousing. Within seconds she was aware of the aching peaks of her breasts beneath her shirt as they rubbed against the rough hairs on Ben's chest, the growing heat in the juncture of her thighs as he subtly pressed her hips against his hardness. Her limbs felt heavy and languid, and yet her fingers were trembling with impatience as she pulled his shirt free of his shoulders and traced the length of his shoulderblade with her lips. The taste of his skin was musky, intoxicating in her mouth.

He laughed deep in his throat and then caught her mouth with his own, and the last traces of sanity left her. Lost to the plundering of his tongue, of his lips, she scarcely felt the cold stone on her shoulders as Ben pressed her back to half-sit, half-lie on the great river rock. His hands slid up between her thighs, parting them, as she fumbled clumsily with his belt buckle, the desperation to feel him inside her growing by the second.

Her breathing matched his, loud, ragged with passion, and she didn't hear Rima's first, plaintive wail. But she heard the second and immediately stiffened.

'It's…it's Rima…'

'Later. Later,' Ben muttered against her hair and as she opened her mouth to protest he kissed her again and again. He helped her free his belt buckle at last and he began to position himself between her thighs. Rima's cry changed to a scream of panic. The high-pitched sound bounced between the walls of the river valley, amplified almost beyond bearing.

It was only then that Emma realised what she was doing.

She must be insane. What other explanation was there? Here she was, pressed up against a rock in the middle of nowhere, allowing a man she barely knew to take her, and Thomas, her poor, saintly husband, scarcely cold in his grave…

She thrust hard with flattened hands against Ben's chest, so quickly that he was taken by surprise and staggered backwards.

'No! I've got to go! She needs me!'

'Oh, for Chrissakes! She'll be all right,' he snarled, but Emma had already gathered her disarrayed skirts about her and was running up the hill, slipping in the dark in her haste. By the time she reached Rima the child was rigid with terror.

'What was it, Rima? A bad dream?'

'*Taniwha*. It came out of the water to get me and you were gone.' Rima snuffled against Emma's shoulder and then yawned.

'There's no *taniwha*, sweetheart.' Emma pulled the blanket up to Rima's chin and lay down beside her. 'And I'm here.'

'But I heard it,' Rima insisted drowsily. 'Down beside the river. I could hear it breathing…' Her eyelashes fluttered and she was asleep within minutes. Lost in thought, Emma didn't stir until Ben put the billycan, now full of water, over the fire. He flung himself down on his bedroll, his face impassive but plainly angry.

'Is she all right?'

'Yes. But…she heard us…'

'I expect she must have.'

Emma looked guiltily at Rima's sleeping face. 'What if she had come to see what the noise was?' she said quietly. 'What if she had…seen us?'

He shrugged. 'She wouldn't have seen anything that she hasn't already seen dozens of times before.' He saw her shocked expression and sighed heavily. 'Oh, for God's sake, Mrs Johnson, you've lived with these people. They don't have parlours or beds with curtains or privies! We might not approve, but that brat has probably seen more of life—real life—than you have in your lifetime.'

'That doesn't excuse what we…what you did!' she snapped, stung by his patronising air.

'Oh, that's going it a bit thick, coming from *you*!' He kicked a small, errant log back into the fire with his booted foot. 'I could have had you any time I wanted! You've been practically begging for it from the first…'

'I have not! How dare you!' She clutched her blanket to her like a shield. 'You…you took advantage of a momentary weakness, that was all!'

He leaned forward intently. 'Momentary, was it? Tell me something, Mrs Johnson. Have you ever been made love to? Properly made love to? Oh, yes—' he waved a dismissive hand '—I know you were married, but old Tom would scarcely have been able to manage more than a quick fumble before he relieved himself…'

With a short scream of disgust Emma shot to her feet, but he was beside her in an instant, his hands on her arms restraining her from flight—or from boxing his ears.

'Why are you doing this to me?' she hissed. 'And to Thomas? What has he ever done to you? You're so loathsome and disgusting and contemptible…'

'And right,' he interjected gleefully. 'I am right, aren't I?' He grinned and if her hands had been free to do so she would have scratched his horrible pale eyes out. 'Why, Mrs Johnson, I do believe you're practically a virgin…'

That did it. With all her strength she used one of the two limbs that remained free and kneed him in the groin. Very hard. She watched him roll around on the ground with considerable satisfaction, not bothering to intervene when he almost went into the fire and she could hear his hair singe.

'Jesus, you've killed me!' he managed at last, when he had his breath back.

'I only wish I had!' she retorted. 'And please keep your voice down, or you'll wake Rima.' He said something completely unrepeatable then, and as he staggered to his feet she took the precaution of seizing a burning branch from the fire and holding it before her. 'One step closer, Mr Morgan, and I'll…I'll…'

'…kill me. All right, all right, I get the message.'

He lowered himself carefully on to his bedroll, his face creased with pain, and for a moment she felt almost guilty. But not for the world would she ever apologise to him.

The moon was hanging heavy and pale gold above the hills, and there was no sound except for the crackling fire and the strange, plaintive cry of a kiwi foraging for its supper close by. In the peace, Emma's rage slowly subsided to a grudging acknowledgement that she might have contributed minutely to the situation. She could have said no from the beginning, instead of encouraging him. What he had said about Thomas was utterly unforgivable, of course, but then Mr Morgan was nothing more than an unmannerly boor. He had no doubt been born a boor, and he would most certainly die a boor. He just couldn't help it. He deserved her pity, not her contempt.

The billycan over the fireplace was boiling away merrily by now. From the tiny, tightly wrapped packages of dried herbs in her medical bag she chose two and sprinkled a little of each into the simmering water.

Camomile and peppermint, her favourite herbs. 'I think we both need a hot drink,' she said aloud.

He sighed and lay back with his eyes closed. 'All right. As long as you drink some first.'

Despite everything she could not resist a smile at that. 'I have some laudanum, if you need it...'

'No, I'll survive.'

When she gave him a mug of tea he met her eyes squarely. 'I should apologise, Mrs Johnson. For saying what I did about your husband.'

After a moment's hesitation she nodded graciously. 'I accept your apology. And I'm pleased to hear you admit to being wrong for once.'

'Oh, I'm not wrong.' He settled himself more comfortably against his bedroll. 'I'm just sorry that I told you, that's all.'

Chapter Seven

A heavy mist clung to them when they awoke the next morning, dampening the bedrolls and beading their hair with fine droplets of moisture. Emma fed the struggling fire and poked cabbage-tree roots into the embers to bake. The tender, sugary roots were delicious washed down with more of her herbal tea, and there were enough roots to wrap in flax leaves and carry with them for eating later.

Ben was uncommunicative and Emma made no attempt to talk to him, apart from a brief word of thanks when he again picked up her luggage and slung it over his back with his own. He walked on ahead, somewhat stiff-legged, she noticed, and he seemed quite indifferent to whether they kept up or not. But they were climbing steadily higher, with the rapids and twists in the river much more pronounced, and Ben frequently stopped to make his measurements and sketches.

After some agonising, Emma had elected to continue wearing her petticoat and Ben's shirt, and as the mist burned off to another hot, cloudless day, she was glad she had put comfort ahead of modesty. She still wore her bonnet, of course, and Rima had woven herself a little flax hat to keep the sun off her face.

What had always enchanted Emma about the New Zealand forest was the feeling that she never walked alone in it. The trees were full of birds, like the fat wood-pigeons that sat placidly on low branches, quite unaware that they were a prized delicacy for the Maori, and the glossy parson-birds whose belltones made the forest ring and— most companionable of all—the tiny fantails that swarmed around, piping excitedly as passing humans stirred up invisible insects.

And the forest was a good provider if one knew what was edible. Emma and Rima both ate as they walked, snacking on bracken-tips and berries they picked on their way. A full stomach, cool, comfortable clothes, beautiful scenery... Emma realised with surprise that she was actually enjoying herself.

They were negotiating a particularly steep bank when suddenly Rima scurried away from Emma's side and grabbed Ben's hand, making him turn abruptly to face her.

'*Ahi!*' she hissed.

He looked at Emma for clarification.

'Fire,' she said, puzzled.

He sniffed the air and then shrugged his shoulders free of the bedrolls. 'Stay here.' He disappeared through the thick bush, seeming to barely disturb the branches as he went. Emma looked down at Rima for an explanation.

'Fire,' Rima said patiently. 'Can't you smell the smoke?'

She couldn't, although Ben plainly had. When he came back he motioned to them to follow him at a crouch. They moved slowly and as silently as possible, keeping at the same height as the undergrowth. Emma thought it an uncomfortable waste of time until she saw the *pa* across the river. It was a war *pa* like the one she had lived near, heavily fortified, with dug-out trenches for defence cut into the riverbank and high, spiked palisades surrounding the *whares* on the top of the hill. The armed guards on patrol were perfectly visible from where she crouched, and a dozen canoes were tied up at the bank, ready to be launched at a single shout of warning.

It seemed to take forever until they gained the next valley, out of sight of the *pa* guards. It was all too easy to pretend that they were the only humans in this exotic wilderness. If it had not been for Rima they would have blundered into full view of the *pa*. The Maoris there may or may not have been friendly, but the threat to Rima's life was still too fresh in her mind, and Ben had the most dangerous tendency to irritate his Maori hosts. They had been lucky to have had Rima's sharp little nose with them.

They stopped by a small pool in the rocks, to drink and eat more of the baked roots. Emma took off her boots and, taking care to arrange her petticoat over her ankles, dipped her feet in the water. It was oddly warm for springwater and Rima lost no time in jumping in with a shriek of ecstasy. She was like a little fish in the water, Emma thought proudly, as she watched the child chasing *koura*, the tiny, freshwater shrimp that were a delicacy for the Maori.

She glanced across the pool to where Ben sat carefully filling in pieces of a complicated-looking survey map. He looked tired, and she hoped that he was not still suffering from her well-placed kick. She watched him as he drew, almost mesmerised by the intent look on his face. His bottom lip was caught between his teeth, his eyebrows almost met in a scowl of concentration. He had not shaved since they had met and his stubble, darker than one might expect from a fair-haired man, was now pronounced. It had rasped against her skin the previous night, and the hairs on her arms prickled at the very memory of how it had felt. The sharp jolt of longing that plunged through her was enough to take her breath away.

Rima, watching Emma watch Mr Morgan, suddenly slammed her hands down into the water, fingers outstretched.

'Rima!' Emma spluttered with a laugh of surprise as the water sprayed over her face. '*Kati rawa*! Stop it!'

Ben leaped up in fury, holding his dripping survey map as far away from Rima as he could.

'You little cow! Look what you've done!'

'She didn't mean it,' Emma said indignantly, getting to her feet, although the smirk on Rima's face indicated just the opposite. 'Don't shout at her—it was an accident.'

'Like hell it was. For Christ's sake, look at this—days of work ruined!'

She looked at the water-splattered pages, blotchy with ink.

'Maybe it's just as well,' she said without thinking. Then she met his look of incredulity and wished the words had never left her lips.

'And what do you mean by that?' he said slowly, each word sharp with anger. 'Oh, don't tell me—I should have remembered. The missionaries are the only Europeans with the moral authority to be here, right?'

Emma bit her lip. 'I…I just don't think you should shout at Rima like that. It's only paper, after all…'

Something that looked like murder flared in his eyes and she took an involuntary step backwards.

'If you had any idea…' he began, when a small, flailing *koura* hit him squarely between the eyes and then dropped to wriggle frantically on the papers in his hand. Ben stood there as if frozen, staring as the creature turned his measurements and calculations to an inky smear. The only sound in the deadly silence was Rima's giggle. Ben threw his ruined papers to the ground.

'Right…'

'No!' As he moved forward Emma plunged into the pool and reached up to grab him. 'Please, no! She's only a child!'

He tried to shake his arm free but she clung doggedly to it, her teeth clenched with the physical effort of restraining him. Her bonnet fell unheeded into the water and her hair tumbled over her face, almost blinding her. But nothing would make her release her grip.

'Let me go!' he snarled. 'I'm going to kill the little bitch!'

Shuddering with panic, Emma pressed closer to the arm she held imprisoned, moving so that her left breast lay under his hand.

'Please,' she whispered. 'I'll do anything. Anything you want me to. Please don't hurt her.'

She tried to see his expression, but his eyes gave nothing away. Her heart pounded under his hand and for a wild moment she wondered if he was capable of ripping it out. Behind her Rima whimpered in terror.

She felt his fingers flex around her breast and she closed her eyes, scarcely able to breathe. He would take her, and it would be violent, but at least his anger would be diverted from the child and she...she would then know what she had always wanted to know about Ben Morgan.

With a curse, he shoved her from him.

She watched him gather his precious papers and disappear into the forest. Her knees abruptly gave way and she sat down heavily on the side of the pool, her breath coming in great juddering gasps as the implications of what she had done—of what she had been prepared to do—dawned on her. The previous night he had told her he could have her any time he wanted, and he had just been proved right. Yet he had walked away from his advantage...

Rima gave a wobbly cheer that was sheer bravado.

'You have chased him away, Hemma! He has gone, with his evil eyes, gone back down the river!'

'Oh, I hope not,' she whispered. 'I don't want to be left here alone.' She shook her head in despair at the little girl. 'What you did was very wrong, Rima.'

'No, it wasn't!' Rima's bottom lip stuck out defiantly, but it was wobbling and her eyes were suspiciously bright.

'Yes, it was. Like stealing the pistols from Tawhai was wrong. Those papers were very important to Mr Morgan.'

Rima considered that. '*Tapu*? Like Tawhai's *kumara*?'

'Yes, sacred, like the chief's *kumara*. But Tawhai can always grow another *kumara*. Mr Morgan may not be able to draw another picture of the river.'

The child bent her head and studied the ripples her fingers were making in the pool.

'I don't care.'

Deciding that there was little point in pursuing the matter now, when tempers were still so frayed, Emma said nothing as she swung her out of the water. Rima's little shift was sopping, and so Emma took it off and replaced it with one of her own shirts. With the sleeves rolled up, the shirt hung down almost to the ground, and Rima stroked the lace inserts reverently, all unhappiness forgotten in the joy of temporary ownership. No doubt it would have more than one tear in it by the end of the day, but it would be worth it if it put Rima in a better frame of mind. Emma could only wish that Ben was as easy to please.

They found him standing on the brow of the next hill, engrossed in yet another measurement, another sketch. As they joined him, Emma gave a gasp of delight. Before them the land flattened out and directly ahead lay three mountains. One was a long, flat, unremarkable protuberance, one was a perfect cone with a gentle wisp of steam coming from the top, and the other was massive, topped with snow even now in the middle of summer.

'The volcanoes are Ngauruhoe and Ruapehu,' Ben said shortly. 'The smaller mountain is Tongariro.'

Emma would have loved to have asked him more, but he shoved his sketchbook in his bag and walked on without a backward look. She hoped he was not going to prove to be as sulky as Thomas had been; if Thomas had been put-out at all, especially over something trivial, he would brood in silence for days. It had always taken her repeated apologies and cajoling before he would deign to speak to her again. On the other hand, she reflected, she always had Rima to speak to, so perhaps what passed for conversation with Ben wouldn't be such a great loss.

They travelled in silence, still following the river as it meandered through dense forest to the west of the mystical, quietly steaming volcanoes. It was mid-day before they stopped to eat the last of the baked cabbage-tree roots. Tussock grass made comfortable seating above an almost vertical gully, at the bottom of which the river flowed dark and riotously. At the end of the gully, framed perfectly for their enjoyment, Ruapehu rose dramatically up into the clouds.

'Give him *karaka*-seed instead,' Rima advised, as she watched Emma unwrap the roots. 'Or *rangiora* leaves.'

Emma shook her head. 'Why would we want to kill him, Rima?'

'Because we hate him.' Rima watched resentfully as Ben took his portion of the roots. 'Wouldn't you like him to die, Hemma? Then we could go back to the tribe.'

'We can't go back,' Emma said absently as she peeled away the thick, fibrous skin so that Rima could eat the flesh inside.

'Then where do we go?'

'I don't know. To Sydney, I suppose. I have a house there, and family.'

Rima's eyes lit with excitement. 'Sydney!'

'Sydney?' Ben echoed.

Emma froze. She had become so used to discussing her thoughts with Rima in Maori that she had forgotten that Ben could well pick up on any English part of their conversation.

'We…we were just talking about where we might go when we…when this is over.'

'Mmm.' He took another mouthful of root and chewed thoughtfully. 'If you're thinking of going to Sydney one day, why don't you start speaking to her in English?'

'Because…because I need to practice my Maori,' she said lamely.

'And because I can't understand you, right?'

She began to concentrate furiously on peeling

Rima's root, remembering what he had once said about her transparent lying. 'I have no reason to hide anything from you, Mr Morgan.'

It was Rima who created the diversion Emma needed. She had been idly tapping a rotten log against a rock, watching the maggots of the hu-hu beetle fall to the ground. The fat, white grubs were a staple food of the Maori, and Rima was always delighted by Emma's revolted reaction to them. Now Rima popped one in her mouth and smacked her lips noisily.

'Rima!' Emma reproved her, as much for something to say as to reprimand her for what she was eating. Rima glanced at her and then thrust a handful of the repulsive grubs in Ben's face.

'Thank you,' Ben said and calmly ate one, biting off the squirming head with the expertise of a connoisseur. When he went to take another one, Rima snatched them back in rage and gobbled them down so fast Emma thought she would make herself sick.

With a shrug Ben got to his feet and took his surveying equipment from his bag. There was a small promontory just below their picnic spot, and it was here that he stood to sketch the gully and the surrounding landmarks. Emma stood to dust herself off, and was about to suggest to Rima that they dig up some more roots when she realised that the child was racing down towards the cliff-edge where Ben stood, her arms outstretched before her, her intentions very clear.

'Rima, no! Ben, watch out!' she screamed.

As if in a dream she saw Ben turn and step aside in one fluid motion. Rima, moving too fast to stop, missed him by a foot and plunged headlong over the cliff. Ben reached out to grab her as she fell, but his fingers closed on empty air.

Emma ran down the bank to the river, heedless of the branches slashing at her face and hands. Below in the swiftly churning water she could just make out Rima's head, pathetically small, bobbing up and down. Around her swirled Emma's shirt, effectively hampering any attempt to swim that Rima may have been able to make.

Scrabbling for a grip on the crumbling bank, Emma tried to think. Perhaps if she could find a long branch to hold out to her... But already Rima was spinning out of reach, missing a boulder by mere inches. Her head disappeared under a white-crested swell, to reappear much further downriver. In a few seconds she would be around the riverbend and gone.

The fact that she could not swim one stroke no longer deterred Emma, and she had already kicked off her boots when she heard the splash as Ben dived in, some twenty yards further downriver. She watched with her heart in her mouth as he swam strongly towards Rima, but suddenly an undercurrent seemed to catch the child and drag her under. As Ben dived to find her, Emma lost sight of him around the riverbend.

It seemed to take an eternity to force her way though the dense bush. An eternity with her heart pounding painfully in her chest, and the only sounds that of her ragged breathing and the hateful roar of the river. She swiped impatiently at her face as her vision became smeared, oblivious to the twigs catching painfully in her hair.

Her path was blocked by a massive fallen tree and she gave a scream of frustration. It took forever to clamber over it, but when she had, and had tumbled down to a small, sandy bank, she was just in time to help Ben pull ashore Rima's limp body.

Rima's small face was white and pinched-looking. When Emma listened to her chest she could hear no heartbeat, no sign of breathing.

'She's dead,' she said flatly, unable to take it in. She had seen so many deaths, had even managed to deal with her husband's and her father's deaths with some measure of composure. And yet, to lose Rima...

'Maybe.' Ben knelt beside the child and pressed firmly on her chest. Then he turned her on her side.

Emma watched in shocked amazement.

'Mr Morgan, please!' she implored him. 'Let her be. She's gone.'

He ignored her and pulled Rima over onto her back. He pinched her nose shut and put his mouth over hers to breathe lightly, once, twice. Then he pulled her over onto her side again.

Rima's body convulsed in a sound that was half-cough and half-splutter as water poured out of mouth and her nose. The sound of the air dragging into Rima's lungs was the sweetest sound Emma had ever heard

Ben gathered the child in his arms and carried her up to where they had left their luggage. Swathed in bedrolls and held close to Emma's side, she slowly regained her normal colour and old cheekiness.

'My throat hurts,' she complained. 'And I'm hungry.'

Emma watched as Ben, still in his wet clothes, coaxed a fire from a hastily snatched handful of twigs.

'As soon as the water boils I'll make you a drink to soothe your throat.'

'Can I have some of the sleepy-stuff?'

Emma frowned in mock disapproval. She had once given Rima a tiny dose of laudanum for a mouth abscess, and the child retained fond memories of the blissful release from pain.

'No laudanum, you little mischief! Laudanum is for when you're in pain, not for when you've had a nasty fright. If your throat is still sore when you wake up tomorrow, we'll think about it then.'

A mug of hot herbal infusion did much to restore all their spirits. Her drink finished, Rima looked up somewhat drowsily at Ben sitting on the other side of the campfire.

'Ka nui to aroha,' she said.

'She said…' Emma began, but Ben silenced her with a shake of his head.

'I understood that. Tell her I accept her thanks,' he said quietly. Then, correctly reading Emma's expression, he gave a chuckle. 'No. I don't understand much Maori. But I know the word *aroha.*'

The word meant affection, gratitude, love. Emma pulled the bedrolls warmly around Rima's head, pleased that the little girl was slowly drifting off to sleep.

'I have to thank you for what you did.'

'Anyone else would have done the same.'

'I don't know that they would have. I do know that you didn't want her with us. And she did try to kill you…'

'Forget it,' he said abruptly. 'You're probably the first person who has ever been kind to her—no wonder she's so possessive. And I can't imagine she'd have had much kindness from a man before. Why shouldn't she hate me?'

Emma felt touched. 'But you objected to her so much…'

'Yeah, I know I did. And I still think the ideal place for her would have been back with her tribe. But we couldn't leave her for their cooking pot, could we?'

She shook her head. 'No, I don't believe they would have done that to her.'

'Well, you should. There may not be much meat on her, but she had to die for stealing from your friend the chief, so why would they have wasted her? What do you think happened to my old friend Eru's body? Thanks to your Missionary Society, most tribes seemed to be stopping the practice now—but it does still go on.'

'Then I have even more reason to be grateful to you,' she said softly. 'But that…that way you brought her back from the dead…'

'She wasn't quite dead, Mrs Johnson.'

'But she looked dead,' Emma persisted. 'Her heart had stopped, I'm sure of it! What did you do?'

'Just got the water out of her lungs and got her breathing again,' he said with a dismissive wave of his hand. 'We did it to calves on the farm that were stillborn. It doesn't always work, but it's always worth a try.'

'Calves!' she said incredulously.

'Yeah.'

'You breathed into the mouths of calves!'

'Well, you see, sometimes when we were a bit short of female company…'

She started to laugh at the sheer extraordinariness, the sheer common sense of the idea. And then she burst into tears.

'Aw, now…' Ben came around to sit beside her and gently disentangled her from Rima's sleeping form. With his arms around her Emma found it irresistibly comforting to cling to him and sob her heart out into his already damp shirt. He held her much as she held Rima, carefully and with great tenderness.

'It's been one hell of a day,' he muttered into the top of her head when the worst of her crying was over. She nodded fiercely. The sooner it was over the better, as far as she was concerned.

Neither of them had the energy to go down to the river to catch eels or a trout for dinner, and so they dug up cabbage-tree and bracken roots and put them in the embers to bake.

The sunset that night was spectacular, lighting Ruapehu with a warm rose glow, but as the heat of the day faded Emma realised that the volcanic plateau they were now on was considerably cooler than the lower reaches of the Whanganui River had been. Rima was still fast asleep, wrapped in both her own bedroll and Emma's, so when Ben suggested that

Emma take his bedroll, it seemed only fair that they should share it.

'Until Rima wakes up,' Emma amended for the sake of propriety, as she sat down beside him and arranged the blanket over her shoulders. The fire took care of warming her bare toes.

'Of course.'

They lay back, not quite touching, saying nothing as they watched the sky darkening. Emma felt inexplicably happy.

'Would you tell me, Mr Morgan, about your childhood?'

She felt him turn his head to look at her. 'Why would you want to hear about my childhood, Mrs Johnson?' The amusement in his voice warmed her.

'Because you understand about Rima—what her life has been like. Was your life like that?'

For a while she didn't think he would answer. Then he said, 'No. Not at all. My mother died when I was very young, but I had a father. And we used to have a lot of money, even given that we were farmers—my family have been in New South Wales for generations, and my mother brought a big dowry out with her from England. It wasn't a deprived childhood, if that's what you're thinking.'

'I'm sorry about your mother,' she said softly.

'Don't be. I don't remember anything about her. Besides, I had lots of replacements.'

The sudden edge to his voice alerted her. Propping herself up on one elbow, she looked for, and found, the blasé gleam in his eyes that always saddened her.

'I remember my mother, and she could never be replaced.'

'Yeah? Well, apparently mine could be. Only my father called them housekeepers, and they all became like part of the family. They even shared my father's bed, that's how close we all were. God knows how many he went through over the years; some of them stayed only a night. They were convict women, mostly, in those days—there are precious few women that aren't in New South Wales. When I was fourteen one of them started sleeping in my bed and that's when my father decided to kick me out and send me as far away as he could. He took me down to the docks and put me on the first ship out. Didn't even ask where it was going.'

'Didn't he care?' she gasped.

'No. And if I'd been him, I wouldn't have, either.'

'How horrid for you.'

'No, it wasn't "horrid" for me,' he said, mimicking the schoolgirlish dismay in her voice. 'I never went hungry, I wasn't beaten or abused...'

'But you weren't loved!'

He threw back his head and laughed. 'Oh, Mrs Johnson. No, of course I wasn't loved. But most children aren't anyway. At least I saw the world, trained as a surveyor and learned how to earn a crust, and I had the best education the school of life can give you. I count myself a lucky man to be disabused of any romantic slop that early in my life. Hell, my father still hasn't been. So save your pity for someone who needs it, please!'

But he didn't fool her, not for a moment. Twice

today he had revealed the man beneath the harsh exterior, and she now knew that the softness of his heart was equalled only by his determination not to reveal it. She snuggled down beside him under the blanket with a small smile. She had better be careful—she could almost come to like the man!

Chapter Eight

It took them another day to follow the river through the high plateau. There were many tributaries to the Whanganui River to negotiate at this point but, after the long spell of dry weather, they were relatively easy to cross.

Emma found that the travelling was more pleasant than she could have imagined. Certainly they never seemed to have quite enough to eat, and she hated having to rely on the inadequate shelter of trees during a shower, and she would have sold her soul for a hot bath. But they stopped so frequently for Ben to take measurements that they never grew too tired, and the scenery was so breathtaking that she was genuinely sorry when they at last lost sight of the quiet volcanoes behind the steep hills.

What was best, though, was the new camaraderie that began to develop between the three of them. Rima's feelings about Ben seemed to have taken a complete about-turn, and she now idolised him, running after him like a small, eager puppy. He was now 'Pen', which was the closest she could come to pronouncing his name, and her English was coming along in leaps and bounds as she struggled to communicate with him. Emma had been a little hurt at first, but then she remembered what Ben had said about Rima having been starved of a man's kindness. Besides, she found Ben's reaction most intriguing. It had always been her experience that only a few men could resist the adoration of a small girl, and Ben was certainly not one of those select few.

To her enormous relief he was able to redraw his ruined maps, without the loss of any vital information. She supposed that he would be paid very handsomely for the completed survey maps—certainly they involved such risks that he deserved a fortune for them.

In a wide, densely forested valley the river divided into two and they followed the southern branch as it meandered back around the volcanic plateau. The river now fell from a myriad of shallow rapids. The contributing streams were mountain-fed and delicious to drink from, ice-cold and crystal-clear.

One evening they made camp on the foothills of yet another mountain range. As dusk fell Emma stood by the campfire, hands on aching hips, staring at the jagged peaks. For the first time in the almost two weeks that they had been travelling she acknowledged to herself that she was tired, and sore from sleeping on the hard ground.

And hungry, she thought wryly, contemplating the task of digging up yet more roots for their dinner. There were no eels to be found in the clear, swift-running river or its tributaries—they preferred the mud. Ben had been surprisingly good at catching *pukakhos* and *wekas*, launching a flying tackle on the hapless birds as they foraged, but now the ground was more open, without the undergrowth the flightless birds loved. Her mouth watered at the thought of bird stew and she shook her head at the futile thoughts. A mug of hot water would keep hunger at bay for a while at least.

'Hemma, Hemma, come quickly!' Rima called, her voice shrill with excitement. Emma found her crouched over what looked like a small fire under a rock, prodding at it with a stick.

'How did you start a fire?' she began, and then realised that it was not smoke but steam rising from the fissure. As Rima continued to dig, bubbling mud began to trickle gently from the ground.

'Geothermal heat,' Ben said, when they showed him. 'We must be very near the lake now.'

Looking more closely at the hills, Emma could see that what she had taken for mist was in fact small wisps of steam seeping palely from under the rocks on the hillsides. Excitement built in her. Over those hills, perhaps, and there would be Lake Taupo. And then…and then what? She had deliberately blocked all thoughts of the future from her mind this last week. Somehow she had been content to simply travel.

She watched as Ben filled a billy with water from the river and showed Rima how the hot mud heated it just as effectively as a fire. He was a kind man, she thought, as well as protective and charming—on occasion—and his sense of adventure was contagious. Since Rima's rescue he had been on his best behaviour, and she had nothing with which to reproach him. And yet sometimes her restlessness was so overwhelming that she found it a struggle to contain it. The strange erotic dreams that plagued her had continued, although she had learned to wake herself up as soon as they started. But sometimes at night, when she lay next to Rima and watched Ben asleep across the campfire, she almost burned in torment. Madness, she told herself, madness! But still she had to fight every instinct that was telling her to go to him. To take his hand and lead him down by the river and finish what they had begun on that other starry night.

Ben stood up abruptly.

'What is it?' she asked.

He frowned, studying the misty hills. 'I thought I heard something. Wait here.'

Together they watched him wade across the river and disappear into the forest.

'Hemma, I am scared!' Rima said, and although Emma tightened her arm around her, she did not trust herself to speak. She felt the small hairs lift on the back of her neck, so strong was the sensation that they were being watched.

He seemed to be gone a very long time. Aware of Rima's growing fears, Emma forced a smile to her lips. 'Let's see if your water is boiling in the mud, shall we?'

When she turned around she was mere inches away from the heavily tattooed face of a Maori warrior. Rima screamed and buried her face against Emma's side. Her terror—and the obvious look of fascination on the warrior's face—gave Emma courage.

'*Tena koe,*' she managed to say.

He grinned widely, white teeth startling against the dark-pigmented decorative whorls on his cheeks.

'*Bon jour, madame.*'

She felt her jaw drop. 'You speak French? English?' The warrior frowned, plainly confused, and so she tried again, this time in Maori. 'Where did you come from?'

He smiled again and gestured towards the hills. Behind him more warriors emerged from behind the trees but she could see that they were clearly a hunting party, not intent on war. They surrounded her, feeling her dress, touching her red hair where it escaped from under her bonnet. Their comments were admiring and curious, and she knew she had little to fear from them. Even Rima began to visibly relax.

She began to worry again when Ben reappeared from across the river, accompanied by another party of Maori warriors. But to her amazement he seemed to be quite at ease with them.

'They're from the lake,' he told her. 'Very friendly. They'll take us over to their settlement in the morning.'

'How do you know that?' she demanded.

He shrugged. 'That's the odd thing—they don't speak English, but they've got a few words of French. There's a Frenchman living on the north side of the lake, apparently. The Maoris don't like him much, but they're prepared to take us across the lake to meet him.' He grinned at her expression. 'I take it you don't speak French, Mrs Johnson.'

'And you do?'

'I do. Remember that ship I told you about that my father put me on in Sydney? I ended up in Marseilles.' He turned away as one of the warriors asked him something in the odd garbled tongue that was Maori-French, and that was almost indecipherable to her. All she knew of the language was that the Whanganui Maori had called the French *Wiwi*.

In the end, they ate very well that evening, on *weka* and *kumara* wrapped in flax and cooked until tender in the boiling mud. The warriors were indeed friendly, and eager to answer any questions. They were the Ngati Tuwharetoa and so she glossed over the time that she had lived with their old enemies down the river. Tactful questioning on her part revealed that they were not planning to carry out their threat to sweep down the Whanganui in their war canoes in the near future. However, knowing the Maori as she did, it was probably only a matter of time before the old grievance—whatever it had been—would resurface.

The next morning they set off for the lake. The Maoris, somewhat amused by Ben's insistence on following the river to its source, watched intrigued as he took his measurements and drew his maps. It was a large, good-natured party to be travelling with, and Emma began to thoroughly enjoy herself.

It was still only mid-morning when they scaled the last hill and saw Lake Taupo lying spread before them, huge and enchantingly azure under the summer sky. Emma thought Rima's eyes would pop from her head at the sight of so much water in one place. There was something distinctly mystical about Taupo, with its gleaming haziness and blue hills. She could just make out the hills across the lake to the north where the warriors told her the Frenchman had built a house. It appeared that Ben's comments that the Maoris didn't like the Frenchman was something of an understatement. The *Wiwi* was *porangi*, the Maoris said. Mad. They spat when they said the word, making her feel most uneasy. Yet the thought of seeing another European face filled her with excitement.

The Maoris waited patiently for Ben to finish before leading the way along the lakefront to the *pa*. Here they were received formally and warmly. Emma, with Rima attached firmly to her skirt, was taken away to sit with the women, and she left with some misgivings. What if Ben said or did something to annoy this tribe? Fortunately, Ben's command of the Maori language was extremely limited, and the Maoris spoke only a little French, so most of the male conversation was conducted in sign-language. From what she could make of the gestures the subjects seemed to be limited to the universal male obsessions of food, fighting and fornication, so she could only hope that Ben managed to avoid giving offence on any of those subjects.

The women of the tribe were as delightful as the Whanganui women had been, and made her just as welcome. They had traded freely with Europeans for some time now, and the evidence of this was apparent in the pots and blankets in their *whares*, and in the European dresses some of them wore. But she could find out little about the Frenchman across the lake, apart from the fact that he was not a recent arrival. According to the women, the *Wiwi* had rejected all attempts by the local tribe to be friendly, and the Ngati Tuwharetoa were now too offended to continue trying.

With mischievous giggles the women pointed out many items of clothing they wore, a cache of clothes pegs and even a washboard. It appeared that they made frequent raids on the *Wiwi*'s washing line as retribution for his slights. She examined a dress they showed her, an exquisitely worked concoction of velvet and lace, of the kind that only very wealthy women could afford and very much in vogue. How odd to see it here, in this dark *whare*, lying on the dirt floor!

'So the *Wiwi* has a wife?' she asked and they nodded and tapped their heads meaningfully. The wife was as crazy as her husband and would chase away anyone who dared to come close. If she caught you—and ai! Was she fast!—she would beat you with a broom. But if you were clever and stayed out of reach she would throw things, handy things, like buckets and shoes. It sounded like a vastly entertaining game, albeit one-sided, and Emma felt a twinge of sympathy for this poor, unknown woman, trying to keep her beautiful possessions out of the grasp of the marauding locals.

'I'd like to meet this woman,' she told them, and they nodded and said yes, certainly, the next day they would take her. It was all being arranged.

* * *

True to their word, a canoe was prepared before dawn and a large contingent of Maoris took Ben, Emma and Rima across the lake. The journey took hours but the warriors made it seem effortless, paddling the huge, ornately carved canoe in time to a rhythmic chant. There was not a breath of wind and they seemed to be skimming over blue glass, so smooth was the water. Watching the dense forest slide by so swiftly was a novel experience for Emma after days of walking.

She had prepared as best she could, washing Rima's shift and the better of her black dresses, and leaving them to hang overnight to avoid creasing. Her bonnet was too badly torn from days of walking through the bush to wear, and so she had been forced to restrain her hair in a neat bun at her nape. She was satisfied that they looked as respectable as was possible, given the circumstances.

Ben was wearing his old moleskin trousers, and the shirt he was wearing—while it had been roomy on Thomas—was rather close-fitting on him. But at least it was clean. He was crouched in the bow of the canoe, swiftly sketching the terrain, occasionally checking his compass. As they approached the north shore he packed away his equipment with movements that had a distinct air of finality about them. Watching him as carefully as she was, she saw the tension leave his shoulders and, when he caught her eye, he smiled broadly.

'You've finished,' she stated unnecessarily.

'I have.' The satisfaction was evident in his voice.

'Have you decided which way you…' she hesitated and then continued '…we should return?'

He was silent as he studied the nearing shore. The spray from the oars had dampened and tangled his hair, and his dark stubble had grown to be almost a beard. He had never looked so ruffianly, as scruffy and as utterly desirable as he did then. She bit hard on her lip and dragged her eyes away.

'I don't honestly know yet, Mrs Johnson. If we go by the fastest route back down the river, we run the risk of these very nice people offering to take us.'

She hadn't thought of that. It would, of course, provide the Ngati Tuwharetoa with the perfect excuse to escort them down the Whanganui with a war-party, and her own tribe would scarcely overlook the provocation. However, the Frenchman must have come by an alternative route, and he would surely have supplies brought in on a regular basis. He would be able to advise them with confidence.

They landed at a long, sandy bay on the north shore.

'Up there is the *Wiwi*,' one of the warriors told Emma. He showed her a well-beaten path through the forest. 'On top of the hill. We will wait here a while if you should decide to come back with us. We could take you to the *Wiwi* ourselves, but…' He grinned and tapped his head in the by-now familiar gesture. She translated for Ben, who nodded and gave his thanks in French.

'After all,' he commented to Emma, 'we may be no more welcome to him than the Maoris. Anyone who would choose to live all alone out here has to be a bit…what's the word they use?'

'*Porangi.*'

'Yeah. *Porangi*. Or a missionary.' He slung their bags over his back and grinned at her scowl. 'Well, let's go and meet this lunatic.'

There were steps cut into the hill, making the climb easy. On the brow of the hill the path widened abruptly and the three of them came to a halt.

'Good God,' Ben whispered. 'It's a bloody chateau!'

Small, neatly pruned bay trees bordered the dirt path, leading to a pair of huge iron gates. Although the gates were closed, and looked to have been for a long time, they presented no obstacle, as there was no fence on either side. Beyond lay what Ben had described as a chateau, and indeed it was obviously intended to be a scaled-down replica of such a building. It had a turret either side, small battlements along the roof line, and long, narrow windows. The veranda at the rear, and the fact that it had been built in wood and not stone, were almost the only acknowledgements that the house was in New Zealand and not in France. Despite its sheer eccentricity, it was a grand house by anyone's standards, and absolutely the last thing Emma had ever expected to see so many miles from civilisation.

They negotiated their way around the iron gates and walked up the path. The garden had been formally set out in the European manner, with low boxwood hedges and carefully measured plantings, but it was clear that the introduced plants were struggling to survive in the acid volcanic soils. Set among the gardens were stone plinths, even an unadorned fountain, and Emma thought it a safe guess that the missing statues had been irresistible to the Maoris.

'So much work,' she said under her breath to Ben, as they approached the wide steps leading up to the front doors. 'But it's all rather...'

'Futile?' he suggested quietly, and she nodded.

The doors were flung open with a flourish as they reached the bottom step, and the man who was without doubt the owner of the house stood there, his arms spread wide in welcome. A man of perhaps fifty, shorter even than Emma, with carefully arranged white hair and small beard, he carried himself with an air of great dignity. Immaculately attired in dark trousers and jacket, he could have that moment stepped straight from a Parisian salon.

'*Bon jour, mes amis!*' he boomed in a voice that was much larger than his frame. 'I am the Baron de Visceni. Welcome to my humble home.'

Ben held out his hand. 'Thank you, sir. My name is Benedict Morgan.'

'Ah, welcome, welcome!' The small man pumped his hand enthusiastically. 'An Englishman, are you not?'

'I'm from New South Wales,' Ben confessed, and the Baron beamed even more widely.

'Delighted, sir, delighted! And this lovely lady...?'

'My wife,' Ben said without a second's hesitation. Emma had no time to object before the Baron swept her hand up to his lips.

'*Enchanté*, madame. My wife will be delighted to meet another lady! Please, both of you, come in! Come in!'

They were ushered in so swiftly that Emma only
just had time to grab Rima before the door shut
behind them. They stood in a reception room that
was two floors high, panelled in dark wood. The
only light came from the long windows, which were
heavily draped in dark velvet. The dusty light shone
dully on a vast chandelier and highlighted the deep,
rich colours of the thick rugs on the polished floor.

A woman stepped forward from the shadows.
Taller than her husband, she had the narrow, stern
face of an aristocrat. Under her plain, beautifully cut
black dress her back was ramrod-straight. Large di-
amond rings glittered on her fingers and at her ears.
Wondering how much notice the Baroness had had
that visitors were arriving, or whether she always
dressed like that, Emma automatically made a small
curtsy. The Baroness's severe features softened per-
ceptibly.

'How kind of you to call,' she said graciously,
her voice as heavily accented as her husband's, as
she extended a few fingers to them both—scented
fingers, Emma noted. 'I am sure you would both
like some refreshments after your journey?' She
spoke as if they had simply been passing by, instead
of struggling to this destination for weeks.

'Thank you,' Emma said gratefully. 'That would
be wond—'

'Oh,' the Baroness interrupted sharply. She had
been turning towards one of the doors leading from
the reception hall but stopped abruptly as she saw
Rima for the first time. Her fine, high-bridged nose
wrinkled as if an unpleasant smell had wafted past.

'I see you have a child with you. Would you care to leave her outside?'

Ben reached over and ruffled Rima's hair. 'This is Rima, our daughter,' he said with a disarming smile. 'I'm sure she'd like something to drink too, madame.'

'Your child?' There was a long silence in which Emma was sure that a multitude of possibilities passed through the Baroness's mind. Eventually she sniffed and nodded. 'This way, please.'

The salon she led them to was as dark as the reception room, with brocaded, overstuffed furniture and heavy curtains. With an elegant wave of her hand the Baroness indicated that they be seated, and tugged on the bell-pull. Emma sat stiffly on a small armchair, taking care to tuck her muddy and battered boots beneath her skirt. Ben took a chair opposite, pulling the stunned Rima on to his knee as if it was the most natural gesture in the world to him. Only Emma knew that it was to prevent Rima from flying around the room exploring.

When no servant had appeared after a minute or two, the Baroness excused herself, and the Baron, insisting that a stronger drink was called for, busied himself with pouring brandy into two large bowls for himself and Ben. While the Baron was thus occupied, Emma leaned forward.

'Mr Morgan…'

'Yes, Mrs Morgan.' And the warning in his eyes was so explicit that her words of protest died. She sat back unhappily. It was wrong to lie, and goodness only knew what would come of this pretence, but she had come to trust Ben's judgement by now.

If he was choosing not to tell the Baron and his wife the truth, then he must have a very good reason for it.

Besides, she reflected, as she watched the Baron press a huge brandy on to Ben, this was a most peculiar situation.

'Now, my friends,' said the Baron jovially as he took a seat. 'This is such an unexpected pleasure. Please tell me how you happen to arrive here?'

Ben took an appreciative swig of his brandy and settled down in his chair, his grip on Rima tightening slightly as she tried to inch her way free. 'My wife and I were looking to farm in this area. We had hoped that there would be some settlements around here but—' he gave an admiring nod at their elegant surroundings '—we had no idea that we would find this degree of civilisation.'

The Baron beamed proprietarily. 'Well, I dare say I could make you a grant of a nice piece of land to break in…'

'We were certainly not looking to infringe upon your own land,' Ben broke in, and the Baron laughed.

'My dear young man! But this is all my land.'

'Oh?' Ben leaned forward politely. 'How far does your land extend, sir?'

For the first time the Baron looked slightly offended. 'How far? How far can you see, Mr Morgan? This is *all* my land. My country. I am the Emperor of New Zealand!'

Chapter Nine

Emma stared unhappily at herself in the gilt-edged mirror. The old, mellow glass threw back a softly flattering reflection, but there was no hiding the ruin that the harsh New Zealand sun had wrought on her complexion. So much for remembering to wear her bonnet all the time—it had not stopped her from tanning. She touched her cheeks and frowned. Freckles! She had not had those since she was a child.

There were pots of cosmetics on the dressing-table, and she turned to look among them for a whitening cream. Then she stopped, her hand hovering in mid-air. This was vanity, one of the sins she had been most guilty of before she married Thomas. Resolutely, she turned from the mirror.

The upstairs bedroom that the surly Maori serving girl had shown her to was huge, panelled in dark wood like the rest of the house, and opulently furnished. The big bed with its ornately carved posts looked inviting after months of sleeping on the hard ground, and Rima had bounced up and down on it most enthusiastically before falling asleep. Emma had covered her with a featherdown quilt. She was almost tempted to lie down beside her—it was still two hours before dinner—but somehow she knew that even a nap would not be achievable in her present state of mind.

Hot water had been brought to the room and she had washed and changed into one of the dresses that the Baroness had very kindly lent her. Dark green, with a collar of ivory lace, it was as lovely as any of the dresses she had owned in her life before her marriage, and it needed only a little pinning to shorten the skirt. The silk felt luxurious under her fingers and she could not resist a little spin to feel its soft weight against her legs.

From the mullioned windows she could see Ben and the Baron strolling in the beautiful, sickly garden. Snatches of their conversation, in French, drifted up to her on the still air. Ben had his head bent down towards the Baron, his face intent, and she wondered what they were talking about. It was odd to have the tables turned on her, and not to be able to understand a word they were saying.

Rima muttered in her sleep and Emma came to stand over her as she slept, tenderness threatening to overwhelm her at the sight of the weary little dark head on the big white pillow. Ben had blithely ignored all the Baroness's pointed comments about the child being happier downstairs with the Maori servants, and so Rima had remained with her 'parents'.

Dragging her eyes away, she turned and ran her fingers admiringly over the collection of small figurines above the mantelpiece, over the gold-embossed spines of the books—all in French—on the bedside table. A vase of full-blown crimson roses, the first she had seen since Sydney, lent their heady scent to the warm air. Under her feet the thick Persian rug felt seductively soft and she curled her toes into its depths in bliss. She could not recall ever being in a house as splendidly furnished as this. It was a house befitting an Emperor, she supposed. It was a folly, a glorious piece of whimsy… And yet something about the Baron's whimsy deeply disturbed her, although she could not say what that something was. The Baron was quite delightful and the Baroness, while colder in manner, had been both gracious and hospitable. Perhaps they were both what they seemed, a charming, eccentric aristocratic couple who had chosen to claim sovereignty over a country that no one else appeared to want. Eventually, of course, circumstances would force common sense upon them, but in the meantime, was there really any harm in their fantasy?

There came the sound of Ben's quick footsteps on the stairs. Closing the door behind him, he studied the luxurious room with a frown.

'I see the Baroness has made you very comfortable here.'

Emma fiddled nervously with the collar at her throat as she saw him look at the only bed in the room. 'I…I believe we're intended to share the room, Mr Morgan—'

'I'll be perfectly comfortable in the chair,' he broke in evenly. Then, as he drew towards her, he screwed up his nose. 'What's that smell? It's not you, is it?'

She looked around her, puzzled. 'I don't know. The roses…?'

'That's them.' To her horror he grabbed the gorgeous things out of their vase and tossed them out of the window. 'I can't abide the stink of the things,' he said by way of explanation. 'Promise you'll never wear rosewater around me, Mrs Johnson.'

'I doubt that I'll ever have the opportunity,' she said, quite taken aback by his odd behaviour. Perhaps the eccentricity of the de Viscenis was infectious.

He stayed by the window, staring down at the garden below, and for the first time she realised that he was distinctly uneasy.

'I don't think we should stay here past tonight,' he said slowly, confirming her suspicions.

She thought of the comfortable bed awaiting her that night. Of the hot water brought to her room earlier, the soft clothes on her back, the thick carpet under her toes, the delicious smell of dinner wafting up from the kitchen. The small moan of dismay that escaped her lips was entirely voluntary.

Ben moved away from the light in the window. 'I take it you like it here, Mrs Johnson.'

'The Baron and his wife have been more than kind.' She came closer, dropping her voice. 'But I don't understand why you're insisting that we say we're married.'

'You don't understand why I didn't introduce you as a missionary's widow I picked up along the

Whanganui River, and with whom I've been sleeping every night this last couple of weeks?'

Emma swallowed her embarrassment. 'I would hardly describe our relationship as that…'

'I'm sure you wouldn't, but I think our hosts would.' He took her by the shoulders and lowered his voice to a tense whisper. 'Listen to me, madam. Charming as our host may be, he hates the New Zealand Company. He hates the English. He hates the missionaries. He hates the Maoris. Have I left anyone out? The only reason we've been asked to stay here is because we're the only white faces they've seen in months and because I'm an honest farmer from New South Wales. Everyone else is out to steal his country away from him, as far as he can see!'

She stared at him blankly. 'But they've both been so kind to us!'

'Because you had the good manners to curtsy to the Baroness and because neither of us had the face to tell them they're both insane. The Baron firmly believes he is the Emperor of New Zealand by divine right.' He gave her a little shake as she made a scornful face. 'Yes, you can humour him, and treat him like some kind of harmless eccentric. Except that I think he might be more than that.'

'What are you saying?'

'That I think he might carry things too far. And that we ought to get out as soon as we can.'

Emma sank down on to the edge of the bed, holding on to the bedpost for support. 'Mr Morgan, why do I have the feeling that you're not telling me everything?'

He sat down beside her, careful not to wake Rima. 'There's a treaty that's being signed this month at Waitangi, in the far north, between most of the North Island tribes and the British Government. Have you heard of it?' She shook her head. 'They were talking about it when I left Wellington in January. There was a lot to be sorted out, and the Missionary Society are interfering in there as well, but there's every reason to believe that it will be signed—if it hasn't been already—and that New Zealand is now a colony of Britain. Which leaves our friend the Emperor without a country to rule.'

She rested her head wearily against the bedpost. It had taken so long to get here. It was as if all the trials and stresses of the long journey had suddenly caught up with her. 'And you want us to leave before he finds out.'

'Yes.'

Cautiously, as if not to frighten her, he took her chin in his hand and made her meet his eyes. His fingers against her skin were warm and calloused and, to her dismay, she felt a strong lurch of desire shoot through her stomach. She could only pray that nothing of her consternation showed in her expression.

'Trust me,' Ben said softly, as if she had any choice in the matter.

Dinner was served promptly at eight o'clock, with an elegance that quite took Emma's breath away. In the long dining-room the crimson velvet curtains had been drawn against the dark, and candlelight glittered on the chased silver utensils that were laid with precision on an ornate damask tablecloth. They took their seats with due formality, assisted by the Maori servants, each of whom was dressed in the smart red livery of the Emperor of New Zealand.

The servants stood in the shadows, unobtrusive and silent. When Emma smiled at the young girl who filled her soup plate the girl deliberately averted her eyes, her expression distinctly unfriendly.

'They're from Auckland,' the Baroness said when Emma asked. 'I wouldn't have any of the local natives in this house. They're all thieves, all of them. But at least none of these servants have relatives living nearby that they can pass stolen property to.' She sighed dramatically and threw an accusatory look in the direction of her husband at the other end of the table. 'You can have no idea of what we have to put up with here. None at all.'

Emma glanced at the servants but, if they had understood the Baroness's English speech, they gave no sign of it. Not, Emma thought, that the Baroness would have cared if they had.

In the hour before dinner, Emma had taken the precaution of requesting cutlery from the kitchen and had given Rima intensive instruction in how to eat at a table. While she was sure that Rima would be well looked after in the kitchen while she and Ben ate, she didn't want to give the Baroness any excuse to separate her from the child.

'If you don't know what to do, just watch how Mr Morgan and I eat,' she had advised Rima, correcting her grip on the fork for the umpteenth time.

Rima had nodded, scowling fiercely with concentration as she pulled apart the piece of bread they had been practicing on with the tines of her fork.

'And Rima…' Emma had hesitated, and then plunged on. 'If the servants should ask you about us, the baron and his wife call me Mrs Morgan. They…they think I'm married to Mr Morgan.'

Rima glanced up at her in surprise. 'You *are* married to him.'

'Why do you say that?'

'You lie with Pen. You're Pen's wife. I don't mind now. I probably won't try to kill him anymore.'

'Good,' Emma had said weakly, wondering how she was ever going to adapt Rima to polite society. 'And do you know what Mr Morgan does, Rima?'

'He makes pictures.' Rima had looked around for the sealskin bag, but Ben had taken the precaution of placing his maps in what looked like a little-used upper cupboard in the bedroom.

'No, he's a farmer. He works in a *mahinga*.' Which wasn't a lie, exactly. He had been a farmer in New South Wales, and might well be again, one day. And it was crucial that Rima not let slip to the other Maoris that he was a surveyor. But Rima had shrugged, uninterested, and begun to attack the piece of bread again.

After the expectations that had been built up by the beautifully laid table, the meal itself was a little disappointing. *Kumara* soup, indifferently stewed duck with more *kumara*, a salad of wilted *puha*— but Emma was grateful for food that she had not had to kill or cook herself and so she took pleasure in dining off the fine, gold-rimmed plates and sipping the finest wines she had ever tasted from the array of crystal glasses before her. For the Emperor's wine collection was, by his own boast, perhaps the best in the South Pacific. With a different wine for each of the four courses, Emma began to feel decidedly mellow as the evening progressed.

She was careful, however, to keep her wits about her and follow the background that Ben had created, that of a would-be farmer and his wife, looking for a desirable place to settle in the central North Island. Fortunately, the Baron did most of the talking, breaking frequently into French. The baroness said little, apart from the occasional sharp admonition in French to the servants. That Emma plainly did not understand a word of their language did not seem to concern either of the de Viscenis.

Rima's presence was also ignored by their hosts, but she was doing remarkably well, requiring only a little help from Emma to cut up her duck. When the final course arrived, of candied fruit and tiny *bon bons*, Rima was almost beside herself with delight.

'Do you eat them?' she whispered to Emma, as an exquisite chocolate-coated confection was placed on her plate. At Emma's nod she took a tiny nibble and a look of utter bliss spread over her face.

Emma raised her head to find Ben watching them both, his eyes alight with amusement. He had shaved, and without the softening effect of facial hair, his face was all harsh masculinity. His smile, then, was all the more potent, and Emma found her breath catching in her throat at the sight. I love him, she thought, and then scoffed at herself for the very idea. Love? She had never been in love in her life. She had become fond of him, that was all. These weeks of closeness, and he had been very kind to her and to Rima…

So why did she feel such a compulsion to touch him? To go into his arms and lay her head on his chest, to kiss him and stroke his beautiful, roughened skin and then…

It was lust. That was all it was. Another vice to overcome, like those of vanity and her love of luxury. She remembered Thomas and felt her resolve strengthen. Ben's eyes left hers and he reached across the table to remove Emma's glass from Rima's hand.

'Wine is not a good idea for little girls.'

The previously full glass was completely empty.

'Rima, no! *Hei aha*? You have water to drink.'

Rima smirked. 'I want some more.' As Emma shook her head Rima glowered and kicked at her chair. It was clear that her period of good behaviour was over.

'*Ka nui tenei*. That's enough, Rima.'

As gracefully as she could, Emma excused herself and took Rima upstairs. By the time they reached the bedroom door Rima was yawning hugely and it was the work of a few minutes to wash her hands and face and tuck her up in bed. Emma sat quietly on the bed for a while, watching the faint flickering of the lamp on the bedside table. Downstairs she could hear the Baron laughing uproariously at something Ben said. From the kitchen came the gentle, domestic noises of clattering plates and the hum of Maori voices. It felt so strange to be in a European household again, and nowhere near as pleasant as she had thought it would be. Again, she felt a niggling sense of unease at the elegant artifice that was the Baron's empire. Something was very wrong, and she was sure Ben knew what it was.

When at last she was sure that Rima was soundly asleep, she went downstairs to find the Baroness waiting for her.

'We shall leave the gentlemen to their brandy,' she said coolly, cutting through Emma's stammered apologies. Emma followed her into the small sitting-room, where a pot of strong coffee awaited them. Admiring the Baroness's embroidery at hand filled a few minutes but, as the Baroness tended to respond to all questions in monosyllables, conversation was a struggle.

'Do you prefer New Zealand to France, Baroness?' Emma asked, taking the cup the baroness had poured for her.

'No.'

'This is a particularly beautiful part of the country, don't you agree?'

'It is wild and full of savages.' The Baroness picked up her embroidery hoop and began to stitch a European landscape with small, perfect stitches. It had begun to dawn on Emma that the Frenchwoman much preferred her own company. She drank her coffee in silence, hoping that Ben would not be long. A small yawn escaped her attempt to stifle it, and at once the Baroness laid down her hoop.

'You are tired, Mrs Morgan.'

'Well, yes, I am a little…'

'Then you have my permission to retire.'

Emma felt as if she should back out of the room, curtsying as she went. In their bedroom Rima was still soundly asleep, but Emma felt far too restless to join her.

After an hour or so she heard the servants moving around the house extinguishing the lights for the night, but there was still no sign of Ben. Outside a full moon hovered, illuminating billows of milky steam. Emma remembered the ornamental hot pools their hosts had shown them that afternoon in the gardens at the rear of the house. One pool, in particular, had been landscaped for bathing. Suddenly the thought of hot, clean water was too tempting to resist. Taking a towel, she made her way carefully down the stairs and past the dining-room, where the men were still talking quietly in French.

She had no need of a lamp to find the pool she was looking for. On one side a small half-wall provided privacy from the house, and the forest overhung the pool on the other side. The night was still, with only the steady bubbling hiss of the hot underground fountains to break the silence. She undressed and stepped down into the pool, easing herself slowly into the hot water until she was sitting on a submerged rock. She felt the heat gradually suffuse through her body, soothing the aches from her tired muscles. Such luxury, such absolute bliss!

After a while it became a little too hot for comfort, and she moved higher up the rock, to where the water was waist-high. The moon had moved higher in the sky, almost eclipsing the stars, and she tilted her head back to watch, marvelling at the soft, magical light it threw over the forest. She could almost believe she was a part of the magic, a mermaid perhaps, or no—a nymph of the forest. She felt wanton and free with the cold air on her breasts and the warm water caressing her legs. She shook her head, loving the feel of her hair falling free down her back. Fleetingly, she wondered what Thomas would have made of this behaviour and, for the first time, found that she didn't care.

She lowered her eyes and only slowly made out the dark outline of a man, seated on the low stone wall around the pool, watching her. With a gasp she slipped down into the water, even as she registered that the man was Ben.

'What are you doing here?' she spluttered.

'Looking for you. I thought I'd better try to find you myself before raising the alarm with our hosts.' He spoke slowly, with the careful precision of the very drunk. 'You have beautiful breasts, Mrs Johnson. Perfectly round. That's rare in a woman.'

She twisted around so that her back was to him. 'You must leave, Mr Morgan,' she told him, but her voice sounded hollow even to her ears.

'Yes, I should. I'm sorry. Only…I can't help wanting you, Mrs Johnson. More than I've ever wanted any other woman, and that's the truth. I want you, and I can't have you, and I think it's killing me.'

Despite the heat of the water a slow shiver of desire ran through her. She stared up at the glowing sky and thought—why not? I want him and he wants me, and it's not as if he was the first… Why should I keep on pretending that I am what I'm not?

Her words came out in a shaky rush.

'If you want me, Ben, then you…can have me.'

The only answer she received was the quiet bubbling of the water.

'Ben?'

When she turned around he had gone, leaving her feeling foolish and frustrated. At least he wasn't there to hear the names she called herself, names she had learned from the dockside taverns of Sydney.

Chapter Ten

As usual, common sense asserted itself with the light of day. She had no idea where Ben had spent the night, but when she and Rima came down to breakfast the next morning he was at the table alone, obviously nursing a sore head.

'Good morning,' he said, rising to his feet. As Emma took her seat he remained standing, his eyes awkwardly fixed on the table before her. 'I…I believe I should apologise for last night…'

'You had far too much to drink, Mr Morgan,' Emma said calmly. 'And I think we should leave the matter there, don't you?'

He opened and shut his mouth, and then nodded. 'Thank you.'

It was a delightful change to have him at a disadvantage for once, and she thought the previous night's humiliation almost worth it. The de Viscenis joined them then, the Baron as expansive and the Baroness as reserved as the day before.

Breakfast was delicious, consisting of coffee and small, hot rolls served with strawberry conserve.

The Baron was more inclined to speak in English this morning, and he chattered away most entertainingly about his library that, he assured Emma, held many English volumes which she was welcome to read at her leisure.

'Thank you,' Ben broke in over her appreciation, 'but as I said last night, we really must be leaving today.'

Emma was certain she saw a flicker of relief pass over the Baroness's rigid features, but the Baron looked positively stricken.

'Leave? But—Mr and Mrs Morgan—have we not made you welcome?'

'More than welcome, thank you, Baron,' Ben said firmly. 'But we must leave.'

The Baron threw his small hands up in a Gallic show of horror. 'Back into the wilderness, Mr Morgan? When I have offered you a portion of country here, a beautiful piece of land? You and your wife can stay here and build, surely? I shall arrange for stock, for seeds to be brought here…'

Ben shook his head. 'Thank you, Baron, but we must go.'

The Baron's mouth pursed truculently, and for a second he looked just like Rima in a tantrum. '*Non!* I forbid it. You will stay here.' His wife opened her mouth to speak but he quelled her with a single look. 'You will stay, I order it. Now, Mrs Morgan, you would like to finish your coffee before I show you my library?'

Perhaps sensing the strained atmosphere between the adults, Rima chose that moment to abandon her struggle with the spoon and to tip the entire contents of the conserve jar over her plate. The Baroness took this breach of etiquette so seriously that it was easy for Emma to remove Rima from the table.

'He is joking, isn't he?' she demanded of Ben when he later joined them in their bedroom. Although the de Viscenis remained in the breakfast-room, she spoke quietly so as not to be overheard. 'He can't stop us leaving—I mean, why would he?'

Ben sat heavily in the armchair. 'He likes us here.'

'He likes *you* here.'

'True.' He got to his feet and lifted Rima away from the dressing-table, where she had been decorating the mirror with face cream. 'Do that again, Rat,' he told her calmly, 'and I'll throw you out the window. Do you understand?'

Rima grunted comprehension and he put her down again.

'I think the Baroness would be delighted to see Rima and me go,' Emma said ruefully, grabbing Rima by the collar as the child ran to look out the window to gauge the length of the drop.

'Yes, I think she probably would,' Ben said absently, his attention caught by some movement on the hills beyond the garden. 'If you can gather together our luggage, we'll leave tonight when it's dark.'

'That's a little rude, don't you think? To leave without so much as a ''thank you'' for all their kindness…'

'It's the only way to get away from them, believe me,' Ben murmured. His hand on the windowpane clenched suddenly into a fist. 'And if this is what I think it is…'

He turned on his heel and left the room. Emma raised her eyebrows in puzzlement at Rima.

'I wonder what the problem is? I'm going to go and ask for a cloth to clean up the mess you made on the mirror, Rima. Promise me you won't touch anything while I'm gone? *Please?*'

But the noise emanating from the breakfast-room put all thoughts of cleaning cloths from her mind. A Maori she had not seen at the house before met her in the hallway, desperation to escape clearly written over his face. Behind him rose a tirade of French and the sound of crashing plates. Ben met her at the breakfast-room door and barred her entry.

'Go back to your room, Emma.'

She peered over his shoulder at the ruin of the breakfast table and the Baroness in tears. 'What has happened?'

'The Auckland papers have arrived.'

'Has…has the treaty been signed? The one you were talking about?' she whispered.

'Yes. Emma, go to your room. I'll be up later.'

Thoroughly unsettled by now, she returned upstairs to find that Rima had tried to clean the cream from the mirror with a bedsheet. She tidied up as best she could, but could find no servants to inquire about fresh linen. When she looked out the window she saw them huddled together under the trees at the far end of the garden, presumably waiting until the Baron calmed down. She couldn't blame them.

Eventually the shouting died down, but there was still no sign of Ben. Bored with being confined to their room, Emma took Rima on a long walk along the lakefront to look at the hot mudpools.

Hours later, Ben came to find them.

'I'm sorry to have left the house,' Emma began, but he cut through her apologies with a shake of his head.

'It was probably just as well that you did.' He lowered himself to sit beside her in the shade of a spreading, gold-flowered *kowhai* tree, from where she could watch Rima frolicking in the lake a few yards away. He looked troubled and tired, and she could not resist touching him lightly on the sleeve in sympathy.

'Won't you tell me what's going on, Ben?'

A smile curved the weary line of his mouth. 'That's the first time you've called me by my first name, Emma.'

It wasn't, quite, but she was hardly going to tell him that. She waited patiently and at last he sighed and looked away, across the lake.

'The Baron declared this country his about four years ago. As he saw it, the British didn't want it, the French were only slightly interested in it, and the Missionary Society had no right to it. He advised all three by royal proclamation, and as far as he was concerned, that was the end of the matter.

'Living out here in isolation, he doesn't seem to have realised that not only did no one take him seriously, but the British didn't like the idea of this becoming a colony of France. Hence the treaty that was signed last week.'

'I see,' Emma said slowly. 'No wonder he's so upset. But there's not much he can do about it now.'

'That's not the way he sees it.' He pointed to where a small canoe was disappearing into the hazy horizon of the lake. 'That's a messenger from the Baron to the tribes of the southern end of the lake. A messenger has already gone to the tribes in the north. They've all been summoned here, to a meeting tomorrow.

'None of the tribes in the area have signed the treaty yet. He proposes to form them into an army to oust the British and the missionaries, leaving himself as undisputed ruler of New Zealand.'

Emma shook her head, caught between amusement and pity. 'Oh, the poor deluded man! The Maoris hate him, Ben! They'll never agree to it.'

'I rather think they will.' He rested his head against the tree trunk and closed his eyes. 'He showed me his cellar last night, Emma. Crate upon crate of rifles, boxes of shot, kegs of gunpowder, even a goddamned cannon, all for the Maoris if they agree to join him against the British. There's not much of an army in the country at the moment— even if they call in the troops stationed in Tasmania it'll take months before they get here. If the Baron acts now, before the British start arriving in real numbers, he can effectively take control.'

'You should have told me all this earlier! All this time I thought he was just an eccentric old man, but *this…!*'

'Emma, last night I talked and talked to him until I was blue in the face. Nothing I said—nothing anyone says—is going to change his mind. He's quite convinced that just arming the tribes will achieve a peaceful surrender from the British, and that when it's all over, everyone will realise he's acting in the best interests of all parties. He's not a bad man, Emma—just a mad man.' He took her limp hand in his and said urgently, 'We've got to get out of here tonight, as soon as it's dark. We'll take a canoe across the lake and travel back down the Whanganui. It shouldn't take more than a week.'

'And the tribes? What happens to them once they have the Baron's guns?'

He looked uncomfortable. 'You know what will happen then.'

'They'll go to war with each other.'

'Emma, stay out of this. It's none of our business!'

'Yes, it is,' she said firmly. 'We must stop it, because no one else is going to be able to. Somehow we must get rid of the ammunition and the guns. The problem is how.'

Ben said nothing, but his mouth was white with anger as he turned away to watch Rima playing contentedly by the lake. Emma continued to think aloud.

'If we threw them in the lake—the guns and ammunition, I mean…'

'Too heavy,' Ben said shortly. 'There's hundreds of the damn things down there. How d'you propose to carry them a couple of hundred yards down to the lake in secrecy?'

'Hmm. The gunpowder is in kegs, though, isn't it? We can roll them down to the lake.'

'God spare me from well-meaning, interfering

missionaries!' Ben snarled and got to his feet, but
Emma had long since learned that his tempers were
short-lived, and she leapt up to stand beside him,
quite undeterred by the rage in his eyes.

'You know I'm right.'

He gave an exasperated sigh. 'Yes, you're right.
You're always bloody right. Just remember to tell
Saint Peter that when I'm banging on Heaven's gate
for admittance, will you?'

She grinned impishly. 'You think they'll let you
in?'

'Not a chance.'

Without thinking, she stood on tiptoe and planted
a kiss on his lips. 'You're a good man, Ben.'

Ben caught her by the waist when she would have
moved away, and kissed her back, his lips passing
swiftly over hers in a kiss that was so tenderly affectionate that she never wanted it to end.

'I wish you'd let me prove just how good I can
be, Emma,' he said. And then Rima was upon then,
splashing them with water and crowing disgustedly
about them kissing, and Emma lost the chance to
reply.

By the time they returned to the house, late in the
afternoon, things had returned to some semblance
of normality. The Baron was closeted in his study,
surrounded by maps of his 'Empire' and when he
heard their arrival he pulled Ben in to discuss mil-
itary strategies.

'Go straight to your room. Say nothing,' Ben
whispered to Emma before the Baron shut the study
door on her, and she could only hope that this time

Ben would be successful in making the Baron see sense. Given the excited light of battle in the Baron's eyes, however, she somehow doubted it.

The Baroness was in the parlour, dusting off an ornately braided jacket that she informed Emma was the Emperor's coronation suit.

'He shall wear it tomorrow, when he addresses his people.' She frowned at a small mark on the ribboned pocket and dabbed it with a damp cloth. 'It is very smart, *non*? I sewed it myself.'

'It's very smart, madame.' Emma motioned to Rima to go up to the bedroom alone and then turned nervously back to the Baroness. Ben had explicitly warned her against saying anything, but she could not stand idly by when the Baroness could prove a powerful ally.

'Madame, this war that your husband is planning against the British…'

The Baroness put down the jacket to stare at her coldly. 'The British know very well that my husband is the legitimate Emperor of this country. This treaty they have signed means nothing. *Nothing!* They have no power here. They cannot usurp him.'

Emma closed her eyes for a moment while she struggled for control. 'Madame, you cannot arm the Maoris! They will turn the guns on each other!'

'I see.' The Baroness carefully laid down the jacket on her escritoire and opened a drawer. 'Of course, Mrs Morgan, you are English. I had thought your loyalty would have lain with your husband, but I am wrong, it seems.'

Emma stared in disbelief at the small pistol that

the Baroness took out of the drawer and aimed at her.

'Please go to the study, Mrs Morgan. My husband will know how to deal with your treachery.'

Ben looked up as Emma opened the study door, his mouth shaping an obscenity as he instantly comprehended the situation. There was a rapid exchange of views in French between the Baron and his wife, and then the Baron looked at them in genuine regret.

'I'm so sorry, my friends. I offered you so much... But I need to trust those around me at a time like this.'

'I understand,' Ben said tightly, his eyes on the barrel pressing against Emma's forehead. 'Look, Baron, you're a busy man. Why don't you just let us go on our way so that you can concentrate on your meeting tomorrow?'

The Baron thought about that. 'I think perhaps you should remain as our guests until after the meeting. Then you may take our message with you out to your wife's countrymen.' The Baroness broke in urgently, but he waved her objections away with a regal hand. 'Please return to your room, Mr and Mrs Morgan. And I do most sincerely regret that this has come to pass.'

As the key turned in their bedroom door, Emma met Ben's eyes apologetically.

'I had to say something to her, Ben! I thought she might see reason, even if her husband didn't! If I'd thought for a moment that she was as insane as her husband...'

He gave a short laugh. 'Oh, she's much worse than her husband. She wanted to shoot you there and then. At least the Baron is still hoping for a happy ending.' He looked around the room. 'Where's Rat?'

Emma collapsed in an unhappy heap on the bed. 'I told her to come up here and she's disobeyed me again! Oh, Ben, why can't she ever do what she's told!'

'Hush! She'll be all right.' Ben sat beside her and pulled her against him so that her head rested on his shoulder. 'She's very good at taking care of herself, and our hosts don't seem to notice her at all. She'll be outside waiting for us.'

Emma allowed herself to melt against his warmth and strength. 'What do we do now?'

'If no other opportunity turns up, I suggest we wait until dark and then climb out the window. This is hardly a fortress they're holding us in.'

'And then we take the gunpowder out of the cellar and take it down to the lake?'

'I do that. You and Rima wait in safety in the forest.'

She rubbed her face against his shirt, breathing in the heady masculine scent of his skin. 'We do that. I want to make sure every last keg is submerged before we leave.'

'You're an impossible woman,' he growled and kissed her. She responded with alacrity, threading her fingers though his hair to hold him close. Whether it was desperation or desire she felt, she had no idea. All she knew was that she had waited long enough. He pulled his head back, his eyes half-closed.

'Emma,' he whispered, and his fingers came up to cup her breasts. 'Are you sure you want this?'

For answer she pulled apart the buttons of her bodice and placed his hands inside. The rough skin of his fingers caught on the tips of her breasts, teasing them unbearably, and she groaned at the delicious pain that shot through her. Yes, she wanted this! And much, much more besides.

Ben rolled her on to her back, pulling at her skirts, and she helped him, tugging impatiently at the impediment to her pleasure. She hesitated for just a moment when she first held him her hand, fearful of his size, but then he was inside her, filling her, stretching her, and all she knew was the plunging ecstasy as he moved, the wildness, the joy as he brought her along with him on a journey she had never known existed.

And then, with a gasp, he was still, leaving her taut and expectant, quivering on the brink of an abyss.

'I'm sorry,' he muttered against her damp hair. 'I couldn't wait. You're so beautiful...'

She could have wept with the disappointment, except that she felt his fingers reach between them and touch her, and suddenly she was bucking and gasping and clawing at his back as the world seemed to explode around her.

Afterwards she clung to him, so overcome that the words of gratitude and affection caught in her throat. He held her close, stroking her hair as if she were a child, waiting as her breathing returned to normal and she slowly came down from her euphoric heights. Only gradually did it dawn on her that they could have been disturbed at any time, and she looked up at him with wide, horrified eyes.

'How could we have, Ben? Here, of all places!'

He smiled his beautiful smile that made her want to start all over again, and helped her sit up.

'I've always found fear makes me amorous.' He tucked her tousled hair back behind her ears with a grin. 'Maybe that's why I've been in a permanently uncomfortable condition ever since we met!'

It occurred to her that this was the time to tell him the truth. Maybe he would understand if she told him now. On the other hand, maybe he wouldn't. Either way, she felt compelled to risk it.

'Ben.' She stroked the side of his face, loving the harshness of the dark shadow under her fingers. 'There are things I have to tell you about me.'

'I know all I need to know, Emma. You're all I ever wanted in a woman and never thought I'd find. You're beautiful, courageous, honest, pure...' He caught her fingers as they stilled and brought them to his mouth. 'We have a lot to talk about, my love. Later, when this is over.'

She shut her eyes on the tenderness in his face. No, she couldn't tell him. She should never have acted so prudishly in the first place! If she had been as open about her desire for him from the very beginning as he had been, if she had not sought refuge in her façade of the prim missionary's widow, then perhaps they would have stood a chance together. Instead, it had all become based on a deceit. She had effectively ruined any chance of a future, and she had no one else to blame but herself.

'Hey, don't cry!' He carefully rubbed away her

tears with his thumb. 'We'll be out of this in no time, I promise you.'

How strange it was to feel so awkward with someone with whom you had just shared the most intimate of all possible acts. To cover her confusion she went to the window and stared blindly out at the dusk gathering over the hills. Somewhere out there in the evening shadows was Rima, alone and no doubt terrified, despite Ben's assertions to the contrary. A movement in the trees beyond the hot pools caught her eye and she leaned forward eagerly. But it wasn't Rima who lifted a starlit face to her and then walked on towards the house, but a heavily tattooed man. Followed by another and another…

'Ben,' she said faintly. 'The garden is full of Maori warriors.'

He leapt off the bed with a muttered curse that made her bristle despite her nervousness, and came to stand beside her. The few warriors had become dozens, all bearing their clubs and spears, moving silently towards the house on their bare feet. It was the most terrifying sight Emma had ever seen.

'I thought the meeting was tomorrow,' she whispered.

'It is, but you know what they're like, Emma. Anything to get a jump on the other tribes.' He smiled slightly as he watched the noiseless progression towards the house. 'I wonder how the Baron is going to handle this?'

They waited tensely, watching in the dark. At last there was a polite knock on the door and the key turned in the lock.

'Good evening,' the Baron said. He looked distracted, his hair untidy and his cravat askew. Waving his hands in the direction of downstairs, he said hesitantly, 'Mrs Morgan, if you would be so kind… I know that you speak the native language, and your assistance would be much appreciated…'

Emma remained standing composedly by the window, grateful for Ben's quiet support behind her.

'Do we remain your prisoners, Baron?'

'No, no! You were never that!' He placed his hand over his heart, his round little features showing his horror at the very thought. 'I only wished to delay your departure!'

'Where is the Baroness?'

'My wife is lying down. Her nerves, you understand… Please, you must come, madame!'

'I think not, Baron,' she told him. 'I do not appreciate being ordered around at the point of a pistol.'

'The pistol was not loaded, Mrs Morgan! We would never have hurt you, never! Mr wife…the strain, you understand…' The Baron wrung his hands in agitation, looking pitifully old and close to tears. Emma felt unexpectedly sorry for him. He had plotted for so long and on such a grand scale. Now his dreams were turning into reality and he was rapidly losing control.

'Go, Emma,' Ben said and then added in a voice that was only for her ears, 'and keep them occupied for as long as you can, my love.'

She followed the Baron down the great, carved staircase to the front door. There, lit by dozens of burning flares, stood a hundred Maori warriors or more. She almost turned and fled back up the stair-case, as no doubt the Baroness had done. She certainly wished that Ben had been there beside her. But somehow she managed to take her place beside the Baron on the veranda, tightly clasping her hands before her.

'*Hai!* Hemma!' A burly warrior wearing the white feathers of a chief in his hair shouldered his way through the crowd, raising his spear in greeting.

'Tawhai!' Her delighted recognition of a familiar face was immediately tempered by the memory of the circumstances surrounding her departure from his tribe. But Tawhai seemed to have forgotten all about Rima as he grasped her shoulders and pressed her nose with his in an enthusiastic *hongi*.

'Tawhai, what are you doing here?'

He feigned innocence at her surprise. 'We have come to visit, to trade peacefully with the tribes of the lake, Hemma. What else would we be doing here?'

Clearly rumours of the Baron's munitions stock-pile had reached well down the Whanganui River. She turned to the Baron.

'What do you want me to tell them?'

The Baron's eyes darted nervously over the crowd of warriors. He licked his lips. 'I...I don't know. Tell them to go away.'

'But you summoned them here,' she pointed out.

'Tomorrow! Not...not tonight!' he said queru-lously.

'And what will be different about tomorrow if they come then?' She waited for his response, worried by the glazed stare that his eyes were taking on. The crowd shifted uneasily and began to murmur. Their patience had a short fuse, but as the seconds ticked on, it became glaringly obvious to Emma that the Baron was losing his already-tenuous grip on reality. At last she turned to the crowd and began to speak in Maori.

'*Haere mai, haere mai, haere mai,*' she greeted them formally. 'The Baron asks you to come to see him in the morning. There are matters he wishes to discuss with you. But not tonight.'

'We don't want to put the Baron to any trouble,' Tawhai said politely, his eyes alight with mischief. 'Please ask him how we can help him tonight.'

She stared at him sternly. 'Tomorrow, Tawhai.'

'Tonight, Hemma.'

'Tomorrow.'

A slow smile spread over his face. 'We would like the guns tonight, Hemma.'

A chorus of agreement greeted this statement. Emma faltered, knowing that to deny any knowledge of the guns would lose her all credibility. Excited shouts emanating from beside the house saved her from having to make that decision.

'Guns! Many, many guns! Come and see!'

A warrior walking around the grounds had found the cellar door at the side of the house. Within minutes the heavy wooden crates were being smashed open with axes and the rifles distributed to every warrior present. There were a few tussles as some wanted more, but as crate after crate was dragged up from the cellar and opened it was clear that there were more weapons than all the gathered men could carry. The shouts of triumph were deafening. Emma looked accusingly at the Baron but he was sitting on the veranda, his head in his hands, lost in his own collapsed world. Oh, where was Ben? She could have screamed at her own helplessness to stop the madness going on around her.

As the first burst of euphoria at their new possessions quietened down, Tawhai came up to her again.

'The powder, Hemma. The powder that makes the guns work. There is none.'

She swallowed. 'You're right. There is none, Tawhai.'

He slowly began to climb the steps to where she was standing on the veranda, and the crowd of warriors fell silent.

'Is it in the house, Hemma? Shall I look for it?'

She fell back, arms wide to block his entry through the front doors. They would go around the back, or climb in through the windows, of course, but the thought of these warriors rampaging through the beautiful house, carrying off everything that wasn't nailed down, was unbearable. 'You will not enter this house! I forbid it!'

Tawhai laughed indulgently. 'Such a little person to forbid me entry! Stand aside, Hemma.'

'Hey! Tawhai!'

All heads turned at the shout. Ben was standing at the end of the veranda, one of the Maoris' flax flares alight in his hand. Tawhai bared his teeth in rage and his fingers tightened around his spear.

'*You!* You vermin who crawls on his belly! I shall tear out your lying tongue with my fingernails! I shall crush your testicles between two shells! I shall break every tooth in your head! I shall…'

There was much more, and Emma could only be grateful that Ben didn't understand Maori. The crowd, however, was watching the one-sided exchange with enormous interest. Ben reached out into the shrubbery with one boot and rolled out a large keg.

'Emma, tell your noisy friend what's in this,' he broke in over Tawhai's invective.

But as silence fell, it was plain that Emma didn't need to. For a long frozen moment all eyes were on Ben, standing very still over the keg of gunpowder, the flickering taper in his hand. Then Tawhai stepped forward and at once Ben lowered the flare to within a foot of the keg.

'*Ben!*' Emma quavered, sure that he was crazy enough to send them all sky-high. The pure terror in her voice was enough to convince any doubting warriors of Ben's sincerity of intention. Like wraiths they backed away into the forest and within minutes it was as if they had never been there.

Emma's knees gave way and she collapsed on to the veranda. Seconds later two thin arms were flung around her neck in a throttling hug.

'Rima!' She hugged the child close. 'Where's Ben?'

'Here.' He bent over beside her, his hands on his knees, breathing hard. 'I've just got rid of the last of the gunpowder and the shot.'

'Where?'

He jerked his thumb over his shoulder in the direction of the rear of the house. 'In the hot pools. I

don't know if it'll have any effect on the underground geothermal water system, but there wasn't
anywhere else close enough. Anyway, we're not
staying here to find out. I took one of the Baron's
rowing boats along the lakefront this morning. If we
get going right now, we should be well clear by
daylight.'

'We can't leave the de Viscenis.' Putting Rima
aside, Emma looked along the empty veranda.
'Where is the Baron?'

'Gone,' Ben said cheerfully. 'About five minutes
ago. Along with his wife, the servants and as much
as they could carry. I saw them heading north into
the forest as I was submerging the last of his kegs
of gunpowder.'

'Oh, the poor things,' Emma said sadly. 'To have
to leave this lovely house and all their dreams...'

'Yeah. And you and me alone with a hundred
armed Maoris, creating just the diversion they
needed to make their escape. You don't owe them
anything, Emma. Especially not pity.'

He was right, she supposed. When she walked
through the house to retrieve their belongings her
footsteps seemed to resound eerily through the un-
inhabited rooms. She felt like a thief as she packed
bread and cheese from the kitchen and took some
warm clothes and blankets from the bedrooms. And
even though she knew it was pointless, she took care
to shut the front doors behind her. No doubt the
mansion that had been intended to be the royal pal-
ace of New Zealand would be thoroughly ransacked
within hours.

They found the small rowboat where Ben had left

it earlier, hidden under some overhanging trees. Across the lake they could see the warriors' flares flickering along the shore. They were waiting until light to make another foray on the house, although Emma was quite certain that Tawhai, for one, would be pleased to know that Ben was leaving.

It was a perfectly still night, which meant that Ben had to row silently and slowly until they could be sure they were out of earshot. Only once the lights on the shore had reduced to tiny flames did Emma dare to speak.

'We can't go back the same way, Ben! It's such a long way, and we've got to get past the Ngati Tuwharetoa *pa*, and then Tawhai's *pa* further down the river…'

'Emma, listen!' he said urgently, worried by the small note of hysteria in her voice. 'Just think about the options. If we head north, we'll run into all the tribes the Baron contacted, and we'd have to cover at least a hundred miles on foot to get to the nearest settlement. The tribes from the south will be staying overnight to sack the Baron's house, which means we have a good headstart on them. We'll be going downriver all the way, which will be fast and damned near effortless. I chose this boat over a canoe because it's light and we can carry it overland if we have to. And, if I've done my job properly, I've got survey maps that show every *pa*, every rapid, every goddamned hill between here and the mouth of the Whanganui River. How can we go any other way but south?'

After a while, she nodded. 'You're right.'

'But?'

'I just can't believe… Oh, Ben, what have we done? Now every Maori in the district is armed, and it's all our fault…'

'No, it's not.' He began rowing again, speaking in bursts between strokes. 'Emma, the guns would have come from one source or another eventually. They'll be traded for land, for a start—what do you think the New Zealand Company uses for currency? But your missionary friends have virtually eliminated cannibalism from the friendly tribes—don't you think they can do the same with warfare?'

'I don't know,' she said woodenly.

'You should have more faith, Emma,' he teased her gently.

He refused her offer to help row, and so she and Rima wrapped themselves in the bedrolls and made themselves as comfortable as they could. Rima was eventually rocked to sleep, but Emma lay silently staring up at the moon trailing across the sky. So much had happened that day. Within the space of hours she had known love and passion and terror on a scale which made the rest of her life seem insignificant by comparison.

What she wouldn't give to be surrounded by normal people again, she thought. People who were sane and spoke English and didn't have impossible fantasies of owning entire countries…

She thought of Thomas's house in Sydney. Thousands of miles to the north-west it was standing under the very same moon, waiting for her return, the safe and secure haven she had always craved. She fell asleep, willing the miles away.

Chapter Eleven

As dawn broke Ben rowed them into the southern outlet of the lake. The swift-flowing current made it virtually unnecessary to row, although Ben still had to use the oars like a rudder to stay clear of the eddies and rocks. They were traveling far faster than Emma had dreamed possible, but the toll on an already-weary Ben was heavy, and she was relieved when he steered them into a quiet little bay around mid-morning.

They secured the boat out of sight under some heavy flax, and Emma shared out some of the bread she had brought from the house. Ben fell asleep before he had finished eating, one arm flung over his face. He had, she realised, been rowing steadily for over twelve hours. Overcome with tenderness, she took the uneaten bread from his inert fingers and pressed a kiss on his forehead.

'Eeeh.' Rima screwed up her face. 'You keep doing that to him! Stop it!'

Just to tease, Emma grabbed her and covered her

with kisses until Rima was a helpless bundle of giggles, wiping her face in mock disgust.

'You like your husband now, Hemma?' Rima asked when they had composed themselves.

Emma lay down beside her, squinting at the cloudless sky between the fern fronds. 'He is a good man,' she said carefully.

'I like him.' She began giggling again. 'I like him because Tawhai hates him! *Hai*, I thought Tawhai would kill him, he was so angry, but Pen didn't care. He is very brave.'

Emma stared at her aghast. 'You were there, when Ben was going to set the gunpowder alight?'

'Yes, I was hiding in the bushes. Pen told me to run and hide by the lake, but I wanted to see what was happening. It was fun, wasn't it, Hemma?'

'No, it wasn't! Rima, why don't you do what you're told? Ben told you to run away because there would have been a great explosion if he had set light to the gunpowder. We would all have been dead!'

Rima scowled. 'Pen would not have done that. He was only pretending!'

'I don't think he was pretending.'

'I do,' Rima said confidently. 'He would not have killed you, Hemma! He likes you now. He didn't used to.'

Not for the first time, Emma wished life was as simple as Rima perceived it to be.

In the afternoon they launched the boat again. Several times Ben deemed the rapids too dangerous to risk, and so they had the opportunity to stretch their legs along the bank, tying a rope to the boat and letting it run the rapids unmanned. To Emma's relief Rima didn't even notice as they passed by the place where she had almost drowned the previous week. Instead she chattered away happily, wildly excited by everything she saw. Ben kept insisting on speaking to her in English, and by now Rima's speech was a slightly confusing muddle of the two languages. Within another couple of weeks Emma was sure that Rima's English would be perfectly comprehensible, which would help her settle wherever Emma stayed. Where that would be was something to which Emma found herself giving a lot of thought.

It was dark by the time they left the great volcanoes behind them and slipped quietly by the *pa* on the hill. The flares on the sentry platforms were reflected in the water, but the moon was partly obscured behind cloud. Ben kept the boat close to the far side, in the shadows, and within minutes they had swept by unseen and safe.

A few miles further down the river they pulled ashore for the night. Rima was yawning by the time they finished their bread and cheese. Emma wrapped her up in a bedroll and lay beside her until the child was fast asleep. When she finally sat up Ben got to his feet and held out his hand.

In silence she took his hand and allowed him to lead her further up the hill. There, on a bed of soft ferns, Ben threw down a bedroll and took her in his arms.

'You're shivering,' he said quietly. 'Are you cold?'

'No.' She steadied her hands against his chest,

feeling the rough hair under his palms. Then she reached up and kissed him, his mouth, his nose, his ears, anywhere she could reach.

'Emma!' He was laughing as they tumbled to the ground, his chest shaking against her breasts.

'What's funny?' she muttered against his skin.

'You're so enthusiastic, I... Oh, God, Emma!' he gasped as her fingers found him. 'Don't do that yet, sweetheart, or this will all be over in ten seconds!'

And he made her wait, ignoring her whimpers of complaint, until he had satisfied her fully. Only then did he take his own pleasure, driving into her until she thought she would die from the ecstasy of his violent possession. As he shuddered in his climax she looked up at his beloved outline blocking out the stars and knew she would never feel as intensely about anything ever again.

Afterwards they lay entwined, their heartbeats and their breathing slowly returning to normal. Emma mentally explored her body, testing the places she ached, wondering how she could enjoy it so. It embarrassed her to have to acknowledge that it was she who was demanding the fast, rough pace of their love-making, even though Ben was more than happy to follow. Surely intimacy between a man and a woman should be more restrained and delicate? What was wrong with her, and why didn't Ben mind?

He raised himself on one elbow and gently pulled back the tangled mass of her hair.

'I love you, Emma.' He kissed her, and for the first time she tasted herself on his lips. Horrified, she wriggled away and began to grope for her clothes. Somehow he had managed to take them all off her. But then, she had torn off his. She was as guilty as he was. Ben put out a lazy hand and wrestled the chemise from her.

'Don't put that on, I haven't finished with you yet. Unless you're cold?'

'No. I'm just not used to…'

'Being naked?'

She nodded, although it was really the intimacy that she found so unnerving. He ran his fingers possessively down her spine.

'Not even with Thomas?'

She tensed at her husband's name. 'No.'

His hand stilled on her thigh. 'It was as bad as that, was it?'

She sat still and silent. It had been neither good nor bad with Thomas. It had been simply an act that her husband had performed infrequently for his relief, and one to which she had submitted modestly, as a good wife should. Never in her wildest dreams had she thought that the same act of union could be like that she had just experienced. Thomas had been almost fifty when he had married her, and he had been proud that he had never lain with another woman. Whereas Ben…

'How many women have you known?' The question was blurted out before she could stop it, but Ben didn't look at all put out by her forwardness.

'A lot when I was younger. Far too many, probably. But I had a bad experience a couple of years ago that taught me a lesson or two. I've been celibate ever since.'

She waited, but he was staring at her, a frown

gathering between his brows. Suddenly nervous, she covered her breasts.

'What's the matter, Ben?'

'Nothing. Just for a moment you looked...'

'Looked like someone else?'

'No,' he said emphatically, but she knew he was lying. She remembered when he had first mistaken her for another woman, someone from Sydney, and once more the feeling of terror gripped her insides like an icy hand. It hadn't been her! It couldn't have been her! Could it?

Ben lowered his head and bit her hard on the hip, and she gasped at the sharp, erotic pain.

'I love how responsive you are,' he whispered against her stomach as he pulled her down to lie beside him. 'I love how beautiful you are. I'm glad I'm the one to have shown you what love can be, Emma. I'm glad I'm the first.'

Oh, Lord, I'm a wicked woman, she thought. I deserve to burn in all the fires of Hell for this. But as she welcomed Ben inside her again she wondered if even eternal punishment wouldn't be worth these hours in Ben's arms.

A heavy mist hung over the river the next morning and they felt safe enough under its cover to light a fire. Rima had caught a giant eel before dawn and they made a hearty breakfast of it sandwiched between two slices of bread.

Rima was her usual ebullient self, boasting about her eel, excitedly asking questions about how far downriver they would be traveling that day. In fact, her spirits were a little too high, Emma thought with a twinge of anxiety. The child was slightly flushed, with glazed eyes, although she didn't appear to have a temperature.

'We'll try to get past your *pa*, today,' Ben told Rima.

'Will you stop and beat up Tawhai?' she demanded breathlessly in Maori.

'Rima!' Emma translated and Ben choked as he swallowed his tea the wrong way.

'No, I think I'll give it a miss, Rima. But thank you for the suggestion.' He finished his tea with a gulp and put his mug in the pack containing their bedrolls. 'Which reminds me that we'd better make an early start of it if we don't want your friends catching up with us, Emma.' She was stamping out the campfire and he eyed her half-drunk mug of tea. 'Can I finish that if you don't want it?'

'No!' she said quickly, but he had already brought it to his lips.

'It's foul!' he exclaimed and then he sniffed it. 'I've smelt this before. What is it?'

'Just…just a tea I make for myself sometimes.' She held out her hand for it but he made no effort to hand it over.

'What's in it?'

'Herbs, that's all,' she said quickly.

'Would they include pennyroyal by any chance?' His expression hardened as he watched the colour rise to her face. 'No wonder Thomas never gave you any children, Emma.'

She snatched the cup from him and defiantly gulped down the revolting brew.

'What medicines I take are none of your business!

What is it to you if I choose not to conceive a child out here in the wilderness? You're not my husband!'

He grabbed her wrist so hard that she winced. His eyes were ice-hard and furious. 'I will be, Emma. One day.'

'You haven't asked me!'

'Haven't I?' He loosened his grip and stood back. 'I thought it was understood. I'm sorry. I wouldn't have slept with you had I not intended to make you my wife.'

'Really? You never married any of the other women you slept with!'

'None of them was you.' He leaned forward and kissed her, hard. 'Be a good girl and throw out the herbs, will you, sweetheart? No decent woman should take that sort of thing.' He picked up Rima, who fortunately had not understood a word of their exchange and ruffled her hair in the way he knew she hated. 'Come on, now, Rat. Into the boat and we'll be off.'

'Ben...' Emma began, but he shook his head.

'Enough, Emma. We'll discuss it no further, do you understand?'

He turned away and missed the stunned look on her face. The words were exactly those that Thomas had said to her on an almost daily basis, over issues ranging from what time dinner would be to whether they would go to New Zealand. The prospect of a lifetime of marriage to Ben loomed before her as little more than a repeat of her first marriage, with the added shackle of children. And the single consolation of Ben's extraordinary love-making to sweeten the union might not last constant pregnancies and crying babies... She followed him down to the boat, the worry and indecision chewing at her insides like a cancer.

The rapids gradually became fewer and then disappeared as the river became deeper, racing between the towering banks. They entered wide, serene valleys where the water ran placid and silver under the sun, and then the river would plunge into secret, winding alleys, the water turning an even darker green than the dense, overhanging ferns. No wonder the Maoris talked of magical *taniwha* and other monsters of the deep on this river, Emma thought, and was a little surprised that Rima slept through most of the journey.

Late in the afternoon they arrived at a point just north of Tawhai's *pa*, where they landed and hid the boat. The *pa* would not have been left entirely unmanned, and it seemed a good idea to pass by under cover of darkness. The morning's mist had returned, thick and drizzly, and they sought shelter under a thick canopy of *rimu* leaves.

'I want to make a few sketches and measurements from the top of the hill behind us,' Ben said. 'What with one thing and another, I didn't manage to survey this area very well when I was here last.'

'Be careful,' she said, and he kissed her and promised that he would be.

'I have some dried fruit left,' Emma said after he had gone and she settled down next to Rima. 'Would you like some?'

'No.' The girl was curled up into a tight ball and Emma instinctively touched her forehead.

'Rima, you're burning up! Do you feel all right?'

'My head hurts. Go away,' Rima grumbled.

For the next few hours Emma sat beside her, watching anxiously as Rima tossed feverishly, her nose and eyes streaming. She strongly suspected that Rima had contracted a cold from someone at the Baron's house. Before the Europeans had arrived in New Zealand, the Maoris had never been exposed to the relatively minor contagions like measles or the common cold, and in recent years Emma knew that many hundreds of Maoris had died from such illnesses. And only a few miles away was the place where Thomas had died and been buried... She hugged her knees and rocked in silent misery.

When Ben returned she told him her fears and he sat back on his heels, his face concerned. 'Do you think we should stay here until she's better?'

'That could take days, and we have no shelter. I even thought of taking her to the *pa*, but I know you wouldn't be welcome there, and Tawhai may not have forgiven Rima.'

'Then we'll keep heading downriver. Once we're past the *pa* it doesn't matter if we travel by day.' He put a reassuring arm around her shoulders and she leaned against him gratefully. 'Three days, Emma. I don't think it will take any longer than that to get to the sea.'

They wrapped the feverish, shivering child in the bedrolls and Ben carried her down to the boat, where they made her as comfortable as possible. He prepared an oil lamp and, as soon as the sleeping *pa* was behind them, they lit it and Emma leaned over the bow, holding it aloft to light their way. A reluctant moon eventually came out from behind the clouds to guide them from the path of any over-hanging branches or protruding rocks. By the time the sky began to lighten Emma was close to exhaustion, but they had covered many miles.

They pulled ashore briefly for a hot drink and something to eat, and then Emma curled up in the bow with Rima, half-dozing as Ben steered their way through the currents. They travelled like that all day and most of the next night. Rima slept and muttered and thrashed around, and all Emma could do was keep her cool and as comfortable as she could. In the dark hours before dawn Rima went into convulsions, and when they finished Emma soothed the tiny, flushed face with the damp edge of her skirt and cursed her own helplessness.

'She'll live,' Ben said shortly, and she glared at him, hating him for his callousness.

'She won't. She's sick, and I can't bring her temperature down. She needs a warm, dry bed, and a room with no draughts. Not...not this!' She indicated the rugged, mist-shrouded banks rising around them with a shaking hand.

'You've written her off before,' was all he said, and she sat silently, knowing that it was wrong to make him the brunt of all her anger and frustration. He had been rowing now for days, denying himself rest, trying to get them downriver to civilisation as soon as possible.

By the next morning the river had widened so much that the travelling was easy. For the first time Emma saw a small European-style house high up on a hill, smoke trickling from its chimney, washing fluttering colourfully on the line. She nearly tipped the boat over in her excitement.

As if on cue, Rima chose that moment to open her eyes.

'I'm hungry,' she announced in her usual imperious voice.

Two hours later they were pulling the boat ashore at the mouth of the Whanganui River. Emma stood on the beach, stamping her feet to regain circulation after so many hours cramped in the boat, amazed at how the small town had grown in just the few months since she had left it. A half-dozen ships from as many nations were tied up at the docks, and new buildings were being constructed on every street.

Ben hoisted a wide-eyed Rima over his shoulder and picked up their bags. Emma looked at him, suddenly overwhelmed as the practicalities of their situation dawned on her.

'What do we do now?'

He grinned. 'That must be the most stupid thing I've ever heard you say, Emma! We go to a hotel, we have a huge meal and a good night's sleep…'

'No, I meant…we have no money!'

'We're staying at the best hotel courtesy of the New Zealand Company. They can afford it. Come on, ladies.'

The best hotel in Whanganui was perhaps nothing compared to those found in larger towns, but the room they were shown to was more than comfortable. Ben deposited their bags by the door and looked around him in satisfaction.

'I'd better get to the offices of the Company with the survey plans. Make yourselves at home, order anything you want. I might be a while.' He caught Emma to him and kissed her possessively, 'Then we'll make our plans, hmm?'

She nodded woodenly, unable to trust herself to make a reply. Growing in her was the conviction that she had to leave him before he bound her to him too closely for her to ever break free. She remembered all too clearly what life with Thomas had been like. She had tasted freedom now, and she was not prepared to exchange one prison for another, no matter how appealing the jailor.

After he had gone the innkeeper's wife brought up hot water and bowls of mutton soup. Emma washed Rima and put her in one of the two beds in the room. With a tummy full of soup, Rima's chatter gradually trailed away and she dozed off, leaving Emma in peace to scrub herself thoroughly and wash her hair. She did some necessary laundering and hung up what clothes she had, but still there was no sign of Ben.

Outside the temperature had dropped and the drizzle had turned to heavy rain. She put another blanket over Rima and moved to stand by the window. The wide main road was rapidly turning to mud. Somewhere out there was Ben. Presumably at the offices of the New Zealand Company, wherever they were.

It occurred to her that perhaps he had gone. After all, what man would willingly saddle himself with a penniless woman and a small child? He would be paid for his work now. He would have money in his pocket, in a town with bars and women and ships going anywhere in the world. He had even taken his bag with him, the one that contained not only his maps but his clothes, too...

He wouldn't do that! a small voice of reason told her, but another small voice asked insistently, What if he had? What would she do now, with no money and no friends in this isolated town?

She let herself quietly out of the room and asked the innkeeper's wife to keep an eye on Rima for a while. Two doors along from the hotel was the bank she knew Thomas had used when they first arrived at Whanganui. It was a long shot, but she at least had to ask if Thomas had left any funds in the bank before they had traveled up the river.

'Mrs Johnson!' Mr Conroy, the bank manager, recognised her immediately, much to her surprise, and she was promptly ushered through to his office. She took a seat, uncomfortably aware of the manager's furtive scrutiny of her bare head and worn clothes. 'Tell me, Mrs Johnson, what can I do for you?'

She studied her splayed fingers on her lap, wondering how friendly he would be if she asked him for a loan. Probably not very, she decided, but what option did she have? She took a deep breath and plunged on.

'My husband died shortly after we arrived at his chosen site on the river, Mr Conroy. I only arrived back at Whanganui this morning.'

He tsked his sympathy. 'So you'd like to return to Sydney, Mrs Johnson?'

'Yes. My husband still owns a house there—a substantial one—and…'

'Much the most sensible course of action, then,' the manager agreed, reaching for a pen and paper. 'How much would you like to withdraw?'

Emma hesitated. She had been about to ask if she could use Thomas's house as collateral. 'Withdraw. Ah…how much is there in my husband's account?'

The sum he named had Emma almost falling off her chair in shock.

'*That* much?' she squeaked.

'Available here in New Zealand, yes, Mrs Johnson. There's no problem in your accessing the funds, as your late husband gave instructions that you were to be given all assistance in the unfortunate possibility of his demise. You will, of course, have to advise the authorities in this country of the circumstances of Mr Johnson's death…'

He talked for a while about probate and wills, but even in Emma's dazed state it was clear that Thomas had prepared fully for her widowhood. Somehow it had never occurred to her that he would.

When she returned to the hotel Rima was still asleep, so Emma undressed and lay down on the other bed. She stared sightlessly at the ceiling, her head still spinning. She thought of her marriage and the dresses she had patched, the shoes she had stuffed with paper, the little luxuries she had denied herself. As the youngest of the numerous offspring of a baronet, Thomas had received what she had assumed was a modest allowance from relatives in

England. His house in Sydney was beautiful but sparsely furnished, and he had never given any sign of wealth in all the time she had known him. And all this time he had been saving every penny for his church at Redemption.

'Oh, Thomas!' she whispered to the silent room, caught between anger at the grandeur of Thomas's dream and guilt at knowing that she would never be able to make his dream a reality. He had wanted her to, she knew, but nothing would ever convince her to go back up the river and start again.

And yet, just months ago, she had never dreamed that she would one day go against his wishes. She had changed so much since his death.

It took time to think it through, but at last she knew exactly what she had to do. If she couldn't build Thomas's church on the Whanganui River, she would leave sufficient money here with missionaries who could. There would still be enough money left over to take her and Rima back to Sydney. She had a house there, she had family, she had work to do among the poor. Thomas would have understood.

She was wrestling with the problem of how to break the news to Rima that Ben was probably not coming back, when the days of sleeplessness finally caught up with her.

It was evening when she awoke, and still raining heavily, the heavy drumming on the tin roof drowning out any sound from the street. As she stirred she became aware of Ben lying behind her, his hand resting on her hip, his shallow breathing indicating that he had been asleep for some time. So he had come back after all. She didn't know whether to be pleased about that or not.

'I'm hungry!' Rima had been watching her eyelashes flutter as Emma woke up.

Emma put her finger to her lips, but already Ben was stirring. He stretched and then slipped a proprietorial arm around her waist, pulling her hard against him.

'Did you complete your business at the New Zealand Company?' she asked, making the question an excuse to move away and turn to face him.

'I did. My plans are now all signed, sealed and paid for in full. In fact, I think they're sailing out tonight for England. I've turned down another job in the South Island. I'd just finished one in the Marlborough Sounds before I took on this one, and I've had enough of living rough for a while...' He stopped and his smile of satisfaction faded. 'What's the matter, Emma?'

'Nothing.' Unable to trust his close proximity, she sat up and swung her legs to the floor.

'Are you still upset that I work for the Company?'

'No. If it wasn't you it would be someone else.' She began to pull on her dress, her fingers cold and refusing to do her bidding. 'I'll go and see if I can order some dinner. Rima, do you want to come with me?'

Dinner was taken with the other hotel guests at the long table in the dining-room. Despite being the only child present, Rima was not as intimidated by the European meal as she had been at the de Visceni home, and Emma had little to correct as far as her table manners were concerned.

With a little judicious manoeuvring she ensured that Ben ended up seated at the far end of the table from her and Rima, thus denying him any opportunity to talk to her. Apart from the other guests' mistaken but necessary assumption that she was married to Ben, she enjoyed the chance to talk with strangers who were, in the main, prospective settlers from Britain. It was only when Rima's chin came gently to rest on her lap, and Ben picked up the sleeping child and carried her upstairs, that Emma knew she could no longer avoid him.

She moved quietly around the bedroom, lighting a single lamp while Ben tucked Rima into bed. Outside the rain still plummeted down, creating an uneasy feeling of isolation from the rest of the world. Emma began to feel apprehensive at what she had to do. When Ben turned towards her, she clutched the edge of the washstand, no longer sure of the continued support of her legs. He stopped when he saw her expression.

'What's the matter, Emma? You've been acting oddly ever since we arrived,' he said gently.

'Have I?' She fought to control her breathing. 'Ben, we really do have to talk.'

'I know.' He sat on the bed, his face so tender that she was suffused with guilt, despite all her resolve. 'Emma, look, there's no easy way to tell you this. I tried to get a special marriage licence today, but it can't be done.'

'It can't?' she said, trying to keep the note of hope out of her voice.

'No. There's all this paperwork and certification to prove that Thomas is dead, and with the country now a colony, it's well-nigh impossible at the moment. So many officials, and none of them wanting to take responsibility for getting anything done! You'll have to swear an affidavit before a justice of the peace, but even so, it could take another six months. I'm sorry, Emma. I know how difficult this must be for you.'

'Difficult? In what way?'

He frowned, surprised at the question. 'Sleeping with me, possibly bearing my children, without the benefit of marriage. A woman like you… It must be an untenable situation for you.'

She gripped the washstand even harder. 'Ben, even if you'd been able to get the special licence, I couldn't have married you. I…I wouldn't have married you.'

He slowly got to his feet. *'What?'*

'I don't want to marry you.' There, it was said! He shook his head, as if he couldn't believe what he was hearing.

'What do you want, Emma?'

'I want to go back to Sydney…'

'Back to *Sydney*?'

His voice cut through her stammering like a whip, silencing her utterly. Too late she remembered her staunch denials that she had ever been in New South Wales, and she felt her heart flutter in fear as he came to stand before her, looming huge in the flickering lamplight. She flinched as his fingers cupped her chin, gently but relentlessly forcing her eyes up to meet his.

'Emma,' he said, his voice softly dangerous, 'this

might sound an absurd question, but I've got to ask it. Were you ever a whore on the Sydney docks?'

Her mouth opened and shut wordlessly, but her silence was more eloquent that anything she could have said. She saw the flicker of hope fade from his eyes and his hand dropped from her as if she was contaminated. He backed away until his boots hit the bedstead, the look on his face holding such revulsion that she wanted to shrivel up and die. She had wanted to spare him this...

'I...I'm sorry...'

'Jesus, I've been such a fool,' he whispered. He reached inside his jacket and pulled out a wad of banknotes. Without looking at them he tore off the top few and flung them on the bed. 'That should see you back to Sydney, Mrs Johnson. I guess you can always turn a few tricks here in Whanganui if it's not enough.'

'I don't *want* your money!'

He picked up his bag and threw it over his shoulder. 'You may as well take it,' he said casually, but his mouth was set in white, bitter lines. 'It's not the first time I've paid for my pleasure, and I doubt it will be the last.'

As he closed the door carefully behind him Emma slid to the floor and buried her face in her hands. Damn, damn, *damn* her past! Would she never be free of it?

Chapter Twelve

Mrs McDuff let out a long sigh of disappointment.

'Another girl. He won't be pleased.'

Emma was silent for a moment, scrubbing off the blood on her hands and arms in the basin on the table.

'How many does this make, Mary?'

'Five girls, now, all living. The boys I've had just don't make it. Maybe it's meant.'

'Maybe.' Emma smiled at twelve-year-old Kate, the eldest girl, who had struggled in with all the clean sheets and buckets of boiled water Emma had needed through the birth, and who now stood quietly beside the table, holding out Emma's towel. Her sisters were crowding at the low door of the tiny house, silently watching the new arrival lying beside their mother in the bed.

'Thank you, Kate. You've been very helpful. Your mother is going to be needing rest for a few days, so are you and your sisters going to be able to manage?'

'Aw, the bairns can look after their father all

right, Mrs Johnson,' Mrs McDuff said. 'He's going to be in a bad mood when he finds out he still hasn't got his son, but he'll come right.' She studied the small, red-faced bundle in her arms. 'Pretty little thing, ain't she? What d'you think we should call her, girls?'

Jenny, who came roughly halfway in the middle of the family, took her thumb out of her mouth.

'Emma.'

Mrs McDuff's prematurely lined face creased with laughter. 'Why not, lass? Emma it is, like all the other new wee lassies born in Sydney this year.' She shook her head at Emma. 'You know we can't pay you until later, Mrs Johnson…'

'And you know I don't mind,' Emma said firmly. The McDuffs would never be able to pay her at all, but Emma had never worked just for the money. She paused to take one last look at the tiny but perfectly healthy baby girl, and felt the familiar glow of content at a job well done. Mrs McDuff had done all the work, of course, but at least Emma had been able to ensure that the baby arrived in a clean, undistressed condition. The McDuffs might have no money, but they were a close, hard-working family, and baby Emma stood every chance of growing up healthy and happy.

Emma tied up her bonnet and picked up her medical bag.

'I'll call by the day after tomorrow to see how you both are, but you know where I am if you should need me earlier. And I've brought a few things that the ladies of the parish make for new arrivals.' There was also cheese, fruit and some treats for the other children in the covered basket she had left on the table, but Emma thought the girls might enjoy finding those for themselves.

In the narrow alley outside the McDuffs' house she checked the time on the watch pinned to her jacket. It was still half an hour before three, so she had plenty of time to collect Rima and her sisters from school. She walked briskly, delayed every so often by patients or parishioners wanting a chat. As her father had been before her, she was a well-known sight in the district, walking through the streets at all hours of the day and night with her black bag. And, while the streets her patients lived in were some of Sydney's roughest, she had yet to meet with anything but goodwill from the residents.

Such had not been the case when her father first started in practice years before—the Sydney Emma remembered then as she worked alongside her father was a much tougher, vicious place. But with the cessation of convict transportation to New South Wales the previous year, there was a new mood in the town now, a sense of optimism and citizenship, as Britain's rejected people earned their tickets and forged new lives for themselves alongside the other settlers. Emma firmly believed that one day the hard work of families like the McDuffs would be amply rewarded in this vast, demanding country of opportunity.

School was still in progress when she arrived at the small, wooden schoolhouse beside the church of St Paul in Carlyle Street. She made herself comfortable on a bench under the trees while she waited. It was sometimes hard to tell when spring arrived

in the southern hemisphere, but the tall oak she sat
under, planted decades before by someone homesick
for England, was not fooled and was gently unfurl-
ing its leaves. All too soon it would be the sticky
heat of summer again. Emma turned her face up to
the soft warmth of the sun and closed her eyes. It
was almost a year to the day since she and Thomas
had left for New Zealand...

She wrenched her thoughts away from that path.
It was all in the past. Now she had a new life, a
wonderful life. A house that she could call her own,
a child she could call a daughter, a life's work that
was more intensely satisfying than she could ever
have thought possible.

The Reverend Collins, who was looking for an
excuse to take a rest from digging a new rosebed
by the church fence, saw her and came over for a
gossip. She moved over on the bench for him with
a warm smile. She liked the Reverend very much—
a kindly, middle-aged man, he had been a fellow-
bachelor and close confidante of her late husband
for many years, and had even officiated at their wedding. Now the two of them were settling into a comfortable relationship, where her money and medical
expertise helped promote the spiritual health of the
Reverend Collins's Sydney ministry. Together they
had made a special mission of alleviating the misery
of the colony's women convicts. For her own reasons, Emma wanted to ensure that no woman was
ever forced into prostitution, and in that she had a
willing and supportive ally in the Reverend.

'Ah, now, Emma, and how are you?' He took off
his hat and fanned himself gently with it, squinting

rather short-sightedly at her. 'And how was Mrs McDuff?'

'Another lovely little girl, James. They're both well. And I called into the Joneses in Burns Street— she's expecting again. Their little one has the croup…'

They talked for a while about their latest project, a hospital to be attached to the Women's Factory, in which they had enlisted the assistance of Governor Darling himself. Emma had persuaded some of Sydney society's leading matrons to assist in the fund-raising, and already there was almost enough in the purse to start building the foundations.

Emma always felt completely comfortable with James Collins. She was certain that he was quietly waiting out her year of widowhood before declaring himself, but she was equally certain that he would take her refusal in the same easy stride that he took all life's little knock-backs.

James reluctantly returned to his digging as the school doors opened, promising to see her on the following day. First out the door, vying with each other to see who could reach her first, came her youngest sisters, Martha and Caroline. Emma reached out both arms to hug the nine-year-olds. Thomas had not wanted to share his household with her sisters and so, after her marriage, she had been forced to accept a request from a childless couple keen to adopt the twins. Now the girls were so happy with the Carsons that Emma had at last reluctantly agreed to leave them where they were. Besides, the Carsons lived only a few doors down the same street as Emma and Rima, so there was endless coming-and-going between the houses. It had turned out to be a very satisfactory arrangement all around.

'Where's Rima?' Emma asked when the first rush of excited chatter was over. 'She hasn't been kept in *again*?'

Caroline rolled her eyes expressively. 'She bit Timothy.'

'Well, he was teasing her about being a cannibal,' Martha stuck up stoutly for their friend. 'Rima says if she's a cannibal then Timothy can be dinner. It's his fault for being beastly to her.'

Emma shook her head in despair. In the seven months since they had been in Sydney Rima had made vast strides towards becoming Europeanised. Her English was almost fluent now, and she exhibited such a voracious appetite for learning that Miss Fenton, the schoolteacher at the church school, forgave her most misdemeanours—cannibalism in the school grounds excepted. But nothing, it seemed, would ever quench Rima's fiery, impetuous personality, and somehow Emma suspected she would never learn how to turn the other cheek.

'Are we coming for supper tonight?' Martha asked, jiggling up and down in excitement. 'You said we could, last week.'

'Of course you are. Charlotte is coming too,' Emma said. Ignoring the twins' pout at the mention of their eldest sister's name, she added brightly, 'She said she had some exciting news to tell us.'

'Prob'ly got her hair done differently,' said Martha.

'I don't know what her news is,' said Emma, giving the giggling Caroline a quelling glance. Martha, like Rima, never needed egging on. 'But she left a note at the house this morning, saying that she wanted all her sisters to be there when she told us.'

The school door slammed loudly and Rima stamped down the stairs, scuffing her boots as she did so. One of her hair ribbons was missing, her dress was torn, and her pretty face was wrinkled into a ferocious scowl.

'I *hate* Miss Fenton!'

'Did she cane you?' Martha asked breathlessly.

'She wouldn't *dare*!' Rima hissed. 'If she tried I would *kill* her, and then I would hang her on the school bell and I would get her cane and I would hit her and I would...'

Plainly Rima had been caned and, much as Emma deplored physical chastisement, she could hardly blame poor Miss Fenton. Taking Rima firmly by the shoulders, she turned her towards the school gates.

'Let's go home, girls. We'll talk about this later, Rima.'

'But—'

'*Later*, Rima.' The prospect of spending the evening keeping the peace between her sisters, and then having to lecture Rima as well, was one that exhausted her. As she propelled the children homeward, it occurred to her that Ben would have known how to deal with Rima, and that compounded her irritation. She had managed not to think of him all day.

Emma loved going home. The honey-coloured brick house that had been Thomas's and was now hers was built on a slight hill to gain the best view of the bay. It was large by Sydney standards, with no less than five bedrooms and a study, as Thomas had intended originally that it be used as a religious retreat, before he fell out with the Missionary Society. Now there was only Emma, Rima and Mrs Stott the housekeeper to live in the big, sun-filled rooms. Occasionally Emma would bring home a patient in need of special care for a week or so, and she was always hopeful that the twins might change their minds and come to live with her, but she was honest enough to acknowledge that she loved the peace and privacy that the big house gave her.

They opened the front door to the wonderful aroma of stew. Although the evening sun still poured through the high windows, Mrs Stott had lit the fires in the dining-room and parlour, and the house was filled with warmth. The girls dropped their schoolbags and pelted outside to play in the large garden at the rear of the house. Emma wearily took off her bonnet. She had been called out to her first patient before dawn, and it had been a long day.

She checked on the progress of their supper with Mrs Stott and then sat quietly before the fire to wait for Charlotte to arrive. She was tired enough to have dozed off, but the prospect of seeing her eldest sister was enough to keep her awake. What was Charlotte's 'exciting news'? she wondered. It had been weeks since she had last seen her sister, and they had quarrelled then, as they always did. Emma loved all her sisters desperately, but sometimes she wondered if Charlotte was even their flesh and blood.

She was, of course, at least in appearance. When

they were younger she and Charlotte were often mistaken for each other if they were wearing bonnets. Only their hair colour was different—Charlotte's was a delicate pale gold that Emma used to envy before she grew to accept her own unfashionable dark red curls. As they had grown older, the differences in speech and dress had become more pronounced, so that few people remarked on their similarity now. Charlotte had always had an innate sense of style and a sparkling vivacious personality that fixed her indelibly in people's memories. In her childhood Emma had longed for just a little of her elder sister's flamboyance, but now there was nothing Charlotte had that Emma would have wanted.

It was growing dark when Charlotte's imperious banging on the door interrupted Emma's reflections.

'Darling!' Charlotte lightly kissed Emma's cheek, leaving a lingering trace of her familiar tuberose fragrance. She carelessly tossed her stylish bonnet on the hallstand and hurried into the parlour.

'It's so cold tonight!' She pulled off her gloves and warmed her hands by the fire. 'Supper smells wonderful. Can I have just a *tiny* little drink? No, don't stir yourself, I know where you keep the sherry!'

She darted around the room in her usual graceful flit that always reminded Emma of the New Zealand fantails. Then she sank elegantly to the rug before the fire with her glass and such an affectionate smile that Emma knew she wanted something.

'You're looking very well, Charlotte,' she said warily. 'What news do you have to tell us? Or would you like to wait until the twins come in?'

'I think I'd better tell you first.' Charlotte smoothed her ringlets in a gesture that struck Emma as uncharacteristically nervous. For the first time, in the firelight, she could see the lines of dissipation on Charlotte's lovely face and she realised that in another couple of years her sister's beauty would be gone, lost to all the drink and the men and hard living. Impulsively she leaned forward to take her hand.

'Are you all right, Charlotte? Is there anything I can do to help?'

'Yes, and yes.' Charlotte hesitated and then said in a rush, 'I'm getting married. Next week.'

Emma hugged her. 'How wonderful! Charlotte, I'm so happy for you!'

Charlotte looked at her oddly. 'Are you?'

'Yes, of course! Why shouldn't I be?'

'Well...' Charlotte pulled a wry face. 'I know you weren't happy in your marriage...'

'I may not have been as happy as I had hoped, but I never regretted it,' Emma said firmly. 'Thomas did care for me, in his way, and he did give me my faith and a sense of purpose in my life.'

Charlotte gave her an odd little smile. 'And of course, he gave you this house. And the annuity. Are you still getting that, by the way?'

The calculating look on her face made Emma heartily wish that she had never let slip about Thomas's financial arrangements to her sister. 'It's paid to me as Thomas's widow for as long as I live, or until I remarry. But I didn't marry Thomas for what he owned, Charlotte. In fact, when we married, I thought this house was all he had.'

'Did you? Well, you're different to me, Em. I couldn't marry a man unless he had something substantial to offer me.'

'And unless you were fond of him, too,' Emma added hopefully.

Charlotte sighed. 'I suppose so. And Edward is rather sweet.'

'Oh, I'm so pleased! Tell me about…Edward? Is that his name?'

'Oh, he's a farmer, with a property out on the Hawkesbury River. His family has been here for generations, but there's not a drop of convict blood in the Morgans. And pots and pots of money.'

'Morgan.' A small dart of shock pierced her at the sound of the name. But it was a common enough name, surely. 'Is…is he from a large family?'

'No, just him now. His wife died over twenty years ago, and he has no surviving children, thank God! The last thing I want is to be a stepmama and start competing for an inheritance with someone's mewling little brats.'

'Twenty years a widower? How old is he, Charlotte?'

'Fifty-four, which is only a little older than your Thomas.' She smiled slightly. 'And probably a damn sight livelier in bed.'

'*Charlotte!*' Emma instinctively checked that the girls had not entered the room unannounced, and Charlotte burst out laughing.

'Oh, you're such a prude! Don't pretend you don't know what I'm talking about. You've never needed physical satisfaction, but I have. It's important to me.'

Emma covered her eyes in despair. 'I've never understood you, Charlotte. Never. How you can do the things you do…'

'Emma.' Charlotte reached over and prised her sister's hands away from her face. 'Look at me! You may not understand me, but you know me. You know what I am. I may be what you call a whore— your late and unlamented pillock of a husband certainly called me that—and I'll admit I ask for payment for what I do. And I've made a lot of money, because I'm very good at what I do. But I only ever do it with men I like and want, because I enjoy it. It's my only skill in life, Emma. Am I so very wrong to use it?'

'Yes, of course you're wrong! Because you lie with men to whom you're not married, and with men who may even be married to other women!'

Charlotte's green eyes narrowed to cat-like slits. 'Is that so? And can you truly sit there with a clear conscience and preach to me? You, of all people?'

'Of course I can't,' Emma whispered, stricken. 'But I did what I did from necessity, Charlotte— you know that. After Father died and left us destitute… I didn't even have anything to feed the twins! There was no one to help us, and you had gone…'

'I couldn't have done anything anyway,' Charlotte said harshly. 'I had money problems of my own then. You seem to conveniently forget that I was sick too, with that accursed fever. I could have died…'

'Father did die! And you could have come home any time.'

'Hardly,' Charlotte snapped. She got to her feet

and poured herself another sherry, filling the glass to overflowing. Her silk skirts swished loudly in the silent room. It was their old argument again, and Emma was heartily sick of it. As always, it was she who made a move to peace.

'Charlotte, we shouldn't fight. Not when you're about to start a new life with a man you love. I'm very happy for you.'

Charlotte put down her glass and looked amused. 'You are happy for me, aren't you? Why? Because I'm going to be respectable at last?'

'Respectability can be very pleasant, Charlotte. I take it Mr Morgan doesn't know about your... manner of making a living?'

'No, he doesn't, and it goes without saying that he mustn't find out, at least until after the wedding. He's been buried in the outback for the past few years, and he doesn't really know anyone in Sydney. I've been very careful since I met him last month, and I don't think he's heard any gossip. None of my gentlemen ever knew my real name anyway.' She finished her sherry and once again Emma saw the calculating look slip into her eyes. 'This is my only chance at a fresh start, Em. He's very eligible, and very wealthy, and he's desperate to marry me. I can't let him slip away.'

'He sounds wonderful,' Emma said softly, 'He must love you a great deal to want to marry you so quickly.'

'Mmm. Well, I won't go to bed with him until I get a ring on my finger, so he doesn't have much choice,' Charlotte said tartly. 'But there is one small problem.'

'And that problem is what?'

'Em, this man is wealthy! You should see his house! He's having it rebuilt, which is why he's in Sydney so often these day, but it's going to be a mansion when it's finished. He could marry any woman he wants. A woman with money!'

'Which is why it's wonderful that he wants you.'

'Em!' Charlotte said in exasperation. 'I've…oh, I've told him that I've got a property.'

'But you haven't, have you?'

'No. Oh, I've got lots of lovely dresses, and even some nice pieces of jewelery that my gentlemen have bought me over the years, but I haven't got a house of my own, Em. That's why I thought that you could perhaps help me out.'

'How?'

Charlotte took a deep breath. 'I've told Edward that this house is mine.'

'Charlotte!'

'Em, I've got to appear as if I've got something of my own! Otherwise he'll just think I'm marrying him for his money!'

'Charlotte, I think you are!' Emma burst out. 'You can't do this! What will he think of you when he finds out the truth?'

'He won't! He thinks Father left this house to me as the eldest child. I'll just tell him after we're married that I've made the house over to my widowed sister, and he won't think twice about it, truly, Em! Look, compared to what he owns, this house is nothing. But I can't go into this marriage looking as if I'm penniless.'

'But if he loves you…'

'He might want me, but he's not a fool!' her sister said sharply. 'You've only got to go along with the pretence for a week, for goodness' sake. And this is likely to be the only chance I'll get to marry someone like Edward. Please, Em, are you going to begrudge me even that?'

She poured another sherry at speed while Emma wrestled with her conscience. Finally Emma said, 'You're basing your marriage on a lie. Why don't you go to Mr Morgan and tell him the truth? If he really cares about you...'

'You don't know a thing about men, do you?' Charlotte hissed. 'If I told him the truth about me, he'd run a mile, or at least as far as the next woman! Men always prefer the fantasy to the reality, Emma, believe me!'

Emma closed her eyes. 'I do believe you,' she said, so quietly that Charlotte didn't hear.

Charlotte began to pull on her gloves, jerking the fabric over each finger in controlled rage. 'There might not be many free women in the colony, but I can assure you there's more than one ambitious mama with a young daughter to marry off, who would snap him up in an instant. However, if you are so determined to ruin my life and insist on the absolute truth, perhaps you could set an example and tell the good parishioners of St Paul's and all your patients what you did before you married Thomas? Or would you prefer me to do it for you?'

'Charlotte, you wouldn't!' Emma whispered in shock, knowing full well that she most certainly would, and would relish the telling. They both knew the power of scandal in a small society like Syd-

ney's in which a large proportion of the population
were either convicts or the descendants of convicts,
and where the reputations of free citizens were jeal-
ously guarded. A respectability earned by a lifetime
of good works could be wiped out in hours and
never regained.

Charlotte watched the capitulation on her sister's
face with a small smile. She hadn't really expected
any opposition from that quarter, anyway.

Chapter Thirteen

Charlotte moved in the next morning, putting Emma's small household in an uproar. Mrs Stott, used to being allowed to run the house as it pleased her, took great offence at Charlotte appointing herself as the new mistress.

'I will not be told by Miss Brown what she wants served for dinner, Mrs Johnson!' Mrs Stott was literally quivering with rage, two bright spots of hectic colour on her bony cheeks. 'I don't care that she's your sister and that she's only staying the week—I will *not* cook this fancy muck she want tonight. Plain, wholesome food I always cook. It's been good enough in the past, and if it's not good enough now, I'm off to where I'll be appreciated.'

'Go, then, I don't care!' said Charlotte tartly as she flounced past them and began to climb the stairs. 'Emma's always been a good cook, haven't you, Em? You won't mind doing something for tonight if this useless old hag disappears back down the hole she crawled out of.'

Emma miserably clutched her medical bag to her

side. She had been hoping to avoid the inevitable spats by going out, but it didn't look as if she was going to be successful.

'I do have some patients I have to see,' she began, but Charlotte's bedroom door had already closed with a bang. She looked at her outraged house-keeper with considerable sympathy.

'I'm sorry, Mrs Stott. Her fiancé is coming to dinner tonight, and I know she wants to make the best possible impression. What is she asking you to cook?'

'She's even made up a menu!' Mrs Stott opened her fist to reveal the crumpled sheet of paper. 'I can't make it out, fancy mumbo-jumbo that it is!'

Knowing Mrs Stott couldn't read, Emma smoothed out the sheet and read through it. 'She wants consomme—that's just a clear broth. A fish dish, a leg of ham, a meat pie, some vegetables, a dessert...' She ventured a conciliatory smile at the housekeeper. 'It's rather more dishes than we would normally have for a meal, Mrs Stott, but nothing that you couldn't produce with one hand tied behind your back. No one has a lighter hand with pastry than you, and you do remember that the Reverend said just last week when he came to dinner that he had never tasted a finer custard tart?'

Mrs Stott sniffed, visibly mollified. 'The Reverend Collins certainly likes his puddings, I'll say that for him. Well, Mrs Johnson, I'll cook for tonight, but any more abuse from her upstairs and I'm off. And you'd better keep her out of my kitchen!'

Emma took her bag and made her escape. She had had a similar scene with Rima that morning, when she had found out that Charlotte was coming to stay. It had taken a combination of threats and bribery to get Rima to go to school and not to stay at home and set boobytraps for the detested Charlotte.

She tried to get home before Rima did in order to peacemake, but she had a great many patients to see, including Mrs McDuff who was running a mild fever, although baby Emma was thriving. When she finally walked in the door she was met with pandemonium. Charlotte had filled the house with flowers in preparation for Mr Morgan's visit and, when Rima had upended a vase while admiring them, she had had her ears boxed. In retaliation Rima had taken a pair of scissors to half a dozen of Charlotte's best dresses. By the time Emma arrived home Rima had wisely taken herself to the safety of the top of the big gum tree in the back garden, and Charlotte was searching for an axe. Mrs Stott had barricaded herself in the kitchen and was refusing to come out.

It took all Emma's diplomacy to calm Charlotte and to talk Rima out of the tree and dispatch her to the Carsons' for the night. Within the hour, however, peace was restored. Charlotte had ordered several crates of expensive wines to be delivered to the house—at whose expense Emma dared not ask—and with a bottle opened and a glass filled, Charlotte quickly cheered up. Obviously, Emma decided, that was the way to keep things calm until the wedding.

Charlotte had also spent a great deal on new cutlery and glassware to make the dining-table look nothing less than magnificent, and Mrs Stott—once she could be coaxed from the kitchen—had worked wonders at such short notice. Silently appalled at what this was personally costing her, Emma sincerely hoped that Mr Morgan would be suitably overwhelmed.

Edward Morgan turned out to be a very handsome man, tall and solidly built, his dark hair just beginning to turn a distinguished grey. Despite his lengthy exile in the rural backblocks, he was very much a lady's man, slightly outrageous and full of extravagant compliments. Only a blotched complexion, slightly shaking hands and a bottomless thirst warned Emma that Mr Morgan was in all probability as much an enthusiast for the bottle as her sister. Still, she supposed that would make them all the more suited to each other.

Having by now fully recovered her spirits, Charlotte looked beautiful in a dress of creamy lace, cleverly cut to enhance her figure. Emma had dressed equally carefully, in one of the sober dark dresses that her wardrobe was full of—she wanted to be as inconspicuous as possible that night.

She took pains to say as little as possible over dinner, planning to excuse herself as soon as she decently could. However, when she began to rise after the final course, she was mortified to find Mr Morgan's hand firmly grasping her knee under the table.

'Please stay, Mrs Johnson,' he said beguilingly. 'It's not often I get to enjoy the company of two such beautiful women of an evening.'

Charlotte's smile became a little steely. 'I'm sure

you've got something to see to in the kitchen, haven't you, Emma?'

Mr Morgan's hand would not remove itself, and so Emma had little option but to resume her seat.

'That's better.' He gave her thigh a little pat. 'Now, isn't this cosy? I think we'll all do very well together here.'

'I beg your pardon?' Emma said frostily, deciding that she did not like Mr Morgan one little bit, as his hand inched further up her leg.

'This is a lovely house, Mrs Johnson.' He smiled widely, showing that he still had most of his teeth. 'You've done a sterling job of looking after it for Charlotte. I know I'll feel at home straight away.'

Now it was Charlotte's turn to look shocked. 'We…we won't be staying here, surely, Edward? Your house in the country…'

'Far too far away for you, my dear little bird of paradise! You'll be much happier here in the town, I know, with all your friends and the shops and all that sort of thing that keeps you ladies busy! There's plenty of room for us all here. Besides—' his fingers moved even higher '—I'm sure Mrs Johnson will enjoy having a man about the house again, hmm?'

Deciding that matters on all fronts had gone on quite far enough, Emma reached for the pickle fork. 'I think there are some details you ought to be made aware of, Mr Morgan,' she said.

'Why, Emma,' Charlotte interrupted sweetly, 'if you're going to tell Edward about your…exciting life before you married Thomas, why don't we go into the parlour and sit by the fire? We may as well make ourselves comfortable.'

For a moment her possible future lives flashed before her. Was it to be the speaking of the truth, social ostracism and utter disgrace, or some obscene *ménage à trois* with her sister and Mr Morgan? Both scenarios were intolerable. Mumbling something incoherent, Emma fled from the room.

After Mr Morgan had gone Emma pulled a blanket around her shoulders and sat for hours on the veranda outside her bedroom. It was a cold night but clear, and the wind from the south brought with it the scent of the sea. The lights in the town below went out one by one, leaving only the odd tavern light and the mast-lights on the ships in the harbour to illuminate the night.

She knew she should sleep—she was desperately tired after a day of hard work—but she also knew that she would do nothing but toss and turn in her bed until dawn. The nights were like that for her sometimes, and had been ever since New Zealand. It was much better to stay up and read, or even to sit like this in the quiet dark, than it was to lie rigid and sleepless in her big bed. Or worse, to dream again and wake up crying, clutching the eiderdown to her in an agony of frustrated longing.

Perhaps she should, after all, take James Collins up on the offer he would make to her in the New Year, when her period of mourning was decently over. Better, perhaps, to live in quiet, passionless contentment than to suffer this torment. She might even conceive. James would make a kindly father, and children would keep her busy and provide an outlet for her love and affection. Eventually she would come to forget the man who had made her burn. The man who had only had to touch her to send her mindless and boneless with lust.

Marriage to James would also give her a desperately needed ally. Whatever Charlotte had planned, Emma wanted no part of it. She would never live under the same roof as Edward Morgan. And at least James knew about Emma's past—there was nothing to fear from him there, nothing Charlotte could do to ruin that for her. Perhaps, after all, that was the only course open to her.

Emma stared unseeingly at the dark harbour, miserably aware of Life simultaneously shutting all its doors of opportunity in her face.

She spent a sleepless night and was feeling wretched the next morning. Even Mrs Stott seemed to sense her mood and unexpectedly left her with a pot of hot coffee before she bustled off to the market. The coffee helped restore Emma's courage, and she was ready to do battle with Charlotte when her sister appeared, tying the ribbons of a very fetching bonnet under her chin as she came down the stairs.

'And what did you think of Edward?' Charlotte said chattily. 'I think it went very well, don't you?'

'No, I don't,' Emma said coolly. 'Please come into the parlour.'

'Said the spider to the fly,' said her sister in a tone of mock-doom. She followed Emma into the small, sunlit room and stood with her arms folded. 'You're not going to be difficult, are you, Em?'

'Difficult? About you and Mr Morgan taking over my house?'

'Oh, that.' Charlotte shrugged. 'Well, it does make sense, doesn't it? I didn't really want to live in the country anyway.'

'I am not going to live under the same roof as that man, Charlotte! He...he's detestable!'

Charlotte smiled sweetly. 'Well, you know the solution, don't you, Em.'

'What?'

'You can leave. And take that horrible little animal you brought back from New Zealand with you. You've got the money, so why don't you just go? Now, then—' she opened her reticule '—I need to go shopping. I'll need some money.'

'Mrs Stott has already gone this morning. Charlotte...'

'Oh, not for food, Em! Be *serious*!' Charlotte said scornfully. 'Can you honestly see me queuing up to buy your fish and beans for you? I've still got my trousseau to buy. How about an early wedding present? Not much—just a few pounds will do.'

'I'm not giving you a *penny*,' Emma said furiously. 'Nor am I going to leave my house so that you and that man can live here! Do you understand me, Charlotte?'

Her sister snapped her reticule shut. 'No, I don't. You're being perfectly beastly about all this, but I'll leave you in peace while you have a good think, and then perhaps you'll see sense.' She turned in the doorway and added, 'And don't worry about the money. Your credit is very good with all the shopkeepers in Sydney, I discovered yesterday.'

As the front door banged shut behind her, Emma knew what it would feel like to murder someone in the heat of passion. She groped for a chair and sat down just in time. She wanted to kill Charlotte and Mr Morgan both. She hated them, hated her sister especially, hated what they had driven her to...

Eventually it occurred to her that she was behaving no better than Rima, albeit with better reason. She took the coffee pot and her cup back to the kitchen with hands that were only slightly trembling and then walked quietly in the garden for a while. It was going to be a beautiful day, and the dew was drying rapidly on the leaves. Rosellas flashed their brilliant colours in the trees. Magpies chased each other noisily across the lawn and rooted enthusiastically among the rows of freshly turned earth she had dug for her kitchen garden.

She turned back towards the house. A few hours of hard work planting her spring vegetables would help, she knew. She had always done her best thinking with her hands in the soil.

As she crossed to the stairs a sharp rap on the front door startled her. So much for her morning's gardening—her patients all knew that she made her visits in the afternoons, but that they could call any time if there was an emergency. She checked that her hair was neatly restrained and then opened the door.

The big, fair-haired man leaning against the veranda post was Ben Morgan. She saw the shock dawn on his face, mirroring her own, and then he sprang forward.

'No, you don't!' He shoved his shoulder in the way as she went to slam the door. It was absolutely the last straw for Emma. Screaming, not caring if any neighbours were about to hear her, she pummelled his chest, kicked his shins, bit his wrists as he tried to restrain her.

'In with you, madam,' he said breathlessly, pushing her back into the hallway and shutting the door.

'Get *out*! I hate you! Get *out*!' she yelled, horribly aware that she was close to tears and knowing that once she started she wouldn't be able to stop. But he held her so tightly that she couldn't free her arms and legs to beat him, and after a while she slumped against him, crying noisily and helplessly. Her hair was all over her face and his, her nose was running, but she didn't care. Ben held her carefully, patting her back comfortingly, making vaguely consoling noises against the top of her head. At last the sobs ceased to rack her body and she lay still against him, sniffing occasionally and feeling, oddly enough, much better.

'I need a handkerchief,' she mumbled.

'Here.' He produced one from inside his jacket and carefully wiped her cheeks. 'Now blow.'

She blew her nose obediently and he put away his handkerchief, studying her blotched, stricken face with a frown.

'Oh, Emma, Emma,' he said softly. 'You were the very last person I expected to see here.'

She gulped defiantly. 'This is my house.'

'Is it?' She could see that the news wasn't welcome to him. He glanced about him, his grip around her waist tightening. 'Then we have some talking to do. Are you alone here?'

'Yes, but…' She turned her head away, but not for the world could she summon the strength to move from his arms. 'I think you ought to go. We've already said all we need to each other.'

'I think not, Emma.' He forced her chin up and kissed her, and it was as if Paradise had thrown its gates wide open to her. She clung to him, drowning in him, desperately clutching at all the pleasure and the pain he offered.

Perhaps he had intended carrying her upstairs, but she was too tightly melded to his body to allow him to pick her up. Dazedly she was aware of them falling on to the stairs, of his hands moving up under her skirts to curve around her hips and protect them from the wooden edge of the stairs. He took her without preamble, there on the stairs, more swiftly and violently than she could ever have thought possible, and so pleasurably that she thought she would faint. As they both gasped out their climax Emma looked up at the portrait of Thomas's father scowling down at them from the wall and wondered at her madness.

'That,' she said, as soon as she had regained her breath and her sanity, 'must never happen again.'

'No,' said Ben with a rueful grin that twisted around her heart. 'My knees are killing me.'

'I didn't mean that.' She pushed at his chest and he slowly disengaged himself, leaving her spread-eagled and splendidly tousled on the stairs.

'God, you're lovely,' he said hoarsely. She pushed him away again when he would have bent to kiss her breasts. Given the opportunity, Ben would make love for hours on end.

'Ben, anyone could come in! I must wash, change my dress…'

He let her go reluctantly and she made her way a little shakily upstairs, every muscle in her legs protesting. In the safety of her room she stared at her flushed face and shining eyes in the mirror, as much appalled at the physical change that love-making had wrought on her as by the thoughtless ease with which she had abandoned all her morals.

The intervening months had not changed a thing, she thought in despair as she went through the routine of her ablutions. Had she not developed any self-control at all? Or was Ben like some delicious addiction to her, something she could never resist, no matter how sensible she was? The best thing—the only thing—to do with an addiction was to remove the temptation, surely? She had to persuade him to leave somehow, and leave quickly. But how the devil had he found her here? He had seemed as surprised to see her as she had been to see him.

Frowning, she came quietly down the stairs. He had his back to her, studying the portraits hanging on the hallway wall, and for the first time she noticed his expensive clothes, certainly not cut by a colonial tailor, and his highly polished boots, devoid of all workman's dust. Ben Morgan looked like a man in the money. Well, she was pleased for him—he had worked hard for it, after all.

He turned at her light footfall, the familiarity of his beautiful, beloved face piecing her heart. 'How is Rat?'

She forced normality to her voice. 'Rima's fine. She's doing well at school. She…she misses you.'

'Hmm.' He turned back to study the Johnson

family portraits. 'This is Thomas's house.' It was a statement, not a question.

'Yes.'

'Not your father's.'

'No.' She looked at him in surprise. 'Why should you think that?'

'I was told it was.' He stood squarely before her, his hands on his hips, studying her still-flushed face as carefully as he had the portraits a minute before. She stood poised on the bottom step, glad of the confidence the extra height gave her. It seemed suddenly inconceivable that only minutes ago they had been achieving the heights of ecstasy together on that same step.

'Emma, I don't know what's going on here, but I'll not beat about the bush. I shouldn't have let you go. It was a mistake. I'd like to start again.'

'Start again?' she repeated blankly.

'Yes. I've forgiven you.'

Somewhere inside her head the red mist of rage began to billow up again. She curled her fingers tightly around the handrail so as not to hit him.

'How kind,' she said woodenly, and he nodded slightly, seemingly unaware of the heavy irony behind her words. Not for the first time, his pomposity struck her as being identical to Thomas's.

'So—I'll repeat the offer I made you in New Zealand, Emma. Will you marry me?'

She took a deep breath. 'Thank you for the kind offer, Mr Morgan, but I wouldn't marry you if you were the last man left on earth!'

His pale eyes narrowed to wintery splinters. 'You'd rather marry my father, is that it?'

Emma was staring at him, quite stunned, when there came the sound of quick, expensively shod feet on the veranda and the front door opened.

'Hello!' Charlotte said brightly, struggling to carry all her parcels in the door at the one time. 'Have we got visitors?' Ben turned around slowly and Emma saw the immediate transformation on her sister's face. *'Hello,'* she said again, and with unmistakable invitation as her eyes slid appreciatively up and down Ben's impressive build. Her lids drooped slightly and she gave a quick little lick of her lips to wet them. Emma realised that she was seeing her sister in hunting mode. Charlotte put her gloved hand out and gave a little gurgle of delight when Ben brought it to his lips. 'I don't think we've met before,' she said throatily. 'Please do the conventions, Emma.'

Wanting to murder them both, Emma said shakily, 'Charlotte, this is Mr Morgan, a gentleman I met while in New Zealand. Mr Morgan, this is my sister, Miss Brown.'

Charlotte carefully retrieved her hand. 'What a coincidence,' she murmured. 'Morgan is my fiancé's name. Are you by any chance related?'

Ben smiled and, only because she knew him as well as she did, a shiver ran down Emma's spine.

'If we're talking about Edward Morgan, then we're speaking of my father. And I take it that you, Miss Brown, are to be my stepmother?'

Charlotte's hand fluttered to her throat. 'I think

there is some mistake. Edward has no surviving children…'

'Just me.' Ben shook his head disapprovingly. 'He always was a careless parent. I arrived from Auckland two days ago, and when my father told me about your forthcoming nuptials, I thought I'd better pay my respects in person.'

Charlotte looked dismayed. 'I had no idea. He told me he had no children at all…'

'We parted years ago, Miss Brown, but don't worry.' He brought his head down to her blonde ringlets and said confidingly, 'He cut me off without a penny. I don't stand to inherit anything that should be yours.'

'Really?' Charlotte said breathlessly, her eyes alight with relief, and Ben nodded kindly.

'Not a bean. You have my word on it. Now why don't you put down all those heavy parcels and the two of us will go and see my father? I want to offer him my heartiest congratulations on marrying one of the most beautiful women in the colony.'

Charlotte dropped her parcels with alacrity and slipped her hand through Ben's proffered arm. 'I've sent the cabbie away. Is that your carriage outside?'

'It is.' He paused at the door, looking down at Charlotte with open fascination.

'What is that fragrance you're wearing, Miss Brown?'

'Just tuberose.' She fluttered her lashes at him beguilingly. 'I always wear it, day and…night. I'm glad you like it.'

'It's very evocative,' Ben said. He spared a quick, speaking look at Emma as he led Charlotte out to the carriage but she was far too angry to give it any attention.

God rot them both in Hell! she thought as she rummaged in the pantry for the vegetable seedlings. They were two of a kind, and they deserved whatever came to them. But the certain knowledge that they would be lovers by the day's end tormented her, and few of the delicate seedlings survived their rough transplanting that morning.

If Ben and Charlotte did indeed become lovers that day, it was a rather rushed affair.

Emma collected Rima from school and was just opening the front door when a carriage drawn by two of the finest horses Emma had seen in the colony trotted briskly up the drive. Rima shaded her eyes against the low sunshine.

'Isn't that Pen?'

Emma hesitated. She had hoped to have time to talk to Rima about Ben's return, but it seemed she was not going to be granted even that small mercy by the Fates on what had turned out to be one of the worst days of her life. As the carriage drew closer Rima screamed in delight.

'Pen! Pen! Pen!' She ran down the steps and only just avoided being trampled by the startled horses as Ben drew them in. She scampered up on to the carriage and flung her arms around Ben's neck, covering him with enthusiastic kisses. Laughing, Ben gave up trying to free himself from her grip and had to climb down and tie up the horses with one hand.

'I see you two know each other,' said Charlotte, watching the exchange with great interest.

Rima glared at her from the security of Ben's arms. 'What are you doing with Pen? He belongs to Hemma!'

'Rima, please let Mr Morgan go,' Emma said sharply.

'Oh, but, Emma, why spoil such a touching re-union?' purred Charlotte, who had given up waiting for Ben to help her down from the carriage and had managed the manoeuvre by herself. She smoothed her crumpled skirts and smiled nastily at Rima. 'And just when did Emma take possession of Mr Morgan, Rima?'

'Why don't you go away?' Rima demanded.

'Rima, go inside!' Emma snapped. 'Go and wash your hands, and Mrs Stott will give you some afternoon tea.'

Rima pouted. 'But…'

'Come on, Rat, let's go inside,' Ben said gently. 'I'd like some afternoon tea too.' Instantly Rima brightened and she happily led him through to the kitchen, talking nineteen to the dozen, her English now fluent enough to allow her to bombard him with her entire store of memories and observations.

'They're very close,' Charlotte observed tartly. 'Ben said you met in New Zealand, but I have to say he was a little vague on the details.' She put her head on one side and looked at Emma knowingly. 'Does he know about your past?'

Emma met her sister's eyes defiantly. 'Yes. Does he know about yours?'

'Why, Emma, if I didn't know you better, I'd think there was something between you and the delectable younger Mr Morgan. But, of course, that's absurd.'

Angry as she was, Emma realised with a great surge of relief that—whatever had happened between Charlotte and Ben—he had told her sister very little about their time in New Zealand. She picked up her medical bag with a shaking hand and turned to go inside. From the kitchen came Rima's shrill chatter and—wonder of wonders!—Mrs Stott's laugh. Obviously Ben was turning on his charm.

'Did you have a pleasant time with Mr Morgan and his son today?' Emma asked as she shut the door behind Charlotte.

Her sister paused by the hallway mirror and frowned at her reflection, adjusting the neckline to better advantage. 'Very pleasant, thank you. Whatever the silly fight was they had years ago, it's all over now. And at least Ben can support himself, so that he won't be a drain on his father. It's a pity he's not done better for himself, though—I'd rather have the son in my bed than his father any day.'

'Charlotte!'

'Well, it's true. He has to be one of the best-looking men I've ever seen, and he can be quite charming, just like his father. But there's something a bit odd about him. A bit…cold. In fact, I wonder if he's not one of those men that prefer other men to women. Very good-looking men can be like that, you know…'

They both turned as Ben cleared his throat, and Charlotte flashed him her most brilliant smile to cover her consternation. 'Ben, darling! Well, I must go and start my packing...'

'You have another three days,' Ben pointed out politely.

'Three days? Where are you going?' asked Emma.

'Oh, didn't I tell you?' Charlotte gave her hair a self-conscious pat and began to sidle around Ben towards the stairs. 'Edward is taking me to England for our honeymoon! I have to thank Ben for that— it was his suggestion.'

They were silent as Charlotte went to her room, and then Ben reached over to take Emma's hand in his. 'Emma, it's imperative that we talk. There's so much I have to tell you.' As she hesitated he took the opportunity to draw her towards the door. 'We'll go for a walk, shall we?'

She was about to acquiesce when Rima came racing out of the kitchen.

'You're not going away again? Pen...'

'I'll be back tomorrow.' He picked her up and gave her a quick kiss. 'Tomorrow, Rat, I promise. I'll take you riding with me.'

'All right.' She gave him a last hug and screwed up her nose. 'Ugh! You smell like her! Like flowers!'

Ben looked at Emma's face and could have cursed.

'Emma?'

'Good night, Ben,' she said, and shut the door on him.

Outside in the late, slanting sunshine Ben curled his hands into fists of frustration. Damn and blast!

All he needed was five minutes alone with her, but between Charlotte and Rima even that seemed an impossibility.

He drove back to his hotel in the dark, lost in thought. He was still mulling over his course of action when he went up to the bare hotel room that was now his temporary home. Once there he took off his shirt, grimacing as he realised that Charlotte's fragrance did indeed cling to the fabric. Bitch that she was! He tossed the shirt on the floor and flung himself onto his bed.

Staring at the ceiling, his hands behind his head, he thought of what to do next. By suggesting the honeymoon to England—at his expense, but Charlotte wasn't to know that—he had successfully brought his father's wedding forward. The next decision was whether to let it go ahead. All it would take would be a quick word from him to either of the happy couple to effectively ruin the day. On the other hand, if he waited, he could ensure he ruined their lives, and that would be far more satisfying. His father deserved no mercy, and his stepmother-to-be deserved even less.

He closed his eyes tightly as he relived that moment in Emma's doorway. When his father had boasted that morning that he was to marry the woman who lived in the big brick house on the hill he had come out of curiosity, wondering what kind of woman would marry a lecherous, alcoholic spendthrift like Edward Morgan. He had not believed his eyes when Emma had opened the door. And then when Charlotte Brown walked in... Her sister! Jesus, why had he not thought of that months ago, in New Zealand? The sisters were like peas in a pod in all but colouring. And character.

God, how he loathed that woman! It might have been almost three years ago now, but he had known her instantly. The wonder of it was that she plainly didn't remember him. But the room had been dimly lit and they had both been drinking that night. No doubt she'd had a hundred men since him. He wondered what she'd done with the money in his wallet. There had been over three hundred pounds there— half of it hard-earned, the other half won in a brilliant streak of luck at the gaming tables. And all of it ready to be handed over to the mortgagors of his family's farm the next morning. For him, losing the money had been two more years of hard, dangerous work. For her, stealing the money probably meant no more than a new wardrobe.

No, he decided, he would say nothing until after the wedding. In fact, he would say nothing even to Emma until his father and his bride were safely on the ship to England. The revenge would be all the sweeter for being slow and savoured.

He rolled over and seized his pillow in frustration, wishing it was Emma's softness he was holding to his face. He had long since given up blaming her for anything she had done in the past. What did it matter if she had sold herself like her sister? Even if she was doing it now—which he doubted—he couldn't love her any less for it. God knew he'd done enough to be ashamed of in the past, and for no other reason than pleasure. Who was he to judge?

He had driven Emma away once before out of disappointment and hurt pride. It was not in his character to make the same mistake twice.

Chapter Fourteen

Charlotte and Edward Morgan were married on the Monday morning, the wedding having been brought forward to enable them to sail out on the afternoon tide to England. Light showers in the morning drove the wedding party indoors, but the ceremony was a private one in the small church of St Paul's, witnessed only by Emma and Ben and celebrated by the Reverend Collins. Rima, Martha and Caroline jiggled about excitedly in the empty pews, but were suitably silent during the service. Emma was proud of them.

Charlotte was a beautiful bride, radiant in dove-grey satin, repeating her vows softly, her eyes fixed lovingly on her husband's face. To Emma's surprise Mr Morgan looked somewhat nervous for such an assured man. He muddled his vows twice and seemed to keep darting quick glances at his son, standing stiffly beside him.

Afterwards they returned to Emma's house for the wedding breakfast; a wonderful spread of Mrs Stott's best 'plain cooking' and a rich fruit cake

Emma had baked for Christmas. Emma was pleased that she had insisted that the children be present— if it had not been for their excited enthusiasm it would have been a rather constrained occasion. She had received a formal peck on the cheek from her new brother-in-law—it seemed there was to be no under-the-table groping in his son's presence—but he seemed oddly out of sorts. Charlotte was play-acting wildly, making an exaggerated fuss of her new husband. And Ben seemed to be offering no more than the bare essentials of courteous behaviour.

Even the Reverend Collins noticed.

'Not the happiest of little family gatherings,' he murmured discreetly to Emma over his glass of champagne, a crate of which had been Ben's donation to his father's celebration. 'What is the problem, do you think?'

'I don't know,' she said quietly. She looked across the loaded table to where the happy couple was busily pouring each other a glass of wine—Mr Morgan senior had perked up quite dramatically after the first toast. Ben, who appeared not to be drinking at all, was making desultory conversation with the Carsons. He looked up and caught her watching him. She quickly averted her eyes, but not before Mr Collins had noted the exchange.

'The younger Mr Morgan is an interesting fellow. Seems rather fond of you, Emma. You met in New Zealand, I understand?'

James Collins knew almost everything there was to know about Emma, but she had not told him about her unforgivable lapses of moral judgement in New Zealand, and no intention of ever doing so. Usually his tendency to harmless gossip amused her, but not today.

Meaningfully she caught Charlotte's attention and indicated the time on the mantelpiece clock. The *Sarah Jane* was sailing in less than three hours time.

She left the girls to help clear the table under the direction of Mrs Stott, and went with Charlotte, Mr Morgan and Ben in Ben's carriage down to the docks. The bridal couple's trunks had all been stowed in their cabin early that morning, and all that needed to be taken aboard was their light hand-luggage. Ben made some transparent excuse to visit the shipping office, and strode off down the wharf without boarding. Mr Morgan expressed a keen desire to inspect the vessel before embarking, which left Emma and Charlotte alone in the cabin.

Emma put the valise containing Charlotte's jewelery and personal effects on the generous double bed and looked around her admiringly. The *Sarah Jane* had caused some comment when she had first entered the harbour three weeks earlier, being one of the new line of bigger and swifter clippers. The master cabin was spacious by anyone's standards, with every imaginable luxury. A huge vase of flowers stood on the mahogany dressing-table, and a bottle of champagne and two glasses awaited the honeymooners on a silver tray beside the bed.

'What a beautiful cabin!'

Charlotte pirouetted in front of the full-length mirror and smiled in satisfaction at her reflection. 'Isn't it? I had no idea one could travel in such luxury. It even has its own dressing-room and bathroom. Still, Edward says he wants no expense spared for his new bride.'

'I hope you'll both be very happy,' Emma said sincerely.

'Oh, I intend to be,' Charlotte assured her. 'All the money I can spend, with a doting older husband—what else could I want? I've got plenty of your special herbal tea, so there won't be any unexpected little visitors while I'm in England, although—' she stood sideways to the mirror and smoothed her tight-fitting skirt over her flat stomach with a frown '—I might just think about having a baby when I return. Just to make sure.'

'Sure of what?'

Charlotte shrugged. 'That I inherit everything. I don't trust Ben. You can tell that he's not happy about me marrying his father, no matter how polite a face he puts on it.'

Emma sat down on the edge of the bed. 'He..he seems quite happy about it to me...'

'How can you say that?' Charlotte reluctantly dragged her eyes away from the mirror and looked archly at her sister. 'You could see for yourself how he could hardly bring himself to congratulate us at the wedding! He must be furious to see his father's money slip out of his grasp—although he's done the most dreadful things to his father in the past! You have no idea! Did you know Edward could never keep his female staff when Ben was a boy? He'd seduce them and then treat them appallingly. Edward was always having to cover for his son. And he hasn't changed. I did tell you that Ben tried to seduce me, didn't I?'

'You told me that you thought Ben had no interest in women...'

'Oh, that was last week! No, he's been most persistent in his advances since then. I had to be really firm with him. In fact, last night I had to virtually fight him off! That's the reason for the sulks this morning. Still, there's nothing he can do now, is there?'

Her husband made his appearance then, apparently satisfied with the seaworthiness of the clipper, and so Emma kissed her sister, said a diffident goodbye to Mr Morgan and went to stand on the wharf. She stood alone, as the *Sarah Jane* was carrying very few passengers, but she still wanted to be there to wave farewell to her sister and her husband when they left. Watching the crew prepare to leave harbour was always interesting, but as the sun began to set behind the clouds the wind picked up, forcing Emma to take refuge behind the customs building.

Ben came to stand behind her as the *Sarah Jane* cast off and pulled away from the wharf. She heard him catch his breath as the sails unfurled, shining ochre in the setting sun. When she stole a glance at his face he was watching the clipper intently, his face oddly exultant.

'I can't see your sister,' he said at last.

'She didn't come on deck,' Emma replied, trying to keep the disappointment out of her voice.

'No, she'll be in the cabin, ripping off my old man's trousers, about now,' Ben said calmly.

Emma longed to slap his face and would have done so if they had not been in such a public place.

'I think your jealousy is demeaning to both your-self and my sister,' she said coldly.

He managed to tear his eyes away from the bil-lowing sails of the *Sarah Jane* and look at her with genuine astonishment. 'Me? Jealous? Of what, for Christ's sake?'

'Of your father. For what he has and...and for Charlotte.'

For a second he looked as if he was going to laugh out aloud, but then he took her firmly by the shoulders and turned her around to face the harbour.

'Emma, what do you see out there on the water?'

'A ship...'

'My ship. Well, to be truthful, I only own a third of her. But by the time she returns to Sydney in a year's time I expect to own another third of her. That's how I managed to wrangle the best cabin on board at such short notice. And that ship is full of the colony's finest merino wool, a goodly portion of which is mine. From my farm. And also on board, of course, is my father and his bride, without a penny between them.'

She shook his hands from her shoulders in irri-tation. 'What are you talking about? Your father has money...'

'About as much money as your sister has.'

'My sister's not...' She stopped as she finally realised what he was talking about. 'But your father is a wealthy man!'

'He used to be, when he inherited the farm from his father. But he drank and whored the lot away. When I got back from England four years ago, the place was in the hand of the mortgagors. I'd brought some money out with me, and I worked like a navvy for a year, and made up the balance on the gambling tables. The day I made the last penny I needed, the whole lot was stolen and I had to start all over again. But I did a survey in the South Island for the New Zealand Company, and that paid for a deposit on the farm and a share in the *Sarah Jane*. The next three surveys I did for the Company—including the one of the Whanganui—paid for the farm outright.' He smiled tightly at her expression. 'It's me who's got the money, Emma—not my father.'

'But he must have some money, Ben! My sister has nothing!'

'According to Charlotte, she owns that big house you live in. Your father left it to her. And if you don't like living in it with her and my father, you have her permission to leave. She told me so herself.'

'But you knew the house was mine! I told you!' A horrible thought occurred to her. 'Why did Charlotte tell you that?'

'Because I asked her.'

'When? Last night, when you were trying to seduce her?'

He stared at her as if she was insane. 'Why the hell would I want to seduce Charlotte? Good God, I'd rather be celibate for the rest of my life than have that poxy bitch in my bed again!' Then his mouth tightened, as he realised that he had said too much, and Emma suddenly felt very sick.

'Emma…' He seized her hand as she pushed past him.

'Leave me alone!'

'You don't understand! Let me explain!' he said desperately.

Acutely aware of the curious stares that their little drama was attracting, she stood still, her eyes fixed on their entwined hands. From the corner of her eyes she could see the rapid rise and fall of his chest. 'What is there to explain, Ben? You've allowed a marriage to take place under false pretences...'

'Yes, I did. And I'm not going to apologise for it.'

'And what happens when they get to England and find they have nothing to live on?'

'Your sister will be off and on to the streets within five minutes, Emma. I'm hoping they'll find out the truth about each other while they're still on the ship. I'd like to think of them cooped up together in the same cabin for months on end, hating each other every minute of the time.'

She glared at him, her green eyes glittering with fury.

'You've had all this planned, haven't you?'

'Yes.'

'But why? I know you've never got on with your father, but....why Charlotte? She was so happy! This was her fresh start! What has my sister ever done to you?'

'She was the one who took my savings, three years ago.'

'And how did she do that?'

'After...after we'd spent the night together. Emma!' He took her by the shoulders, wishing he could kiss the pain away from her face. 'I was a different man, then. I didn't know you, I didn't know you were her sister. I... Oh, God, Emma! She took three hundred pounds off me!'

'You slept with her,' she whispered so faintly that he had to bend down to hear the words.

'Once. Years ago. And after her I couldn't bring myself to take another woman. Emma, you've been the only woman I've been with in three years...'

'Since my sister? Should I be grateful?'

'Charlotte took everything, don't you understand? Three hundred pounds...'

'Oh, to hell with your three hundred pounds!' she shouted, heedless of who should overhear them. 'It's only money!'

He stared at her uncertainly. He had known she wouldn't take it well, but he had not expected this. 'Emma, be reasonable. I've forgiven you for your past...'

'You thought I was her, didn't you? In New Zealand, you thought I was Charlotte!' she hissed. She wrenched herself free, a look of such contempt on her face that he would have willingly taken back every word if he could. She walked away, her head high under her black bonnet. He thought of running after her but they were already the subject of open speculation among the sailors and dock workers. And even if he stopped her, what could he say to make her calm down when he didn't even know why she was so furious with him in the first place? With the greatest reluctance he decided to let her go. Later, surely, she would see sense. Surely.

For the best part of a week Emma filled her days with a rigorous regime of work. She embarked on a frenzy of spring-cleaning, her vegetable and herb gardens were tended to within an inch of their lives, and a rise in the number of patients presenting themselves with a feverish type of cold kept her busy every waking hour.

The only boost to her spirits in that week came with the delivery of the printed edition of her Maori dictionary. She took quiet pride in being able to donate these to the Missionary Society, for distribution to those missionaries working in New Zealand. If their availability helped overcome some of the problems she and Thomas had faced on their arrival among the Maori, she would consider her time in New Zealand well spent indeed.

It was the nights that she dreaded, when she had only to close her eyes for an image of Ben and Charlotte entwined to imprint itself indelibly on her memory. At first she had tried to rationalise the situation to herself. She had turned Ben's proposal down, so why should she care who he slept with now or in the future or in the past? She had had a lucky escape; shouldn't she be grateful to have avoided involvement with a man who would betray her without a second's hesitation and who was, moreover, capable of the most outrageous acts of vindictiveness? But the unfamiliar emotion of jealousy had wound itself so tightly around her heart that no amount of common sense would budge it.

She took what practical steps she could. She wrote two letters immediately—one addressed to the hotel Charlotte was to stay at upon disembarking in Southampton, and one to Thomas's bank in London, requesting that the next instalment of her annuity be paid instead to her sister, Mrs Edward Morgan. The letters were sent on the *Castletown*, the next ship out of Sydney but, while she knew the *Sarah Jane* was to spend two weeks in Cape Town, she worried that the following, slower ship would still be too late. However, the captain of the *Castletown* had promised to ensure that her letter to Charlotte reached her sister, and she could do no more.

Emma could only hope that Ben's wish did not come true, and that Charlotte and her new husband remained in blissful ignorance of the state of their finances for the duration of the journey. No matter what crimes Ben might accuse his father of, no one should have to endure Charlotte in a tantrum in an enclosed space for six months.

Early one morning Emma saw Rima off to school and then wearily pulled on her apron. It was one of those beautiful days typical of early October, when the sun was melting off a sharp frost and already there was real heat in the air. Mrs Stott was noisily clattering the bread tins and singing tunelessly to herself in the kitchen. Emma decided against disturbing her by making a pot of tea, and instead took cleaning cloths and a tin of beeswax and lavender oil out of the linen cupboard. This past week she had washed and repaired every curtain and itemof linen in the house, had beaten every rug thoroughly, had washed every window upstairs and down, inside and out. Polishing the woodwork and furniture should ensure that she was fully occupied this morning.

As she began work on the dining-table, she wondered how long it would take before she allowed herself the time to think again. Mindless work was all very well, and certainly led to an immaculate house, but she knew Rima and her sisters were feeling neglected. Ben had fortunately appeared to have returned to his farm on the Hawkesbury River. Rima was missing him desperately, but had soon learned that talking about him would earn her nothing but a sharp reprimand from Emma. It really wasn't fair to her, and Emma felt guilty every time she saw the hurt look on the child's face. She would have to allow Rima to see Ben, if that was what they both wanted, despite her own feelings.

If she had not been working close by, Emma would not have heard the timid tap on the front door. The child squatting, terrified, on the doorstep was little Jenny McDuff. Automatically, Emma bent and picked her up.

'What's the matter, Jenny? Is it baby Emma?'

Jenny nodded and then took her thumb out of her mouth to cough.

'You don't sound too well yourself, sweetheart. Let's have a look at you.' She carried her into her study and opened her medical bag. Jenny shook her head violently.

'Mam said come quick.'

'I will. I'll come right away,' Emma soothed, while every instinct she possessed told her to examine the child in her arms. 'But quickly, Jenny, open your mouth while I have a look inside, will you? I just want to see what's making you cough.' She looked and then put Jenny down while she found a small spatula. 'Just another look, Jenny, while I put this on your tongue.'

It was a struggle to maintain her calm, professional composure. At the back of Jenny's reddened throat was a network of fine, greyish-white mucous. She had seen it before, in London, and had prayed that she would never see it again.

'Jenny, I want you to stay here.' She threw the spatula into the fire. 'Lie down here on the sofa and rest. I'll bring you a rug to keep you warm.'

'But me mam…'

'I'll tell your mother that you're here. She'll understand.' Almost running, she went into the kitchen and poured hot water into a basin. While she scrubbed her hands and arms she gave rapid instructions to a most unimpressed Mrs Stott. Jenny was to have blankets, warm water to drink, and be allowed to sleep in peace. Mrs Stott was not to move her, and if she touched the child she was to wash her hands immediately. Likewise, anything Jenny touched was to be thoroughly washed. Anyone who came to the door, even Rima—especially Rima—was to be turned away.

'As if I haven't got enough to do!' Mrs Stott said crossly, dusting the flour from her hands. 'And what's wrong with the little madam, I'd like to know, that we've got to treat her like the Queen of Sheba?'

Emma moved to the door and shook her hands dry. She sometimes had her doubts about the cleanliness of Mrs Stott's kitchen towels.

'I think she has diphtheria, Mrs Stott.'

'Oh, the good Lord help us!' The housekeeper backed away. 'So she'll die here, in this house?'

'Not if I can help it.'

'I'm not staying in a house of pestilence!'

'Then go,' Emma snapped.

'I will, don't you fear!' Mrs Stott began to untie her apron, 'I'm not going to catch no nasty disease from some slum brat! I'm going to stay with my daughter.'

'Do as you please. Although I've yet to see an adult die from diphtheria. It only seems to kill children, the youngest children. Just remember that if the McDuff family have it, most of the children will have been exposed to it too.'

Mrs Stott stopped in her tracks, obviously recalling that her daughter's house was located no more than a block away from the McDuffs'. And her daughter had small children. Emma could not spare the time to argue further with her. She tucked a blanket warmly around Jenny on her way out and ran down the hill and through the streets to the McDuffs', her heavy black bag bumping against her legs at every stride.

Please God, let me be wrong, she prayed all the way down to the town. In London she had seen the disease wipe out entire families of children. They had died horribly, fighting for breath, and it had been the only time she had seen her tough, seasoned father break down in tears. She thought of all the children she had nursed through childhood illnesses and accidents, and knew she could not bear the loss of even one of her children.

But one look at baby Emma, rasping desperately

for breath in her mother's arms, her tiny face scarlet
with the effort, and Emma's worst fears were con-
firmed. Six-year-old Peggy was ill too, although the
tell-tale network of membranes had not yet developed in her throat.

'Kate,' she summoned the eldest girl, somehow
managing a reassuring smile. 'Your mother and
baby Emma and Peggy are going to come to stay
with me at my house. Jenny is there already. You're
going to have to manage by yourself for a while.'

Kate nodded, and Emma resisted the urge to hug
the poor, brave, terrified child. Nothing was known
about the spread of the disease, but her own gut
feeling was that physical contact was the only con-
ductor. She was not about to be responsible for
spreading the infection any more than it had already.
She gave careful instructions about the need for absolute hygiene, and the importance of not coughing
on each other or sharing spoons or cups. Mrs
McDuff clutched baby Emma to her, looking alarmingly close to collapse herself.

'What is it, Mrs Johnson? What's wrong with me
bairns?' Emma told her as gently as she could of
her suspicions, and Mrs McDuff nodded politely,
either unaware or unwilling to accept the implications of her diagnosis.

She sent Mrs McDuff and her daughters to her
house, with implicit instructions not to stop and talk
to anyone on the way, but she herself went straight
to St Paul's. James was there, digging in the garden
as usual, and she stood a safe distance away at the
gate and soberly told him of her fears and what she
wanted him to do. The authorities had to be told,

even the Governor, and every doctor in the colony had to be alerted. Quarantine had to be imposed, schools closed… She faltered in her recital, waving James away when he would have come to take her arm.

'I'm all right, James. I just… Oh, I wish I were wrong! But I don't think I am.'

'I'll take care of it, Emma,' he said, and she looked into his kind brown eyes and knew that she could trust him to carry out all her instructions. She had heard nothing of any similar contagion in the town but, because of her sex, few of Sydney's doctors would bother themselves with informing her or, in turn, take a warning from her seriously. If the information were to come from a respected churchman like the Reverend Collins, however, it would be an entirely different matter.

'What about Rima?' he asked. 'Shall I tell her to go to the Carsons' after school?'

'Yes. She and the twins will have to stay there in quarantine until…until this is all over. Until we at least know what this is.' For a moment the magnitude of the problem loomed before her, but then she squared her shoulders. She had a lot of work to do.

At home she found Mrs McDuff and her daughters shivering on the doorstep because Mrs Stott would not let them in. Emma not only let them in but made them comfortable in the best guest-room, tucking Peggy into bed beside Jenny, and lining a drawer with a soft shawl for baby Emma, now fitfully asleep.

Mrs Stott was scandalised.

'I'm not cooking for them, Mrs Johnson! I told you I don't want them in this house, filthy things that they are…'

'And I've told you you're free to go!' Emma said wearily. Almost puce with rage, Mrs Stott's mouth snapped shut and she did just that. Even before the front door slammed behind her and her luggage, Emma had pots of water boiling over the fire and was checking supplies in the pantry. She put the loaves of risen bread in the oven and then carried a jug of cooling boiled water up to her patients. The two older girls had fallen asleep, but baby Emma was awake, snuffling unhappily into her mother's shoulder.

'This is for the girls to drink,' Emma said quietly, setting the jug and glasses beside the bed. 'We should try to get as much fluid into them as possible. The baby is better off if you can nurse her as frequently as possible.'

'Can you give them any medicine, Mrs Johnson?'

Emma saw the expression of anxious hope on Mrs McDuff's face and busied herself by opening the window a few inches.

'Until we know for sure what it is, Mary, all we can give them is warmth and fresh air, and as much boiled water and good food as we can get into them. And Mary, since you'll be my guest for a few days, please call me Emma.'

Mary McDuff smiled tremulously. 'I heard your housekeeper leaving.'

Emma nodded tiredly. 'We'll manage, Mary.'

'I can cook and clean, Mrs Johnson. We won't be a burden on you, I promise.'

Emma didn't like to tell her that she would more than likely be fully occupied with her children should their condition worsen. She was on her way back down to the kitchen when she heard the second knock on her door that morning. She opened to a frantically worried dock-worker, his two-year-old son scarlet-faced and coughing in his father's arms.

By the end of the day there were six children in her bedroom, and three frightened parents. James Collins came in the evening, bringing the news that children all over the town had come down with the disease, and there were already two reported deaths. The consensus was that it was, indeed, diphtheria.

'Oh, dear God.' Emma leaned against the veranda post, beyond which she would not allow James. 'How are Rima and my sisters? Have you seen them?'

'They're well, and Mrs Carson has promised me that they won't be allowed to leave the house until you say they may.'

'Good. It's also important that they have not contact with anyone who may be carrying the disease. Adults delivering foods, other children…and they must never share any cups or plates, or…'

'Emma,' he said in gentle reproof. 'We don't know how this disease is passed! There's no reason to go around spreading unnecessary fears. You have to be sensible about this, my dear. The children will die, or they will live. Ultimately, we're all in God's hands.'

She raked her fingers through her tangled hair in frustration. This was an argument she had often had, this belief of hers that contagious diseases were not necessarily airborne and therefore avoidable by methods like the burning of herbs. Emma believed it quite possible that infections could travel by means of body fluids like blood or saliva. Her father had held the same views, and it was from him that she had developed the automatic habit of absolute cleanliness in case she, the healer, should inadvertently become the carrier of infection.

By the following afternoon her little hospital contained another seven children. Sick children filled every room, with one baby sleeping in a sling she made between the legs of the upturned, still-unpolished dining-table. Emma turned away healthy children accompanying their sick siblings, with explicit instructions to their parents about washing their hands and anything the ill child may have touched. Within her own house she insisted that the rules be followed precisely. A few of the parents muttered about the futility of it all, but most complied without complaint. Some of them had the infection themselves, but they would most certainly suffer from it no more than they would from a bout of influenza.

During the night little Andrew, the dock-worker's son, died and the condition of several of the other children worsened. Emma sent Andrew's grief-stricken father to tell the undertaker. Then, so tired that she could hardly move, she wrapped the small body in a sheet and sat with it on the front steps while she waited for the undertaker to come.

It had been a still, cloudless day. Her garden was

filled with healthy new buds and plants and the sweet, earthy scents of growth. A kookaburra watched her beadily from her front fence, leaping from paling to paling, occasionally letting loose a raucous chuckle. Emma scarcely noticed him. Her ears were tuned only to the coughs and cries coming from the house behind her, and the colours and perfumes of spring left her entirely unmoved.

She heard the steady clop of hooves and stood up, the small body in the white sheet in her arms. But it was not the undertaker, but Ben who rode up her driveway and came to a stop before her.

'Emma? Are you all right?' He swung quickly out of the saddle as she staggered back and almost fell onto the veranda, still clutching Andrew's body to her. She nodded, not sure whether the feeling that swept through her at the sight of him was happiness or misery. He was more tanned than she had seen him, and under his broad-brimmed felt hat his face was set in grim lines.

'Who's that?' he asked, indicating the sheet.

'Andrew O'Shea. He was only two.'

'Best to put him down on the veranda, Emma. The undertaker was a few streets away when I saw him,' he said gently, and she sat down because her legs would not support her any longer. He stood silently for a while, leaning against the balustrade, watching her bent head.

'You've got a full house here, I understand. I came to town to ask if you wanted me to take Rima and your sisters out to the country. We've no sign of the disease out there.'

She shook her head slowly, as if even that simple

action was tiring. 'If they leave Sydney, they could take the disease with them.'

A fretful cry reached them from upstairs, and he watched her flinch.

'Why are you doing this, Emma? Why don't you leave it to the doctors?'

For the first time she showed some animation. 'Ben, I know I can't call myself a doctor. But I've spent my whole life learning how to take care of the sick! All these children are my patients. They can't afford medical care, but I'm free, and I can do just about anything a male doctor can do. And if you're suggesting that I should just walk away from them and let them die without at least trying…'

He put up an apologetic hand. 'I'm sorry, Emma. I didn't know. I knew you had some medical knowledge, but… We never really did learn much about each other, for all the time we spent together in New Zealand.'

'That's true,' she muttered.

'Yeah. Perhaps we're not as different to Charlotte and my old man after all.'

She lifted her chin defiantly. 'Perhaps you're right. Neither of us have been completely honest with the other, have we? We could have saved ourselves a lot of heartbreak if we had been.'

'It's not too late, Emma.'

He spoke so softly, his eyes were so bleak, that for one mad moment she thought about winding her arms around him and saying that he was right, the past should all be forgotten. But almost immediately common sense took control again and, besides, she was too tired to do anything so energetic. The un-

dertaker's black carriage was turning into her driveway and she picked up little Andrew's body again.

'You must go now.'

'Let me take the child for you.'

'No. Not unless you want to stay on here, because
then you'll be contagious.'

'I don't care.'

She put out a hand to restrain him. 'I care. I don't
want you here.'

He waited while she handed the small, white-
wrapped bundle to the undertaker. After he had
gone, Ben said, 'Then tell me how I can help.'

Emma shrugged and turned to climb the steps.
'You can't.'

She supposed that he left after she shut the door
on him. Perhaps she shouldn't have been so rude,
but it was the only alternative to collapsing into his
arms in floods of tears, and she didn't want to do
that again.

Late that afternoon she was called downstairs by
one of the mothers, who had opened the door to a
pile of boxes and bags, and a small, pock-marked,
villainous-looking man.

'Yes?' she said curtly.

He thrust an envelope at her and waited patiently
as she read the note inside.

'Meet Matthews. If you won't accept my help,
accept his.'

It was signed by Ben. She folded the note and
looked at Mr Matthews in consternation. 'I don't
understand. Why are you here?'

He lifted his bony shoulders. 'Mr Morgan said I

had to stay, missus.' And before she could move to block him, the ugly little man had pushed past her with the first of the boxes from the veranda—which she now saw contained vegetables and groceries—and found his way to her kitchen.

'You can't stay here,' she said as firmly as possible, following him back as he collected the second batch of groceries.

'I have to, missus,' he said dolefully and shut the kitchen door on her. One of the mothers called for her urgently and she ran upstairs. She'd get rid of him later, when she had time.

An hour later she smelt something absolutely delicious emanating from the kitchen. An hour after that a yell brought her and some of the mothers downstairs, where a huge pot of the most wonderful vegetable stew with herbs and dumplings awaited whoever wanted it in the dining-room. Emma joined the others in eating it, suddenly starving after days of not eating properly. When she went into the kitchen later to thank Mr Matthews, the bench was immaculately clean, with the dishes washed and put away, but there was no sign of the little man. Later, from the upstairs window, she saw him in the garden, furiously chopping wood by lamplight.

Well, she thought, turning away to check on one of her small patients. Maybe angels come in all shapes and sizes.

Another night and day passed, with no further deaths in Emma's house. All the children were severely ill, but for the first time she could see a slight improvement in the condition of some of them.

Only baby Emma, just weeks old, was losing her battle for life.

That night Emma took the baby from her exhausted mother's arms and held her quietly in a chair by the sitting-room fire. She sat alone, the only sounds the crackling of the fire and the almost inaudible rasping breaths, each one more laboured than the one before, the most pitiful sounds Emma had ever heard. She closed her eyes and prayed for a miracle. When she opened her eyes, Mr Matthews was standing in the shadows in the other side of the fireplace.

'I'm losing her,' she said helplessly.

Mr Matthews glowered and shifted from one foot to the other. 'Mr Morgan would know what to do, missus.'

She gave a small, humourless laugh. 'Maybe he would, Mr Matthews. He saved my daughter's life once, when she drowned.'

'Ah. Breathing into her, eh? We do that on the farm, time-to-time.'

'Yes,' she said slowly.

'Can't do that with this young 'un, missus. Don't she have something across the throat, what's strangling her?'

'Yes, a mucous membrane.'

'So you've got to break it, eh?'

By mutual accord they went into the kitchen and, after rummaging in one of the table drawers, Mr Matthews held up a bamboo straw. Rima had loved drinking lemonade through it.

Emma nodded. 'That'll do. We need to boil it now, to make it clean and pliable.'

It took ten minutes to boil water, and another twenty until the straw was pliable. In that time the baby was visibly struggling and Emma was losing confidence. She took the boiled straw in her fingers, waiting for it to cool, and looked at Mr Matthews helplessly.

'I can't do this…'

'Wotcha got to lose? It's gonna die, anyway.'

Just then the baby stopped breathing. Not allowing herself to think any longer, Emma held her so that her head tipped back and carefully inserted the straw down the tiny throat. She felt the momentary resistance of the membrane and baby Emma jerked slightly. After a second Emma gave the tiniest of puffs down the straw. Under her fingers she felt the baby's lungs fill and empty. She did it again and again, until baby Emma managed to breathe all by herself.

'You done it!' Mr Matthews crowed. Emma put the straw back into the boiling water.

'For now. She'll probably start to strangle again.' She sat down on a chair by the kitchen table and watched baby Emma struggle to survive. After a couple of minutes Mr Matthews put a cup of tea beside her and pulled up a chair on the other side of the table.

'It's a little battler,' he observed of the baby.

'Newborns usually die very quickly of diphtheria. Their air passages are so small. It's a horrible disease.' She dragged her eyes away from the distressing sight and took a much-needed gulp of tea. How, she wondered, had Mr Matthews known that she always took her tea black and unsugared? She looked at his ugly little face with its permanent scowl and he looked right back.

'How long have you been employed by Ben...I mean, Mr Morgan?'

'I ain't an employee, missus. I'm working off me ticket.'

She tried to stop the look of shock on her face, but knew that he had seen it. 'So...you're a...'

'I'm a convict, missus, yes. I got another eight years to go.' His villain's face looked almost sympathetic when he added, 'You're quite safe, missus. Mr Morgan wouldn't have sent me otherwise.'

'I...I suppose not. Can I ask what...?'

'Mr Morgan never asked me what I got time for,' he said firmly, as if that was supposed to explain everything.

Emma finished her tea and let him pour her another. If he was a murderer, he would have been hanged instead of transported, she thought. Presumably Ben knew something about this peculiar little man that she didn't, or perhaps he thought the man's history didn't matter. And perhaps he was right.

'I was on Morgan Station while it was under the mortgagors, and it was only his father there,' Mr Matthews went on, as if he had never interrupted her. 'Proper mess the place was then. Different now the old man's gone.'

'How is it different?'

Mr Matthews wagged his head. 'Well, you see, missus, old man Morgan is a rotten drunkard. Has been for years. Some days he sobers up and you think he's all right—even a nice sort of bloke. Then he hits the bottle again and he's back to living like a pig in his own filth. When young Mr Morgan bought the farm back off the bank, I thought he'd break down when he saw the state his old man had let the place fall into. He gave him money to go away, but within the month the old man was back, looking for more. He'd spent the lot on drink and wimmin. There was one hell of a fight, and the old man ended up roped into the horse trough until he sobered up. Darned cold night that, too. Then Mr Morgan gets all soft and gives the old man some more money, but this time he tells him he's got a year to make something of himself. Then Mr Morgan goes off to New Zealand, and the old man goes and finds himself a rich young wife.'

'My sister,' Emma said quietly. 'Poor, poor Charlotte.'

Mr Matthews nodded. 'She'll have her hands full, all right. But you can't expect Mr Morgan to keep his father, missus. The old soak'd run through every penny he was given and then some.'

Emma regarded him with interest. 'Can Mr Morgan ever do anything wrong in your eyes, Mr Matthews?'

'No, missus.' His eyes dropped to the baby in Emma's arms. 'She's stopped again.'

They had had to revive her twice more that night, but when the morning came, and a sleepy Mrs McDuff came running downstairs in a panic looking for her daughter, baby Emma was still alive.

Emma rejected Mr Matthews's suggestion that she go to bed, but she did agree to sit for a while in the parlour. He put something warm and delicious laced with whisky in her hands and, when she woke up four hours later greatly refreshed, she had been covered with a rug and the fire had been built up.

She lay quietly for a while, listening to her household. Upstairs, for the first time, she could hear the sound of childish voices. If baby Emma survived, and if the other children continued to improve, the only death would have been little Andrew's and, distressing as it had been, it would be a far lower mortality rate than she would ever have thought possible.

Someone—she could guess who it was—had arranged flowers on the table before the window, and the scent of fresh-baked bread was filling the house. Despite his sinister appearance, Mr Matthews had turned out to be an angel in disguise. He had the strangest ability to anticipate what she needed before she even thought of it herself. She stretched her cramped arms and smiled. Perhaps he was a psychic who read minds. Any moment now he would know she was awake and would come in with a hot drink…

'Ahem,' said Mr Matthews behind her chair, and he handed her a cup of freshly brewed coffee.

'Thank you,' Emma said, bemused. 'How is…?'

'Fine, missus.'

'And—?'

'They're fine too, missus. Now you sit there awhile and call me if you need anything.'

She watched him go back to the kitchen and shook her head in disbelief. Thank you, Ben, she thought. But I hope you don't want him back.

Chapter Fifteen

The little church of St Paul's was packed for the Christmas Eve service. Candlelight twinkled off the polished wooden pews and the silver on the altar. Huge arrangements of roses, lilies and golden wattle-flowers filled the air with heavy, cloying perfume. Beside the altar the Sunday School were performing a Nativity Play, complete with Mary, Joseph, a well-tethered sheep, three wise men—two of whom were Emma's little sisters with cottonwool beards—and four shepherds. One of the shepherds looked perilously close to tears; she had originally had the coveted role of Mary until it was decided at the last minute that Rima could not be trusted with a wise man's gift, a shepherd's crook or the sheep. Now Rima sat proudly cuddling baby Emma, who was tired of being the Christ child and was grumbling crossly. Every time she rose to a wail Rima gave her a little shake and Emma, close at hand in the front row, was poised to whisk the baby away should Rima become too rough.

Ben, slumped in the back pew between two

equally burly farmers, watched hungrily. In the usual course of his life he avoided churches like the plague, and would normally have spent Christmas Eve working and Christmas Day drunk. But he thought he would go mad if he didn't see Emma again, and the knowledge that this service would be particularly well-attended had driven him in to town that night.

Emma looked beautiful in a plain gown of peacock blue with a small, matching bonnet. It was the first time he had seen her in a colour that was not brown or black, and he recalled that her year of mourning would have ended that month. Beside her sat Matthews, staring fixedly at the ceiling in obvious boredom. Ben knew he would be running through the menu for Christmas Dinner or mentally itemising a grocery list. When he had sent Matthews to Emma, he had been confident that she would not send him packing—everyone needed a Matthews in their lives. Keeping him there gave Ben the security of knowing that Emma was safe and cared for, as well as a line of information about her and her household: a weekly meeting of the two men at a local tavern saw to that.

When the baby began to wail in earnest, Emma rose gracefully to her feet and prised her out of Rima's arms with a minimum of fuss. Rima grumbled something and kicked the crib, but Emma paid no attention. Almost immediately the baby was contentedly lying on her shoulder, watching the second row of worshippers with big, sleepy eyes.

In all his twenty-eight years, Ben had never given fatherhood a second's serious consideration, apart from how to avoid the possibility. But the sight of Emma's perfect profile against the candlelight was doing odd things to his imagination. She was watching the vicar reading the service with her usual serenity, one hand automatically soothing the baby on her shoulder. It should have been his child, he thought suddenly. His and Emma's. A woman with as much love to share as Emma should have a dozen children. That was why it had come as such a shock to find that she had been practicing contraception like a whore. Which, of course, she had been.

Oh God, he thought miserably as everyone else in the church got noisily to their feet to sing a carol. I should never have said anything to her. I didn't need to know. It wasn't important. None of it was bloody important. All I want is Emma back again.

He had dreaded the moment when the congregation would file out, but one of the farmers beside him was deep in conversation with another man in the pew in front, besides which Emma was kept occupied in handing the baby back to its mother, calming the aggrieved Rima and the deposed Mary, and marshalling her sisters. Only Matthews, following glumly behind, saw him and gave him a quick nod, but he could be trusted not to give him away.

He sat quietly while the church emptied and the sound of people wishing each other a Merry Christmas faded into the distance. When he judged it safe he got to his feet and retrieved his hat. But his escape though the church door was blocked by the vicar, standing there watching him, his round face tilted inquisitively.

'Mr Morgan, isn't it, sir? How nice to see you again!'

Ben mumbled an insincere greeting and crammed his hat onto his head.

'What a pity—you've just missed Mrs Johnson. But if you hurry along Carlyle Street you're bound to catch up with her. She has her sisters staying with her for Christmas, you see. In fact, I'm calling in myself soon— why don't we walk up together?'

'No,' Ben said hurriedly. 'I must be going.'

'Oh, what a pity,' Mr Collins said with real distress. 'I'm sure she'll be most disappointed. But I'll give her your regards, shall I?'

Ben felt like throttling the little man with his dog-collar. 'Listen, Vicar, I'd appreciate it if you didn't say anything to Mrs Johnson about seeing me here tonight. All right?'

Behind the twinkling eyes, something hardened. 'And why should I do that, Mr Morgan? After all, you are family, are you not?'

'Hardly,' he muttered.

'But you are! Your two closest relatives are married to each other...' He watched the expression on Ben's face with interest and continued, 'And when Mrs Johnson and I marry, I too will join the family. Isn't life wonderful, the way that we humans join and blend together, all ultimately joining in one great family of the universe...'

He twaddled on, while Ben felt as if he had been punched in the gut. Stumbling back into a pew, he sat heavily, his hat falling from his fingers as he struggled for breath.

'When are you marrying?' he demanded at last,

interrupting Mr Collins's musings on the nature of universality.

'Oh, we haven't set a date yet. There's no hurry, after all. And this has been a most stressful time for poor Emma, what with her sister marrying so suddenly, and the dreadful epidemic and now Christmas and her sisters. Such a busy time of year, I always think, but one in which we must take time to reflect on all that God has given us and which we must be grateful for…'

'So she's agreed to marry you?' Ben said abruptly, stunned by both the revelation and by the fact that Emma could possibly choose this verbose little man over him.

Mr Collins sat down beside him and patted his shoulder consolingly, albeit very carefully. 'I see you're a little upset, my friend. Yes, I'm a very lucky man. She's a fine woman, the best a man could wish for.'

'Even with her past?' The words were spoken in anger, but even as they left his lips Ben could have cut off his tongue in shame. How many times had he told himself that Emma's past was unimportant? And yet here he was, desperate to spoil her chances of a future with Mr Collins. How despicable and low could he get?

Mr Collins let out a long, soft sigh. 'I see that you know about her time as a prostitute. Did she tell you herself?'

'Yes, she did,' Ben said miserably.

'Well,' said Mr Collins after a pause, 'believe it or not, to me it is not important.'

Wordlessly, Ben shook his head.

'You see, Emma's father was a wonderful man, a great doctor, but quite impractical. He left his daughters with nothing when he died. Nothing. Emma struggled on for a while, but life here is very harsh for a woman, let alone one with small children to support. Certainly she was trained as a doctor by her father—although I can't agree that it's a suitable thing for a gently raised young woman to do—but of course she couldn't charge for her services. It's no wonder she gave in eventually and went on to the streets. Even if it was just for two nights before the Reverend Johnson found her and showed her the error of her ways, and took her and her sisters under the wing of the Church.'

'Poor Emma,' Ben said quietly, trying to imagine what it would have been like for her, alone and frightened on the streets, and yet still determined to look after her sisters, no matter what it cost her. And he had been so quick to despise her...

'Still, it could have been worse,' said Mr Collins cheerfully. 'She has never really spoken to me of those two nights, but I gathered that...well, she was too frightened to...' He cleared his throat delicately. 'I understood from the Reverend Johnson that when they married Emma was still...ahem...'

Ben stared at him incredulously. 'She never took a customer?'

'It appears not...'

'So what is she so guilty about?'

Mr Collins blinked in surprise. 'A sin is no less for being committed mentally and not physically, Mr Morgan. Emma chose to set aside her principles for gain. Whether she committed fornication or not, is beside the point. She intended to, which is the greater sin, surely?'

The answer Mr Collins got was so short, sharp and breathtakingly obscene that he got quite a fright. Ben got to his feet, his face pale with fury.

'I guess that's bloody typical of Emma. She flagellates herself for years over something she never even did, while you and that dried-up, bitter old monster she married mouthed sanctimonious abuse at her to ensure she stayed submissive and guilty! Oh, for God's sake! I'm going to see her now and tell her…'

'Tell her what?' Mr Collins caught at his sleeve as he went to push past.

'I'm going to tell her I've made a mistake.'

'And will she be grateful? Will she welcome you with open arms, Mr Morgan?' He saw Ben hesitate for the first time, and pressed his advantage. 'She's happy now, Mr Morgan. Happy for perhaps the first time in her life. She has her little family around her, she is looking forward to being my wife… You saw her tonight, how peaceful she looks. How can you possibly think of destroying her happiness?'

'She won't be happy with you!' Ben burst out.

'Why? Because you won't be happy without her? That's a very selfish thing to say, Mr Morgan. And besides, if Emma preferred you, she would never be so untrue to herself as to accept my hand, would she?'

For one dreadful moment he thought Mr Morgan would hit him, but then the big man got to his feet and strode out, his booted feet resounding loudly on the polished floor. Mr Collins let out his breath carefully. Thank heavens for that. He felt a little guilty at his white lie, but he had had to deter Mr Morgan from pursuing Emma somehow! After all, the reprobate had been quite openly infatuated with Emma's sister—he remembered the undertones at the wedding very clearly. And now to turn his attentions to poor Emma...

No, she didn't need a hot-headed, ungodly lout like Mr Morgan upsetting her now, just as her life was beginning to flow so placidly.

He removed his vestments and blew out the candles. There was still just enough light to see by as he shut the church door, but even so he was startled when Emma's man, Matthews, loomed out of the dusk.

'What is it, Matthews?' he demanded, more abruptly than he intended, but something about the man's ill-favoured appearance and the looks he gave him always unsettled him.

'Mrs Johnson says to see if you still want to eat, or are you going to hang about here all night.'

Mr Collins forced a smile. 'I'm sure she didn't use those words, Matthews. And I'm coming now. I'm looking forward to one of her delicious meals!'

'I do the cooking,' Matthews snapped and stalked off. Mr Collins watched him leave with relief. What Emma saw in the insubordinate scoundrel he would never know.

Emma stood and rubbed her aching back. She had been working off the excesses of Christmas Day by weeding and cutting back the exuberant growth of her herb garden since shortly after dawn, determined to complete the task before the day grew too hot.

At the end of the garden, under the shade of the big gum trees, the girls were playing on the swing, shrieking with laughter as they egged each other on to swing ever higher.

She called a word of caution to them before making her way back to the house, picking her way through the flowerbeds so neatly tended by Mr Matthews. The big kitchen was invitingly cool with the stove fire low—there was no need to cook when they had enough food left over from Christmas Day to see them through to the end of the week. Mr Matthews was sitting at the kitchen table, drinking tea and gloomily staring at a plate of buttered bread and honey.

Emma sat down opposite and poured herself a cup of tea. She was about to take a sip when she saw that the look on Mr Matthews's face was even more morose than usual.

'Did you go out last night, Mr Matthews?' she asked. Although he was still under sentence, she never bothered to ask where he went on the occasional nights that he disappeared. He was so indispensable to her life now that it would have been churlish to have begrudged him some time to himself, even if he was like a bear with a sore head on his return. 'Would you like me to make up a remedy for you?' she asked solicitously.

'No, Missus. *I*'m not sick.'

'Oh?' She looked at him quizzically over the top of her teacup. 'Who is?'

'Mr Morgan, that's who,' he said glumly.

Emma felt her whole body freeze in shock and she only just managed to put her cup in its saucer without spilling it. 'What's wrong with Mr Morgan?'

'Dunno. Heard last night from a bloke what works on Morgan Station that Mr Morgan's sick.'

'You don't mean injured?'

'Sick.'

'Oh,' she said faintly. She dealt with sick people all the time, but somehow she had never imagined Ben as one of them. She had seen him injured of course, even unconscious, but even then she had felt the indomitable strength of his life-force and known he would swiftly recover. He couldn't be ill!

'Real, *real* sick,' Mr Matthews went on for emphasis. Then, looking at her suddenly white face, he amended hastily, 'Well, *pretty* sick. As I hear tell.'

'Who's looking after him? Is there a doctor out there?'

'No doctor, missus. And he's too sick to bring in, poor bloke.' He shook his head sadly, even while watching Emma to see how far he could push it. 'All alone out there, no one to care for him...'

Emma stared into her cup as if the tea leaves would provide her with some solution. 'He's a strong man. I'm sure he'll survive.'

'Mebbe.' Mr Matthews poured himself another cup. ''Course, I'll be needing some time off, missus. For the funeral and that.'

Emma warred with herself. She was quite sure that Mr Matthews was exaggerating, and yet he had never been anything other than truthful with her until now. And what if he was right and Ben was dying? And what if it was in her power to help him and she didn't?

She got to her feet.

'Could you please take the girls to the Carsons and ask Mr Carson if we can have the loan of two of his horses please, Mr Matthews? Tell him we'll be back tonight.'

'Long trip out there, missus. You won't be back until tomorrow earliest.'

She hesitated. She could hardly spend the night away from home and not have it remarked upon. Mr Matthews picked up her cup and his and put them in the washing bowl.

'Mind you, if we get there and he's gone and carked it already, then you might as well turn right around and come home. Then you'll be back to-night,' he said over his shoulder.

Emma was left with no choice but to pack a small bag with overnight essentials along with her medical bag. Barely an hour had elapsed before they set off towards the distant mountains in the west.

She had never traveled any distance inland before, but the road was excellent and, despite the heat, they made good time. This was one of the earliest farming districts in New South Wales, and the holdings were substantial. Broad-verandaed houses, some of them quite grand, sat amid the orchards and vegetable fields from which Sydney and Parramatta drew their supplies. Further inland the rolling hills became dotted with sheep. It looked peaceful and prosperous, although Emma knew well of the floods and bush-fires that had swept over the terrain even in the few years that she had lived in New South Wales.

Trying to put her fear for Ben to the back of her

mind, she thought of New Zealand, remembering its moist, secretive greenness with nostalgia. She had so loved its vivid colours and lushness. This vast country was very different, with its sun-baked shades and strange animals, and the eerie quiet that could settle on it sometimes. But the feeling of unreachable horizons was the same. She would not have given up either for the teeming, dreary slums of London.

She was not used to prolonged periods in the saddle and, though they stopped several times to eat and drink, and once to cross the Hawkesbury River on the ferry at Stempleville, the discomfort of getting off and on a horse was quite unpleasant after a while. Her legs and back were aching by the time Mr Matthews rode off the main road and up through a valley. The track was bordered either side by golden poplars, and rose gently through well-watered paddocks. Fat sheep stopped grazing to watch them pass and a raucous flock of magpies shouted abuse from the fence-tops.

The house stood proudly on the side of a hill, its roof glinting in the late afternoon sun. Built on one level, a deep veranda gave the house an elegant line while sheltering it from the vagaries of sun and rain. Emma remembered that Charlotte had described it as a mansion, and in truth it was impressively large. But as they drew closer she saw the piles of timber and bricks from the Sydney brickworks stored to the rear of the house. It looked as if the renovation work had been halted for some time.

Emma dismounted by the front door, fighting against cramp as she slid from the saddle. She untied her medical bag and looked rather dubiously around her. The house seemed oddly quiet and empty. Perhaps…oh, surely she wasn't too late!

Mr Matthews was occupied in taking the tired horses around to the stables behind the house, but she caught his sleeve.

'Where is everyone?'

'Dunno, missus. What with the holiday and all they could be gone.'

'And left him alone?' she demanded, outraged.

She heard the front door open and when she looked up Ben was standing there, staring at her with such genuine astonishment that she immediately knew that he, at least, had not been a party to Mr Matthews's deceit.

'Emma? What are you doing here?' He was in his shirtsleeves and braces, his feet were bare and mud was splattered all over his moleskin trousers. His hair was tousled and he had not shaved in some days. He looked tired, but perfectly well.

'You're not sick,' she said coldly, feeling an uncomfortable combination of relief and anger at having been duped.

'I'm sorry,' he said blankly. 'Should I have been?'

'I was told you were dying.'

'Were you? I was just cleaning up after coming in from work.' He lifted the towel in his hand in explanation. 'Is that why you're here, Emma?'

She glared at Mr Matthews, who shrugged. 'Guess I shouldn't listen to gossip,' he said dolefully. He led the horses away and Ben looked at Emma for clarification.

'I hate that man,' she said with feeling, and then lifted a hand to her head as a wave of dizziness swept over her. She felt Ben's arm around her waist, but tried to resist the temptation to lean against him.

'I'm all right,' she said breathlessly, as he scooped her up in his arms and carried her up the stairs, shouldering the front door open as they passed. She closed her eyes, giving herself up to the sensation of his arms around her, the thud of his heart under her fingers, the heat of his breath against her hair. She opened her eyes as he sat her down carefully in a hard, high-backed chair, in a large, strictly functional kitchen at the shady rear of the house.

'Would you like a cup of tea?' he asked.

She blinked, trying not to feel foolish at the prosaic question. 'Thank you.'

He moved around the kitchen with surprising knowledge for such an undomesticated man. She stole surreptitious looks around her as he poured boiling water into a large, battered teapot. Clearly the kitchen was the hub of the house, and she guessed that most meals would be taken here, at the kitchen table. Despite the elegance of the building, this was a working farm, with a heart. She found herself feeling oddly at home.

'Do you… Are there other people who live here?' she asked, eager to make neutral conversation.

'There's a staff of four in the house, and then the farm workers. But they've taken the two days off over Christmas to go into town or spend with their families. Usually it's pretty rowdy in here.'

'Oh.' She cast about for another topic. 'The house is nice, Ben. Very large.'

'Yeah. It was going to be much larger, but I rather lost interest in it a few months ago, when… Well, one day I'll get it finished. At the moment we're concentrating on building up the stock levels. We've had an excellent spring and summer so far, so we've achieved a lot.'

He put the teapot and two mugs on the table and sat across from her, his face lit with a slight smile.

'You've had a long ride. You must be tired.'

'I am, rather.'

He poured the tea carefully. 'Very nice of you to come.'

'I was told you were seriously ill. I would have done the same for any patient.'

'Would you?'

'Yes.'

'I see.' He blew on his hot tea. 'So I'm not to regard myself as any more important than any of your other patients?'

'You can't expect that of me, Ben.'

'I guess not. Not when you're marrying Mr Collins soon…'

'I'm not…' She caught herself, seeing the triumph flare in his eyes. She was not going to give him that satisfaction! 'I'm not sure that that is any of your business,' she finished coolly.

'So you're not marrying him.'

'I might.'

He shook his head with slow deliberation. 'I don't think so. My spy tells me that you're involved in nothing more exciting than charitable works with the Reverend James Collins, despite what fantasies the good vicar might nurture.'

'Your spy...? Oh!' she gasped. 'You mean Mr Matthews? Is that why you gave him to me? To spy on me?'

'Well, I don't do anything nice for anyone unless there's a good reason for it, Emma. You know that.'

'Yes,' she said coldly. 'I've learned that lesson well.'

'Hmm.' He took her hand as it rested on the table and turned it over to study the palm. Her hand looked so small in his, so white against his deeply tanned fingers. Then he gently but firmly bit the soft pad under her thumb and she gasped as a bolt of pure lust shot through her.

'Emma,' he said softly, 'will you come to bed with me?'

The reverberation of his bite throbbed through her, reminding every nerve-ending of how his body felt next to hers, in hers, above hers... She had never been able to deny him. God help her, she never would.

'Yes,' she whispered.

'Good.' He put her hand down with a little pat and said briskly, 'So we can take it that you're not going to marry Mr Collins. Now drink your tea up before it gets cold. I think there might be some bread about, and I know there's some cheese in the safe. Then I'll show you around the house and farm before it gets dark.'

She got unsteadily to her feet, flushed with humiliation and need.

'Forget it, Ben. I'll take a fresh horse, if you can

spare it, and if you can't I'll walk. I'll walk all the way back to Sydney before I spend a night here with you. How dare you play your horrible games with me! How dare you! You…you use everyone!'

'Emma!' She evaded his grasp and stormed out into the huge hallway. Plainly remembering the violence of her temper, he avoided touching her, but blocked the front door before she could reach it. She was enraged to see that he was laughing at her.

'Get out of my way!' she shouted.

'No. You're staying here with me.'

'No, I'm not! You're not touching me!'

'Emma,' he dropped his voice, 'you've already agreed to go to bed with me.'

'That was a mistake!' she snapped.

'No, it wasn't. Neither of us has an ounce of will-power where the other is concerned, Emma.' He moved closer, his eyes and his voice softening. 'I can't think of anything but you, sweetheart. You're like…like an obsession. And you might as well face it—you feel the same about me.'

She found herself shaking. 'To my shame, but then, what else would you expect from a whore like me?'

'Emma!' He took her arms so firmly that he hurt her, but she was too upset to resist. 'Enough of that! Who gives a damn what happened in the past? Whether you or I had one lover or a thousand, it shouldn't change one thing about the way we feel about each other!'

She stared into his eyes and realised what she saw there.

'You know, don't you? Who told you? James?'

'Yes,' he admitted reluctantly.

'So now you've decided that because I'm not quite the whore you thought I was, you'll have me back?'

'Dammit, Emma, I asked you to marry me months ago! Long before Mr Collins took it on himself to interfere. You can't have forgotten that, surely?'

'No, I remember it very clearly. You said you forgave me.'

'Emma…' He went to slide his arms around her waist but she made herself rigid, jamming her elbows into his chest to keep the distance between them. 'I was still angry with you then. But it didn't take long to realise the mistake I'd made. How could you possibly be honest with me, when I'd never given you the chance to trust me? You're the best, most beautiful thing that's ever happened to me. I see you in every other woman's face, in every sunrise and sunset. You're my life, Emma. I love you.'

'Oh, Ben,' she said huskily, close to tears, but as he went to pull her against him she dug her elbows in his chest again.

'What's that for?'

'I bet you rehearsed that.'

'I did not!' he said, so indignantly that she almost relented. 'Ow. Now what?'

'My sister. What you did to her was unforgivable, Ben. I lie awake at nights…'

'Thinking of me?'

'No! Well, sometimes… No, I think of Charlotte,

on the other side of the world, probably deserted by your father, penniless…'

He let out an exasperated sigh. 'Will it make you happier to know that I gave instructions to the captain of the *Sarah Jane* to let them back on board again if they wanted to come back to New South Wales? I've got no doubts the two of them will be back here within the year, demanding we support them in the manner they wish to become accustomed to. Why don't you give your sister your house, if you feel so strongly about it?'

She considered that. 'I don't know if I feel that charitable…'

He tested the pressure of her elbows against his ribs and found the first sign of compliance.

'Why don't we go to bed?' he suggested hopefully. 'I do my best thinking there.'

'Really?' She looked at him askance, biting back her laughter. 'I do my best thinking over a cup of tea.'

'And *I*'ve had to go and make a fresh pot,' Mr Matthews complained from the kitchen doorway. 'You two ready to come and share it?'

Ben and Emma looked at each other.

'I think so,' said Emma.

'Good,' said Mr Matthews, and turned back towards the kitchen with a loud sniff. 'It's taken you long enough.'

* * * * *

MILLS & BOON®

Makes any time special

Enjoy a romantic novel from
Mills & Boon®

Presents™ *Enchanted*™ *Temptation*®

Historical Romance™ *Medical Romance*™

MILLS & BOON®

Next Month's Romance Titles

$\heartsuit$

Each month you can choose from a wide variety of romance novels from Mills & Boon®. Below are the new titles to look out for next month from the Presents™ and Enchanted™ series.

Presents™

THE PERFECT LOVER	Penny Jordan
TO BE A HUSBAND	Carole Mortimer
THE BOSS'S BABY	Miranda Lee
ONE BRIDEGROOM REQUIRED!	Sharon Kendrick
THE SEXIEST MAN ALIVE	Sandra Marton
FORGOTTEN ENGAGEMENT	Margaret Mayo
A RELUCTANT WIFE	Cathy Williams
THE WEDDING BETRAYAL	Elizabeth Power

Enchanted™

THE MIRACLE WIFE	Day Leclaire
TEXAS TWO-STEP	Debbie Macomber
TEMPORARY FATHER	Barbara McMahon
BACHELOR AVAILABLE!	Ruth Jean Dale
BOARDROOM BRIDEGROOM	Renee Roszel
THE HUSBAND DILEMMA	Elizabeth Duke
THE BACHELOR BID	Kate Denton
THE WEDDING DECEPTION	Carolyn Greene

On sale from 5th February 1999

H1 9901

Available at most branches of WH Smith, Tesco, Asda, Martins, Borders, Easons, Volume One/James Thin and most good paperback bookshops

MILLS & BOON®

Medical Romance™

COMING NEXT MONTH

VALENTINE MAGIC by Margaret Barker

Dr Tim Fielding found it impossible to believe that Katie didn't want a relationship, but she was determined to remain independent and *definitely* single!

THE FAMILY TOUCH by Sheila Danton

The attraction between Callum Smith and Fran Bergmont was potent, but as a very new single mother, she needed time before risking involvement again.

THE BABY AFFAIR by Marion Lennox

Jock Blaxton adored every baby he delivered, so why didn't he have his own? Having his baby wasn't a problem for Tina Rafter, but Jock?

A COUNTRY CALLING by Leah Martyn

A&E wasn't easy, and dealing with Nick Cavallo was no picnic either for Melanie Stewart, so it surprised her when they became friends—and more?

Available from 5th February 1999

2 FREE

books and a surprise gift!

We would like to take this opportunity to thank you for reading this Mills & Boon® book by offering you the chance to take TWO more specially selected titles from the Historical Romance™ series absolutely FREE! We're also making this offer to introduce you to the benefits of the Reader Service™—

- ★ FREE home delivery
- ★ FREE gifts and competitions
- ★ FREE monthly Newsletter
- ★ Books available before they're in the shops
- ★ Exclusive Reader Service discounts

Accepting these FREE books and gift places you under no obligation to buy, you may cancel at any time, even after receiving your free shipment. Simply complete your details below and return the entire page to the address below. *You don't even need a stamp!*

YES! Please send me 2 free Historical Romance books and a surprise gift. I understand that unless you hear from me, I will receive 4 superb new titles every month for just £2.99 each, postage and packing free. I am under no obligation to purchase any books and may cancel my subscription at any time. The free books and gift will be mine to keep in any case.

H9EA

Ms/Mrs/Miss/Mr................................Initials ....
                                                                    BLOCK CAPITALS PLEASE

Surname ....

Address ....

....

....Postcode................................

Send this whole page to:
THE READER SERVICE, FREEPOST CN81, CROYDON, CR9 3WZ
(Eire readers please send coupon to: P.O. BOX 4546, DUBLIN 24.)

Offer not valid to current Reader Service subscribers to this series. We reserve the right to refuse an application and applicants must be aged 18 years or over. Only one application per household. Terms and prices subject to change without notice. Offer expires 31st July 1999. As a result of this application, you may receive further offers from Harlequin Mills & Boon and other carefully selected companies. If you would prefer not to share in this opportunity please write to The Data Manager at the address above.

Historical Romance is being used as a trademark.

JoANN ROSS

a woman's heart

In *A Woman's Heart*, JoAnn Ross has created a
rich, lyrical love story about land, community,
family and the very special bond between a man
who doesn't believe in anything and a woman
who believes in him.

MIRA®

Available from February